Rachel's Blog

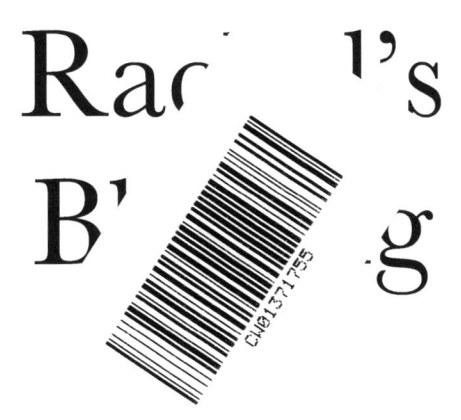

By

Ashley Winter

** Love in South Africa - Book One **

This is a work of fiction. Similarities to real people, places or events are entirely coincidental.

RACHEL'S BLESSING

Second Edition. November 17, 2017

Copyright © 2017 Ashley Winter.

Written by Ashley Winter.

To keep up with latest releases please sign up to receive Ashley's newsletter.
[Find Ashley on Facebook](www.facebook.com/loveinsouthafrica)
www.facebook.com/loveinsouthafrica

Titles by this author

"Love in South Africa" Series

Rachel's Blessing (Book One)
Deborah's Choice (Book Two)
Tanya's Hope (Book Three)
Gemma's Joy (Book Four)
Katherine's Fear (Book Five)
Suzanne's Chance (Book Six)
Isobel's Mercy (Book Seven)
Jennifer's Dream (Book Eight)

Acknowledgements

To my husband Grant, thank you for always believing in me and supporting my dreams. Isn't it amazing that we have each other to laugh with through these crazy parenting years. You are seriously one-in-a-million. I love you.

To my sons, Jake, Kurt, Angus and Chase. Wow, how boring would life be without you four! I love you forever. Special thanks to Kurt for drawing my vision of Hlala Nathi, and to Angus who loves hearing about my plots.

To my incredible family who have encouraged me and read every draft, how could I do this without you? Mom, Bells, Kerryn, Dad… thank you! I love ya'll loads!

Glossary of South African Terms and Expressions

Ag – Expression used when considering something (Afrikaans)
Beshu – A traditional animal skin apron worn by Zulu men on special occasions.
Biltong – Spiced, dried meat, often beef or game.
Boet - Brother (Afrikaans)
Braai - noun. Apparatus used to hold the coals and *braai* the meat on.
Braai – verb. To grill or roast meat over open coals.
Bru – Brother (South African slang)
Bushveld – Subtropical woodland eco region of Southern Africa
Checked – Seen (South African slang)
China – Friend (South African slang)
Chick – Girl (South African slang)
Eina – Ouch (Afrikaans)
Eish – Zulu expression of surprise
Hlala Nathi – Stay with us (Zulu)
Howzit – Hello (South African slang)
Ja – Yes (Afrikaans)
Ja nee – Yes no (Afrikaans, Commonly said together, implying 'yes well')
Lapa – Like a *Rondavel* without side walls
Nee – No (Afrikaans)
Oom – Uncle (Afrikaans)
Oukies – Guys, chaps, blokes (Afrikaans)
Rooi rok bokkie – Girl in a red dress (Afrikaans)
Rondavel - Round rural outhouse with a thatched roof.
Sokkie – Traditional Afrikaans dance
Smaak – Like (Afrikaans)
Takkies – Trainers (South African slang)
Verstaan – Understand (Afrikaans)
Vrek – Die (Afrikaans)
Wors – South African sausage

Reserve
Guest cabins
Lapa
Janice's home
Reception
Hlala Nathi
Game rangers' cabins

CHAPTER ONE

Rachel had never felt so alive. She pulled back the curtains in her *rondavel* and looked deep into the African *bushveld*. The morning sun cast brilliant golden streaks across the frosty savanna. The acacia trees were filled with noisy birdlife, and shook as large flocks vacated and flew into the pinky sky. Coming here had been a good idea. The *rondavel* had been assigned to Rachel a couple of months ago, when she'd arrived from Wales to volunteer at the orphanage on the outskirts of Pietermaritzburg, South Africa. It was rustic and quaint, and smelled of the dried thatched grass that was used to make the roof. She loved it.

With a tune on her lips, Rachel waltzed over to her wardrobe and chose an outfit for the day. A pair of blue jeans, a deep purple jersey and a pair of leather boots would be perfect for a busy day of caring for babies and children. She smiled at her reflection and pulled a brush through her wavy blonde hair. She hadn't felt this happy since Tomos had asked her to marry him. She remembered his chiselled face, the twinkle in his eye as he knelt before her on the beach at dusk. It was perfect. Everything was perfect... until the Welshman announced in the middle of the cake-tasting, that he just wasn't ready to settle down, and probably never would be.

"*I can't do this Rachel,*" he said with a giant piece of fruitcake in his hand.

"It's okay, I'll choose the cake. It's not a big deal."

"No. I mean I can't get married. Rachel, I'm sorry." Rachel felt the panic and insecurity rise up sharply within her. She felt instantly dizzy. Perhaps he was just a little nervous?

"It's just cold feet Tomos, it will pass," she said shakily.

"No Rachel, it's not just cold feet. I'm a loner, independent. Marriage is not for me, never will be."

There was no long explanation, hardly even a drop of emotion. The sales lady had thrown Rachel an awkward look, cleared the cake and scurried from the tasting room.

And just like that, Rachel's life had been turned on its head. The devastation had been so real that it was hard to believe so little time had passed. After two soul-searching months in Africa, she felt new hope, but the longing to be married remained. She was thirty-one now and more than ready to settle down. Tomos was an adventurous free spirit, and Rachel was instantly attracted to the unpredictable spontaneity in him. But he was also a bit of a loose canon, and she could now see that he lacked maturity and wisdom in many of the decisions he made. She had definitely been caught up in the moment, lost in the fantasy. Their break-up had most definitely been for the best.

After talking things out with her parents, Rachel's dad had suggested a change of scenery to help her gain a new perspective. When Rachel had found the orphanage online, he encouraged her to go for it. An African adventure to clear her mind and rejuvenate her soul was just what she needed. Time away from the routine hustle and bustle, and most importantly, time alone with God. Rachel tied her hair back into a ponytail and applied a touch of make-up. She grabbed her key, locked up and strode towards the awaiting babies in the main house.

"Good morning Suzanne!" Rachel beamed as she bounded into the large kitchen through the back door.

"*Howzit* Rach! You look pretty. How about some coffee?" Suzanne turned off the kettle and poured the boiling water into a row of bottles on the counter. Rachel had only known the orphanage co-manager for a couple of months, but already felt a connection with her that went deeper than just manager-volunteer. Despite the number of children scurrying around, they'd managed to have a few meaningful conversations. These deep chats were part of the reason that Rachel felt such peace and had healed so quickly. Most importantly, they'd renewed in her a hunger for God again. Suzanne was a God-fearing woman, wise and no-nonsense. In her fifties now, she'd never married, but had a daughter when she was fairly young. Now she dedicated her life to serve God as a substitute mom to anyone who needed her, including Rachel for the months she was there.

"Oh yes please! And thank you! How did the babies sleep?" Rachel leaned up against the kitchen counter to face her.

"Well… your two slept very well, but the new little one… she was awake every two hours." Suzanne took two bottles in each hand and shook them vigourously.

"Oh poor baby, and poor you too!"

"I'm okay. I'm quite used to living off no sleep!" Suzanne placed the bottles on the counter and popped the covers off the teats.

"Where are they?"

"Your two are still in their cots, waiting for their milk. Here you go." Suzanne handed Rachel two of the bottles.

Rachel could hear the gurgling sounds coming from their bedroom as she made her way down the hall. She'd been put in charge of the 12 month old twins' morning routine, and she loved it. Vusi and Nandi were babbling and sucking on their fists as Rachel entered the small room. She opened the curtains wide and let the sunshine in. The large main house was divided into many small rooms so that the babies wouldn't wake each other in the night and during their daytime naps. Vusi and Nandi had this room all to themselves.

"Good morning!" she sang, as she handed each baby a bottle. Both babies loved their morning milk, and it was gone within a few minutes. Rachel carried them over to the playpen in the main living area and returned to the kitchen for their breakfast.

As she dished up the oats that Suzanne had prepared, she couldn't help but wonder how it would be when she was a mom, waking her own children in the mornings. This time caring for the twins had intensified her longing for a family. She'd tried hard to imagine Tomos as a father, and couldn't really. That fact had confirmed over and over that he wasn't the right man for her, no matter how much fun they'd had together. She wanted a family man.

Rachel could hear the babies' babbling grow louder and louder as she approached with their food. She strapped them into their highchairs and placed a bowl of oats in front of Nandi. Nandi was getting really good at feeding herself with a spoon, but Vusi had made such a mess when Rachel first attempted it, that she hadn't tried again since. She'd then decided she would be feeding Vusi his breakfast until the day she left. Thinking of leaving brought a sadness Rachel hadn't expected to feel when she'd first arrived. Africa, even with all its problems, got under your skin like nothing she'd experienced. The people, the climate, the wildness, the way of life... it made her feel intensely.

After breakfast time, Rachel wiped the babies' hands and faces and took them out of their highchairs. They spent the morning crawling around the living room, playing with toys, singing songs, reading books and practising their walking. Both babies could crawl, but only Vusi was interested in trying to walk. Despite Rachel's encouragement of Nandi, she could crawl so fast that it seemed like learning to walk was a waste of time for her. Rachel gave the babies an early lunch and then it was time for their nap.

This was Rachel's time to relax. She strode past the kitchen, grabbed a packed lunch from Thandeka, the co-manager, and headed outside to where the other volunteers were gathered on the grass. Thandeka was one of the warmest people Rachel had ever met. She exuded love and affection, and the children flocked to her. She would sing the most beautiful traditional Zulu songs to them, and they loved joining in with clapping and dancing.

Though there was a chill in the air, it was so heavenly soaking up the African winter sun that nobody seemed to notice. Rachel found the two ladies who were staying in the neighbouring *rondavels* and sat with them to eat. She'd only made it through her first sandwich when she heard one of the children scream.

"Snake! Snake!"

Rachel was up on her feet instantly. The child pointed to the garden, panic in her dark eyes. Suzanne came running out, mobile phone in hand. "Don't panic guys. Oh okay, I see him. Just come away from there all of you." She gestured wildly with her hand. "I'm going to call the game ranger. Don't cry my baby." She held the little girl with one arm and dialled the number with the other. The volunteers gathered the children away from the snake and listened to one half of the conversation with worry.

"Eric, is that you? It's Suzanne here, we need your help please, quickly. There's a snake right here in the garden by the kitchen door, it looks like a black mamba. What colour? *Ja*, it's dark brown. Okay I'll try and see." Suzanne crouched down and squinted her eyes at the slithering reptile. "Yes Eric, the mouth looks black inside. Okay, it is a black mamba? Come quickly."

CHAPTER TWO

"Okay careful now boys, careful!" called Uncle Kobus.

"Slowly!" shouted Johan. "We're almost there!"

"Okay now, close, close Eric!"

Eric swiftly closed the gate behind the new female rhino that they'd just offloaded into the temporary enclosure.

"Great work boys!" Uncle Kobus smiled as he perched his hands on his hips. "Beautiful! Aren't they just majestic, boys?" Sweat dripped down the side of Uncle Kobus' face and he wiped it with his sleeve. It was more of a statement than a question, but Johan and Eric had to agree.

"*Ja...* they are incredible," Eric said with wonder and a renewed appreciation for their size.

"These beauties are going to be a huge asset to the lodge boys. People will drive from far to see this pair. Let's pray that they start to like each other a bit more, so we can have some calves." And with that, Eric's uncle took off his cap, bent his head and prayed out loud. It was a desperate time for the species. With the White Rhino population in South Africa in a steep and steady decline due to poaching, successful breeding programmes were paramount to their continued existence. And if anyone had the determination and faith to make this programme a success, it was Uncle Kobus.

He had inherited *Hlala Nathi* Game Reserve when his father had passed away, and it had always been his father's dream to have a Rhino breeding programme at the park. Having lost his wife to cancer soon after they were married, Uncle Kobus had never remarried, but had dedicated himself to what he believed he was called to: conservation. He'd become a father figure to Eric when his brother André, Eric's dad, was killed. Uncle Kobus had stepped in and taken Eric under his wing. He'd paid for him to study animal behaviour and conservation at the local university, and then employed him as a ranger at his reserve. He'd also taken in Eric's mum, his deceased brother's wife, and built her a home in the reserve. Eric had immense respect for him.

As Uncle Kobus reached the end of his prayer, Eric felt the vibration of his phone in his pocket. He turned away and took the call.

"Listen *oom*, I'm sorry I'm going to need to get going. Suzanne at the orphanage has a black mamba in the garden."

"*Ja* of course, go! Go quickly, and be careful my boy."

Eric jumped into the Land Rover and raced to the main house to pick up the tongs and bag. Then he headed straight for the neighbouring orphanage. He prayed as he drove. It wasn't ideal to attempt to capture a mamba when you were this exhausted. Black mambas were extremely venomous, one bite could kill you within twenty minutes. Eric felt the increase in his heart rate. "Breathe Eric, you've done this before, you can do it again," he whispered to himself. He should've asked Johan to come along to help him, but he couldn't turn back now. It was too dangerous to leave the snake there for a moment longer with all those children around. He had prayed, and now he would trust God to help him.

***

Suzanne ended the call and strode to where the children were huddled. Rachel took a group and distracted them with games on the lawn, far enough away to be safe, but close enough to keep an eye on the action. No one wanted to miss the moment the game ranger caught the snake.

After about fifteen minutes, a Land Rover arrived and parked near the garden. A young blonde man dressed in khaki jumped out the car with a large hessian bag and a pair of tongs. He located the snake and quickly checked to see that no children were nearby. And that's when his eyes fixed on hers. Rachel froze. She could not look away even though she was desperate to. She swallowed.

"Excuse me!" Eric waved the tongs at her. "Please take the children further back, these snakes are fast and unpredictable!"

Rachel felt her cheeks burn hot and red. She quickly composed herself and did as she was asked. She had totally misread him. Hopefully the gorgeous man hadn't noticed how she had been staring at him so brazenly.

***

Eric could hardly breathe. "Listen mate," he spoke quietly to himself, "just focus now, just don't mess this up. She's beautiful, and she's watching you. Don't look like an idiot, and don't get yourself killed."

Eric tried to push the image of the blushing beauty out of his mind for just a few minutes, but it was proving difficult. Was it just his imagination or had she been staring at him? Did they really have a moment there? Wow she was beautiful!

"Focus!" This time he said the word a little louder and shook his head. Eric approached the snake with caution. Slowly he edged closer and closer to it until he could reach it with the tongs. Suddenly he lunged the tongs around the snake's neck and came in close to grab it with his other hand. He was careful to place the mamba in the bag safely, and tied the drawstring as tight as he could. Eric exhaled a long breath. Still holding the bagged snake, he leaned against the side of his car and wiped the sweat from his brow. Now what? He had to meet her, he couldn't just leave it like this. He dared to look over his shoulder in her direction. She was sitting on the grass playing and laughing with the children. The epitome of loveliness.

Suzanne approached. "Thanks Eric, it's a relief to know that snake is tied up in that bag!"

"That's no problem Suzanne, you know we are always here when you need us."

She took a step closer and slipped her hands into her back jeans pockets. "Listen we are having a *braai* and barn dance tonight at the *lapa*. Why don't you join us? It'll be our way of saying thank you."

Eric shook his head. "Oh no, please don't worry Suzanne. I've got so much on at the reserve, and you have enough mouths to feed around here."

"No, I insist Eric. All the volunteers will be there, we have plenty meat. It's going to be great fun."

All the volunteers... even the blushing beauty. Perhaps he could spare a few hours after all.

"What time?" He grinned as he opened the boot of the car.

"We start the fires at 5pm," she said, a hint of triumph in her voice.

Eric laid the bag down carefully and slammed the boot shut. "That's perfect, thank you Suzanne. I'll see you later."

Suzanne was grinning at him a little too widely and a little longer than necessary. Had she noticed the brief but intense interaction between him and the blonde volunteer?

"*Ja* see you later." Suzanne leaned in close then and whispered, "And wear something nice see, some aftershave too… and brush your hair." She winked at him over her shoulder as she sauntered off.

Eric looked down and chuckled softly. "I'll see you later."

***

Eric hauled a pair of black jeans from his wardrobe and flung them onto the mounting pile on his bed. His mind was a mess. How could a girl he hadn't even met yet, affect him like this? His heart rate had still not come down, and he couldn't for the life of him decide what to wear. And for a 'top of the pile' kind of guy, that was saying something. Suzanne hadn't helped with her closing comments either.

Eric heard Johan's motorbike come to a stop outside his cabin. The door was flung open and the man himself sauntered in.

"Hey *boet*, what's going on here? Are you having a clean out or something?" he asked in his Afrikaans accent. He perched his hands on his hips and gawked down at his friend. Johan was tall and large, with the body of a rugby player. It was no surprise that his dad had wanted him to pursue a professional rugby career. Though he was extremely talented, he'd never played more than club rugby, and didn't want to. Johan's passion was wildlife conservation, and he was living his dream at the reserve.

"No man, I've just been invited to a *braai* at Suzanne's."

"A *braai*? At Suzanne's? Is it black tie or something *bru*?" Confusion etched across his forehead.

Eric frowned. "What? No... I..."

"You what huh? You trying to impress someone? Is there something you're not telling me *boet*?"

"Look *bru*, I'm running out of time here. Please just help choose something half decent."

"I'm now your style guru huh? Okay, calm down and let Johan have a look."

Eric used to hate it when Johan referred to himself in the third person, but after years of trying to change the habit, Eric had decided to just let it go. It had since become rather endearing.

Johan took the pair of black jeans off the top of the pile and held them up. "Jeans *boet*, you can't go wrong with a pair of nicely fitted jeans. And now the top, okay let's see... this blue hoodie is perfect for a *braai*." Johan flung the garment Eric's way.

"*Bru* this hoodie is like fifteen years old!"

"My *china*, you've hardly worn it, it looks like new."

"That's because I hate it!" Eric balled the hoodie and threw it in the general direction of the bin. "Never mind, I'll choose. Thanks anyway."

Johan chuckled. "Wow, I've never *checked* you so tense before *boet*. What's her name?"

"What? Who?"

"This girl you're trying to impress, what's her name?"

"*Bru*, I don't know."

"What? You don't even know her name and you've got it so bad. *Eish*. I'm going to have to pray for you *boet*."

Eric took a deep breath. He wasn't in the mood for Johan's jibes. He pulled on the pair of jeans Johan had suggested, and then yanked a white button-up shirt off a hanger. It was the one he only wore to weddings and funerals.

"No man, you can't wear that! That shirt screams out 'I'm trying to impress you!' *Boet* you have to play it cooler than that."

"It's on now, I'm not changing it. Cheers *bru*, I've got to go." Eric stopped at his bedside table, slapped on some aftershave and grabbed his keys.

"Oh *howzit* Eric, don't you scrub up well." Another wink. "*Ja* please." She nodded. "I need a man around here! Do you mind?"

"I'd love to." Eric felt the relief down to his bones. He blew on the embers and watched the flames roar. He quickly added a few dried twigs and then more charcoal. When the fire was ready for *braaing*, Suzanne brought down the trays of marinating meat, and Eric got started.

When it was time to eat, everyone grabbed a paper plate and formed an informal line. Eric knew Rachel was in the line somewhere, and before he knew it, she stood in front of him, plate in hand. Now was his moment. He needed to make an impression. He decided to go big, or go home!

"And what can I get for you, beautiful?" He grinned, not believing he'd actually said that.

"Uh… steak please, gorgeous." She blushed a deep shade of red, put a strand of hair behind her ear, and looked away.

Eric balked. Then a smile grew on his shocked face. "I'm Eric."

"Rachel." She smiled back. Her British accent was beautiful and made him feel a little unsteady.

"You're the snake guy…"

"*Ja*, that's me." He laughed and lifted a piece of steak in his tongs.

"Well, it was very impressive."

"Thank you." He placed the meat on her plate and found her eyes. They were green with tiny specks of brown.

"Thanks."

"How long are you here for?"

"I have three weeks left, and then I'm heading back to Wales."

"Oh, are you Welsh? Born in Wales?"

"No, I was born in England actually, and then moved to Wales as a teenager."

She was going home in three weeks. This was a bad idea, a very bad idea. If he had any sense at all, he'd end the conversation politely and forget all about the blonde beauty.

"Let's find a seat, let me just grab a bite to eat."

Eric dished up a plate of food for himself and found Rachel seated on a nearby bench. She smiled as he joined her.

***

Rachel hoped she was coming across a whole lot calmer than she felt. The man was even more attractive close up, strong jaw, straight nose, just the right amount of stubble, and a smile that reached his deep blue eyes and set them alight.

Eric took a seat next to her and started tucking into his meat. Why did he have to smell so good? She smiled to herself watching him. Rachel really enjoyed the South African culture. It was down-to-earth and genuine. All South African men seemed to love their meat, and Eric was no exception.

"So what do you do for a living?" he asked, busy now on his piece of *wors*.

"I'm an accountant, I have my own business from home. It's not as exciting as being a game ranger, but it pays the bills." Rachel stabbed a piece of potato and bacon from her potato salad and ate it.

"No, no, accountancy is very exciting. What a rush!" He teased, taking another bite of *wors*.

"Haha, very funny. Not all of us are cut out for what you do."

His dancing eyes held hers for a moment. "And what is it you think I do all day?"

"Oh I don't know... catch poisonous snakes, dodge charging elephants, hand rear lion cubs, that sort of thing."

Eric laughed and Rachel loved the sound of it.

"Well today was interesting because we just got two rhinos. My uncle, who owns the reserve is going to set up a breeding programme."

"Wow, that is amazing." She nodded, cut off a piece of steak and popped it into her mouth.

"But most days, I drive tourists around the reserve and teach them about the animals. It's a real privilege to work out in the bush." He stuck another piece of *wors* in his mouth and turned to her. "So... tell me something about you. What brought you to South Africa?"

Did she have to answer that question so early on in the conversation? "Uh... I just needed a change of scenery."

"Oh? Any particular reason?" His eyes searched hers.

"I had a bit of a bad break up, but don't worry, I'm so so over it!"

Eric laughed. So did Rachel. It seemed he also knew she didn't have to make that fact quite so clear. They moved on to chatting about their families. Rachel could've stayed right there talking to Eric for hours, but Suzanne stood up and addressed the crowd. "Okay guys, it's time for the barn dance! If you all could come through this way please."

She led everyone through to the attached barn, which had been cleared out especially for the occasion. A caller, in full cowboy dress, stood waiting to teach the first dance. The *Ceilidh* was a traditional barn dance in Wales, and Rachel loved going along to them. She was going to enjoy this!

***

A barn dance? Seriously? Now what? Eric's legs were made for running fast, not for moving to a rhythm. The crowd filtered into the barn and the caller took charge teaching the moves for the opening dance. Maybe it was time to leave quietly. Eric managed to edge himself right to the back of the group. He looked over at Rachel near the front. Her face was beaming. Clearly this was her thing. The thought made his palms sweat. Should he stay and be with her? He'd most likely make a fool of himself. Or should he leave now and retain some semblance of dignity?

Before he could make the decision, the caller assigned him to the first group of six. He then used this group to demonstrate for the others. Eric had not exactly been paying attention. Soon the music was blaring and they were hopping and swinging this way and that. Eric had to seriously keep his wits about him just to stay upright. He caught Rachel's eye during a particularly difficult swirl. She had her mouth covered she was laughing so hard. Nice. Real smooth Eric.

It wasn't long before all the groups of six joined in. By then Eric had had more than enough. Just as he turned to find a seat in a dark corner, the caller mixed up the groups and called him back.

"Hey you over there? You in the white shirt!"

"Me?" Eric frowned and pointed to himself.

"*Ja* you. I need you in this group over here please."

Rachel's group. He couldn't help but wonder if Suzanne had whispered something to the insistent caller. The caller explained the next dance, and the hillbilly music pumped through the speakers. Eric's heart was in his throat as he met the beautiful blonde face to face in the line. She looked amused, her cheeks flushed. He linked arms with her, spun her around, and returned to his position. Then he had to join hands with her from behind and promenade her around the room. Eric was desperately trying to hold it together, but he could feel the sweat running down underneath his 'I'm trying to impress you' shirt. Her hair tickled the side of his face. She was so close he could smell the faint perfume in her neck, and see the tiny flecks in her dark green eyes whenever she looked back at him. After a few more swirls and spins, the dance was over. Eric sighed in both relief and disappointment. He'd never been so physically affected by a woman before. Everything about her drew him in, enticing him to want to know her more. He'd never believed in something as crazy as love- at- first- sight… until now.

***

"The last dance for the evening is the *sokkie*. It's a traditional Afrikaans dance. I'll demonstrate." The caller took his wife in his arms and ran through the steps. "Okay gentlemen or *oukies*, grab yourselves a lady, or *bokkie*, as the Afrikaners would say! This is a classic, '*Rooi rok bokkie*' by Die Cambells! Enjoy!"

Rachel had seen the dance done, but never danced it herself. She scanned the room and found Eric pouring himself a drink in the corner. She longed for him to look over and catch her eye. An upbeat Afrikaans song thumped from the speakers as couples moved onto the dance floor. Rachel felt disappointment settle in her. She turned and headed for the door.

It was slightly quieter outside, but soft strains of music still poured out from the open barn door. The cold night sky was peppered with stars. Rachel had never seen the Milky Way as clearly as she did in South Africa. She found a bench and sat down, her heart still pounding from the dance with Eric. She sucked in the crisp air and exhaled slowly. Eric appeared in the doorway. Her heart had hardly had a chance to slow down before it started hammering at triple pace again.

"Are you all danced out?" he asked with a half smile as he leaned against the doorframe.

"No, I just needed some fresh air."

"Care for a *sokkie*? I'm not very good, but we can try?" He was irresistible.

"Okay. Out here?"

He took a couple steps towards her and held out his hand. "Under the stars? Absolutely."

Rachel smiled up at him and took his hand. It was warm and a little clammy. He placed his right hand on her back, and together they moved to the music. The cold vanished as Rachel felt her body grow warmer. He was close, so close she could feel his breath in her neck. Every now and then, his stubbled cheek grazed against hers.

"Is this okay? I'm not really sure what I'm doing here, just trying not to stand on your toes." He looked down and laughed softly.

Rachel smiled. "You're doing great," she answered as they swayed. This was definitely not a *sokkie*, but Rachel didn't mind one bit. Her heart was pounding so hard, she was sure he could feel it. And then too soon, the music stopped. They froze, but didn't let go.

"Can I see you again?" Eric's voice was husky in her ear.

"I'd like that," she whispered.

He let go of her hand and stepped back. "Thank you for the dance. I uh… better get going." He kept his eyes on her, took a few more steps back, then turned and disappeared into the night.

Rachel felt dizzy. She edged back towards the bench, sat down and ran her hands through her hair. What had just happened? She felt closer to the game ranger after a few hours than she ever had to Tomos. She needed to think. She fetched her coat and keys from the *lapa*, and headed back towards her cabin.

***

Eric floated towards his Land Rover with a silly smile pasted on his face. He'd actually pulled it off, and more than that, he'd made real progress. She wanted to see him again. He tried hard to forget about the fact that she was leaving in just a few weeks. He knew he'd ultimately regret letting himself get in this deep, this fast, but he couldn't help himself.

So on the drive back to the reserve, Eric prayed. He'd wanted something special like this with someone for so long, but there seemed to be some huge obstacles to overcome if that someone was Rachel.

As he pulled up to his cabin, he saw Johan's lights were still on. Should he tell Johan what had happened? No, he wasn't in the mood to be reminded of how heartbroken he'd be once Rachel had left.

After a quick shower, he pulled on a pair of shorts and was fast asleep within minutes. And then he could see her face, smiling, laughing, they were dancing, their bodies brushing against each other. And he never wanted it to end...

CHAPTER FOUR

"Eric! Wake up *boet!* It's 8:55! Eric!" Johan banged on the door impatiently.

Eric bolted out of bed and scrambled for his khaki trousers, shirt and dark green jersey. He'd overslept. Thank goodness for Johan. Uncle Kobus did not tolerate his employees being late for work, nephew or not, and the first game drives started at 9am sharp.

"Johan I'm coming *bru!* Wait for me!"

Eric was still tucking in his shirt as he climbed into the Land Rover alongside Johan. They sped down towards the entrance and pulled up outside the reception building in a cloud of dust.

"Boys, you are late!" Uncle Kobus marched towards them with his hands on his hips.

"Sorry *oom*. It's my fault." Eric flung the door open and hopped out.

"Get moving! There's a whole crowd of visitors signed up for game drives this morning and this afternoon."

Winter time was particularly busy at the reserve as the grass was short and the animals could be spotted more easily. Johan and Kobus fetched the land cruisers, while Eric collected the cooler box of soft drinks from his mom, Janice, who worked at the reception desk. Once both vehicles were filled with passengers, and the safety procedures explained, they were off for the morning.

Eric usually loved taking visitors around and educating them on the animals and conservation, but today he was there in body only. His mind was where it had been for the last day, on Rachel. What was she doing now? And more importantly, when was he going to see her again? He hadn't gotten her number and now he was kicking himself. He'd been so ecstatic she'd agreed to spend more time with him that he couldn't think straight after that.

"Excuse me, Eric? Is that a springbok?" asked a woman with a pair of the smallest binoculars Eric had ever seen around her neck.

"*Ja*, that's a springbok alright."

"And what's that one? Is that a Kudu?" She pointed beyond the springbok to a larger buck.

"No, that's a Gemsbok, their horns are straight. The Kudu's horns are curved."

"Please can you show us the new rhinos?"

And so the day passed in a blur of activity. Before Eric knew it, it was the evening and he still hadn't spoken to Rachel. After a quick shower, he collapsed on his bed with his phone.

Johan breezed in then and sat on the edge of Eric's bed. He looked eager to chat. "So I've been waiting the whole day to hear about last night *boet*." He pulled his foot up onto his knee and shook his leg.

Eric leaned back against the headboard. "Okay…" He sighed, his impatience only barely veiled. "What do you want to know?" Eric rubbed his eyes and looked at Johan.

"Who is this girl, *boet*?"

"She's a volunteer from Wales. Her name is Rachel."

"And how long is she here for?" Johan narrowed his eyes.

"She leaves in three weeks, and I know what you're gonna say -" Eric held up both hands.

"Three weeks! Is this a good idea *boet*? You look terrible!"

"Johan, please man. Just leave it!" Eric huffed.

Johan frowned. "You've got it really bad and she's leaving *boet*. Then what, huh?"

"I know. Look I know, okay?"

"You gonna be heart broken, and Johan is going to have to comfort you."

"Don't worry *bru*, I won't come knocking on your door. I promise." Eric flung his legs down to the floor.

"You say that now, but come three weeks time, you're gonna be in pieces over this *chick*, *boet*. This is your best friend warning you now. You're not thinking with your head here *china*."

"I'm just taking one day at a time *bru*. I've never met a girl that makes me feel like this. I can't just *ignore* this feeling."

"Okay well, I hope you know what you're doing *boet*. You know Johan only wants the best for you. So what's she like? You had a really good time with her at the *braai* hey? When do I get to meet her? Invite her for a game drive, better still, a night game drive."

"Listen *bru*, you really need to find a lady of your own. You can't be living out these fantasies of yours through me."

"Don't worry about me *boet*, I'm more than okay as I am. The Lord will provide the perfect lady for me when the time is right."

A night game drive was actually a genius idea. But he'd have to run it by Uncle Kobus first, and that meant telling him about

Rachel. Eric wasn't too sure he was ready for that, but the thought of a romantic drive alone with the beautiful blonde through the bush at sunset was more than enough to convince him.

***

It had been two days since the *braai*, and Rachel had still not heard from Eric. She was going crazy waiting for the phone to ring. She found her gaze continuously drifting to the windows, hoping to see his car pull up in the driveway. As she entered the kitchen of the main house, she found Suzanne in her usual morning spot, cooking oats and mixing milk bottles.

"Hi Rach. How's it going? You're looking a little down today. Is everything okay?"

"Morning Suz, yeh I'm okay thanks."

"He hasn't called yet has he?" she asked over her shoulder as Rachel slumped into a chair at the kitchen table.

"No, he hasn't," Rachel answered with a deflated smile.

"Well I know why. He hasn't got your number, has he? Now he has to work up the courage to call me for it." Suzanne took a large spoonful of oats and plopped it into a bowl, then went back for another spoonful.

"He could've come around though, and he hasn't." Rachel drummed her fingernails against the tabletop.

"No that's not it Rach. Janice, Eric's mom, told me that they have been swamped with visitors since those rhinos arrived there at the reserve. All the rangers are working very long hours at the moment. I imagine it won't be long and they'll have to hire more." Suzanne pulled open the nearest drawer and retrieved a handful of plastic baby spoons. Then she took two bottles in her hand and shook them.

"Oh I see, well that makes sense. Still…"

"Don't worry Rach. I saw the way he looked at you, he'll contact you soon enough. I've never seen that man so rattled in all my life."

Rachel smiled and took the two bottles Suzanne handed her. Her hungry babies awaited! They were sure to put a smile on her face.

***

It was a warmer than average winter's day and Eric relaxed under the shade of a nearby tree. Bruno, Uncle Kobus' Staffordshire terrier had claimed a spot next to him and was softly snoring. Eric was on his lunch break between game drives, and he was just as exhausted as he was hungry. Thankfully his mom had handed him a sandwich and drink as he'd arrived back at reception. More visitors were starting to gather at the land cruisers for the afternoon drive through the reserve. It had been a relentless couple of days, but now he took the opportunity to do what he'd been desperate to do. With pen and paper ready, he sucked in a deep breath and dialled Suzanne. Hopefully she'd go easy on him.

"Hello, Suz here."

"*Howzit* Suzanne, it's Eric."

"Eric!" she said loudly, almost as if she wanted those around her to hear it was him on the line. "I've been expecting your call." He could almost see her winking at the eager crowd pressing in.

"Okay Suz… just give it to me please."

"What's that Eric? What would you like me to give you?" There was no way she was going to make this easy for him.

"Her number please. Suzanne I don't have long, I need to go soon."

"Whose number would you like Eric?"

"Rachel's… come on Suz, just give it to me."

"Oh Rachel's number! Why would you want *her* number?"

"Suz, I'm warning you."

"I'm sorry. It's against our policies to give out the contact details of our volunteers."

"Suz, don't make me come over there! I promise you, the next snake you find, you'll be on your own, catching it with your tiny *braai* tongs..." He could hear her mock sigh.

"I hate snakes. Have you got a pen?"

"Just give it to me!"

"Which one do you want, I have SA and UK?"

"Both!"

Suzanne rattled off the numbers. "You owe me big time!"

"I know." Eric smiled and ended the call.

***

Rachel stood in the doorway grinning.

"Keep your phone on you girl!" Suzanne winked and waltzed passed carrying a tray of baby food. Rachel followed with the twin's breakfast and got them settled in their high chairs. She passed Nandi her bowl and spoon, and started to feed Vusi his oats. Rachel smiled the second she felt the vibration in her pocket. She pulled it out. Unknown Caller. It was him, it had to be.

"Suz can I..."

"Yes, yes of course, go!" Suzanne waved her hand at the doorway.

Rachel walked quickly towards the privacy of the twin's bedroom. She shut the door and cleared her throat.

"Hello."

"Uh Rachel… hi, it's Eric. We met the other night at the *braai*? I hope you don't mind, I got your number from Suzanne."

"Hi Eric, no of course not. It's good to hear from you." Rachel sat on a chair in the corner of the small room and pulled her legs up under her.

"I've been meaning to call, the last two days have been manic at the reserve."

"Yeh I heard you've been inundated with visitors to see the rhinos."

"You heard right, and it's been amazing, but I think we might need to hire a few more rangers soon if they keep coming like this."

"I'd love to see them... the rhinos that is."

"Well actually, that's why I'm calling. I uh… was wondering if you'd like to go on a game drive sometime? I'll have to check the schedule with my uncle and get back to you with a date though."

"I'd love to. Wow."

"You would? Okay great! I'll sort something out and get back to you."

"Sounds good." She smiled.

"Okay well, I have to go. It's time for another round of animal sightings and endless questions for me!"

"Bye Eric, chat soon."

"Bye Rachel."

Rachel's grin froze to her face. She walked back to Suzanne, phone in hand, eyes big.

"And?" Suzanne looked up from wiping a baby's face.

"Game drive!" Rachel squealed.

"That's my boy." Suzanne smiled and nodded. "When?"

"He's going to get back to me with a date after he's checked the schedule."

Suzanne's eyebrow lifted. "What he means is, he's going to have to get it past his Uncle Kobus." Suzanne sighed. "Let's hope he's feeling generous! He's from the old stock… might even insist on a chaperone!"

"What? Seriously?" Rachel frowned.

"Let's just hope Eric catches him in a good mood."

CHAPTER FIVE

"*Oom* can I talk to you please?"

"*Ja* my boy, come and sit. Let's talk."

Eric had plucked up the courage to ask Uncle Kobus about taking Rachel on a game drive. He thought after lunch would be a good time, when Uncle Kobus was well rested and well fed. He found him sitting in his usual lunchtime spot with Bruno - a bench dedicated to his deceased wife, under his favourite acacia tree.

"*Oom* I just wanted to ask your permission to take a friend on a game drive one evening."

Uncle Kobus frowned. "Why? What's this about Eric? Who is this friend?"

Eric's heart rate picked up pace. "It's just one of the volunteers from the orphanage *oom*."

"Okay, does he have a name? And why can't he go on a planned drive with everyone else?"

Uncle Kobus leaned forward on his knees, his eyes fixed on his nephew.

And here it came. Eric rubbed his forehead. "Her name is Rachel."

Uncle Kobus nodded slowly and didn't say a word. Eric could feel the sweat start to run down his back. For goodness sake he was a grown man, he could take a girl out for a drive, surely!

"I am hearing this right Eric? You want to take a lady out for a drive, at night, on your own."

"Yes *oom*, it will be fine. I know the roads very well and I'll have the radio comms too."

More silence.

Eventually Uncle Kobus looked at him, his face pained. "Do you think that's wise my boy? You're putting yourself in a compromising position, and what about her reputation? And yours? At night?" He shook his head. "No my boy."

"Nothing's going to happen *oom*, we hardly even know each other."

"You can't go alone, and that's the end of the story." He held his eye. "You take Johan with, or you don't go."

Eric sucked in a deep breath and looked away. Uncle Kobus had done so much for Eric and his mom over the years, but at that moment, Eric had never been more frustrated with him and his outdated ideas. There were no grey areas with Uncle Kobus, it was either black or white, and he lived his life firmly on the straight and narrow. Eric resigned himself to the fact that it was going to be his way, or the high way.

"Okay *oom*, I'll take Johan then. Can we go on the Sunday night?"

"Yes, after evening church on Sunday."

"Okay, thank you *oom*."

***

"Listen *bru*, you sit in the back with your mouth shut. And your eyes too, even better." Eric shot his friend a warning look and changed into fifth gear.

Johan couldn't stop laughing and it was starting to get on Eric's nerves.

"Now just what are you planning to say and do, that Johan can't hear or see, huh?"

Eric clenched his jaw and kept his gaze firmly on the road ahead. It felt like forever since he'd seen her, and this was not quite what he had in mind. If only it was a normal car with a boot, he could stuff Johan in it. Unfortunately, in the land cruiser, Johan would have a beautiful, elevated view of their entire date and be within earshot the whole time.

The big man shifted in his seat. "I'm not going to interfere *boet*, this is embarrassing for me too hey. I don't want to be the spare wheel."

"Man, you need a *chick* so bad!" Eric banged his palm on the steering wheel and shook his head. He dug his hand into the side door compartment and pulled out an iPod and a pair of huge headphones. He tossed them in Johan's direction. "You're wearing those, the whole night. Now scoot to the back."

"What? No blindfold?" he shot back.

Eric laughed. "Consider yourself lucky."

***

Rachel didn't know what to do with herself. She'd been dressed and ready to go for an hour already. Now she sat on her bed with a magazine, anxiously listening out for the sound of Eric's Land Rover. She'd longed for this time alone with him, and the past few days waiting for Sunday night had felt like weeks.

She'd wanted to wear something feminine, but the night was clear and the temperatures had dropped substantially. In the end she'd chosen black jeans, a grey mohair jersey, and her dark grey woollen coat. She'd left her hair down and wore a colourful knitted slouch beanie.

Rachel heard the sound of tyres on gravel. Her heart thumped hard. She grabbed her keys and phone, locked up and headed for Eric's Land Rover. Eric jumped out the car as he saw her coming.

"Hey, Rachel." How she loved his accent. Was he as nervous as she was?

"Hi." Rachel slipped her hands into her coat pockets.

"Are you ready? Warm enough?"

"Yeh, all ready!" She smiled.

Eric looked back at the car briefly. "Um one little hitch, or should I say 'hitchhiker'..." He laughed nervously.

"Oh, what's that?"

"We have a hitchhiker; I'm so sorry Rachel. It's a long story, but Johan is going with us tonight. He's going to be on his best behaviour."

Rachel couldn't help but feel disappointed that they wouldn't be alone for the evening. She did her best to hide it. "Oh, who's Johan?"

"He's my best friend, neighbour, co-worker... and more recently, my chaperone." He grinned apologetically, waving a hand back at the car.

"Okay well, the more the merrier!" She tried to sound upbeat, but she wasn't sure Eric was buying it. Eric ushered her into the front passenger seat and Eric turned the vehicle back towards the reserve.

***

"Hello," came a lone voice from the back seat.

Rachel looked back over her shoulder. "Hi. I'm Rachel."

"Johan."

He sounded so awkward, Eric thought it was no wonder he was still single. The man needed help.

"It's nice to meet you," said Rachel.

"And you too."

Eric hoped that that was where their conversation would end. For good.

"So do you like it here in South Africa?" asked Johan.

Eric gritted his teeth.

Rachel turned back to look at him. "I really love it, I wish I could stay longer. The beauty, the people, the weather. It's the most amazing place I've ever been to."

"And have you travelled much?" Johan asked.

Eric turned around and glared at him.

"A little. I've been to France, Spain and Austria."

"Oh wow, that's amazing." Johan sounded genuinely impressed. Eric was getting less impressed by the second.

"And you? Have you travelled outside South Africa?" Rachel asked.

"No never. I'm keen to though, so if I get the chance, I'll take it. Wales looks beautiful too; Eric told me you're from there. All I know about Wales is Welsh rugby."

"Yeh, I was born in England, but I've been living in Wales for many years now."

"That's nice man."

Surely that was the end of their little chat. Johan sank a little lower into his seat and put the headphones on. Eric breathed a sigh of relief.

They arrived at the reserve and moved on over to the open land cruiser. Eric made sure Johan was as far away from them as possible. Fortunately this model had four rows of seating, so he hoped Johan would be out of ear- and eyeshot. He leaned over to the seat behind and grabbed the little blanket he'd brought for Rachel to cover herself with. "You might need this."

"Oh thank you!" She smiled and quickly tucked it around her legs.

***

A thousand butterflies flew around inside her. She looked over at Eric in the diminishing light and studied his handsome profile. He looked over at her briefly and smiled, making her stomach flip. Johan had gone into a world of his own in the back and Rachel was grateful for some sort of alone time with Eric. The sun was setting now, casting golden hues over the plains. The *bushveld* was alive with the sound of crickets and frogs, and somewhere in the distance, Rachel could make out the sound of hyenas.

"So, what would you like to see?" Eric looked over at her briefly.

"Anything! Everything!" She clasped her hands together on her lap.

"Okay then, let me introduce you to my favourite characters first, while we're right here."

Eric took a sharp turn off the dirt road and into the bush. He slowed the land cruiser right down as they approached a huge acacia tree. There beyond the tree, Rachel could see a family of elephants. Their beauty, their size, their majesty was overwhelming. There were about seven of them, some adults and some calves. Eric looked over at them with pride.

"This is my favourite family. Thandi is the matriarch." Eric spoke softly as he pointed to the largest female toward the back of the group. And she doesn't take nonsense." Rachel smiled. "That's her sister Nontu on her right, and her calf, Phila, just behind her on the left."

Rachel felt a new appreciation for what Eric did. It was hard to believe that this was how he spent his day, almost every day. It was like living in a parallel universe.

"And those two on the far left are Nontu's offspring, Mandla and Nosipho. That loner lurking at the back is a bull we call Lucky. He hangs out mostly on his own unless he's looking for some female company. And at the moment, he's pretty interested if you know what I mean." Eric raised his one eyebrow and Rachel laughed.

"Okay! So who does he have his eye on then?" Rachel leaned out the window.

"Well, his first choice would be Thandi, but he'd settle for Nontu if she'd be willing to look his way. He's actually got a pretty good reputation with the ladies, hence his name."

After watching the family interact for a little while, Eric put the land cruiser into gear and turned back towards the gravel road. The stars were just starting to appear in between the now rusty colours the sinking sun was casting. The thorn trees had turned into black silhouettes. Rachel was overcome by the beauty.

Eric drove slowly over the bumpy road and glanced at her now and then. When she caught his eye, he laid out his hand, palm up on the seat between them. Rachel's heart turned over. Slowly she scooted closer and placed her hand in his. It was comforting and exciting at the same time, and she loved the feeling of being this close to him. He closed his fingers around hers, and Rachel remembered their intimate dance, his breath floating over her neck. And she longed for more.

CHAPTER SIX

Eric wished he never had to let her go. Her hand felt so right in his, and he tried to forget that she was leaving so soon. After a few more sightings of buck and hyena, Eric reached the outskirts of the reserve, and drove along the border. It was a little trickier driving with one hand, but it was a price he was more than willing to pay. He loved seeing the wonder in Rachel's eyes with every new sighting. It was as if he were seeing the animals for the first time himself.

Something caught Eric's eye. The fence. Eric let go of Rachel's hand and slowed the vehicle to a standstill. "Johan!" He turned to get his attention. Johan caught his eye and pulled the headphones down around his neck.

Johan frowned. "What's wrong *boet*?"

"This fence, it's been cut."

"What!" Johan stood and quickly climbed over to the front of the vehicle.

"You are right *boet*, that's a massive hole, big enough for a car to get through."

Eric grabbed his radio. "Uncle Kobus, come in. It's urgent. Uncle Kobus."

"Yes Eric, what is it? Over."

"A huge hole has been cut in the fence *oom*, big enough for a vehicle to pass through. On the east side. Over."

"I'll be there now. Have you got your rifles? Over."

"Yes *oom*."

"On my way; be careful my boy."

From the light of the land cruiser, Eric could make out one set of foreign tyre tracks. This was recent, he'd driven this road just this afternoon. These guys, whoever they were, had done this tonight, and were most likely still in the reserve.

Eric looked over at Rachel, his eyes intense. "I'm going to need you to get in the back and lay low."

Johan grabbed his rifle and replaced Rachel in the passenger seat. He handed Eric his gun. Eric laid it on the seat beside him, put the vehicle into gear and edged forward, following the tyre tracks he could see in the dirt. Eric was now extremely grateful that Johan was with him, he only wished that Rachel wasn't. He breathed a silent prayer and drove deeper into the bush.

***

Rachel had never seen a gun in real life before. She'd climbed into the seat behind the men and wrapped the blanket around her shoulders. Being in an open vehicle was not a good thing right now. Far in the distance Rachel could make out a small Land Rover. "Eric there." She pointed.

"*Ja* I see it. Get down now Rachel. They're probably armed."

Eric accelerated the vehicle and charged towards the Land Rover. The Land Rover picked up speed and raced to get away. Rachel was amazed at how skilfully Eric could handle the big land cruiser on this bumpy terrain. They were gaining on them despite being in a more cumbersome vehicle. Soon they were just metres away. The Land Rover turned back towards the direction of the east fence, and throttled to get away. Rachel hoped Eric and Johan would just chase them off the reserve and not try to apprehend them themselves.

A gunshot fired. And another.

"Get down now!" Both men shouted.

"Eric, let them go. They're headed for the fence; just let them go," said Johan.

Rachel could see the stress in Eric's face as he looked at his friend. "One of the tyres is hit *boet*." He slowed the vehicle considerably and followed at a distance to make sure the men were in fact leaving. Then he grabbed the radio from the seat next to him. "*Oom*, they've gone. They got away, back through the fence. Over."

"Are you all okay? I heard gunshots! Over."

"*Ja*, our tyre has been hit though. Over."

"Where are you now? Over."

"We're about five hundred metres in from the east side fence. Over."

"I'm five minutes away. Over."

Eric and Johan climbed out the vehicle and detached the spare wheel. After jacking up the front of the car on the driver's side, they unbolted the flat wheel and replaced it with the spare. Rachel's hands shook in her lap. Those bullets had been aimed at Eric, and his side of the vehicle. There could've been a very different outcome tonight. She felt a tear slip down her cheek as the reality of what had just happened became clear. Uncle Kobus arrived as Eric tightened the bolts on the new spare wheel and placed the flat in the back of the land cruiser. He marched over towards them.

"Are you all okay?"

"Yes *oom*, we're fine now." Eric looked over at her, his eyes full of concern. He hopped up onto the seat next to her, wrapped her in his arms and stroked the back of her head.

"Johan, did you get a registration number?" Uncle Kobus turned towards him.

"No plates *oom*."

Uncle Kobus took a deep breath and nodded. "Okay, well, we have a fence to repair. And it can't wait until the morning." He turned to his nephew. "I'm not sure Eric… do you want to take Rachel home? Johan and I can do this."

"If you sure you don't need me *oom*, I think I should take her now."

"*Ja*, go my boy, take my car. We'll take care of this."

***

Eric settled Rachel into the passenger seat of Uncle Kobus' Land Rover. She still hadn't said anything. He leaned over and pulled her towards him, so that she was sitting right up against him. He turned her face to look into her eyes. She looked emotionless.

"Are you okay Rach?"

"Yes." She nodded, but he could feel her body shaking next to him. He squeezed her knee and started up the Land Rover. Leaving his hand right there, he drove towards the orphanage.

"Wow, that was intense," she whispered.

Eric was relieved to hear her voice. "Not quite what you had in mind for our first date then?" Eric teased and glanced down at her in the darkness.

"A high speed car chase in the thick of the African bush at night? Um, not quite."

Eric laughed. "Sorry, I'll try harder next time."

Rachel snuggled into his left arm and put her head on his shoulder. Eric struggled to concentrate on the road. All he could feel was the warmth of Rachel's body against his, and her hair in his neck. He could smell her shampoo, and it was not helping him focus.

When he finally pulled up in the drive at the orphanage, Rachel didn't move. Eric turned off the engine. He looked towards her, still lying on his shoulder, and kissed the top of her head. He brought his other hand over to stroke her hair and the side of her face with his thumb. Her skin was soft, warm, inviting. Slowly he kissed her temple, then tilted her chin up with his finger. He grazed his face down until his lips found her cheek, and finally her mouth. When he felt her respond, his heart galloped up his throat. His breathing increased and he pulled away briefly. She slid her hand up onto his chest and snuggled closer. Eric searched her eyes and pressed his lips to hers again.

***

Rachel could feel the trembling in his warm fingers as he stroked her face. He looked into her eyes and kissed her again, more urgently this time. Then he pulled back and dropped his hand onto his thigh. He leaned back, closed his eyes and breathed in slowly. Had she done something wrong?

"I'm going to have to be very careful around you." His voice was low and rough, his gaze straight ahead..

"Why's that?" she whispered.

"Because I've made a promise." He looked down at her tenderly.

Rachel searched his eyes for an explanation. It hurt when he looked away.

"I've promised the girl I marry some day, that she would be the only one."

Rachel frowned, trying to understand.

"The only one... I'm intimate with." Eric turned back to her, searching her eyes to see if she understood what he was saying.

Understanding dawned in Rachel, and she nodded. She breathed in slowly, trying to temper her longing. This fact however, only made him more irresistible. He was saving himself for marriage. How could she not want him even more now?

CHAPTER SEVEN

As the days passed and the time drew closer for Rachel to leave, Eric found himself more and more irritable. He and Johan had been tasked with the job of overseeing the installation of an electric fence around the reserve. Uncle Kobus had been quite shaken up by the shooting incident, and had hired a company to do the installation. He asked Johan and Eric to keep an eye on things and make sure the installation went smoothly. Uncle Kobus was convinced that the men were poachers who were after his rhinos' horns. He'd told Eric that he was wondering now if starting this breeding programme was a bad idea, as he didn't want to endanger the lives of those who lived and worked on the nature reserve. Eric wasn't sure how to respond, it had been Uncle Kobus' life dream. They had to keep the faith, believe that this would work, and that the electric fence would make life a whole lot safer for them and the animals.

"Johan if you just tighten that section a bit, the pole would stay erect." Eric pointed to the area he meant. They'd reached the section of fence that had been cut. Johan and Uncle Kobus had done a temporary repair job on the night, but the section needed to be properly replaced before the installation company got to there with the electric components.

"Eric I'm telling you, I've tried doing that and it's not working." He frowned back at his friend.

"Why is this suddenly now so complicated? We've done this a thousand times. You must be doing something wrong." Eric waved his arm at him.

"Eric, I know what I'm doing, I'm going to install the next section and then that bit will tighten up," he said, eyes fixed on the wire cutters in his hand.

Eric placed his hands on his hips. "For goodness sake Johan, you just tried that and it didn't work! You don't have a clue what you're doing!"

Johan's eyes turned wide. He stood and faced his friend. "*Boet* what is wrong with you? I've never seen you so tense. Not even when the poachers were shooting at you."

"Just... focus on the fence okay." Eric gritted his teeth and crossed his arms.

"Okay *boet*, whatever you say." Johan shook his head.

Eric had never raised his voice at Johan before. What was wrong with him? He needed to cool off and think.

Finally Johan got the new section of fence up and Eric started to relax. As they drove back to the main house in his friend's Land Rover, Johan wanted some answers. "So what was that all about?"

"Look, I'm sorry Johan. I haven't been feeling myself lately." Eric had his elbow out the window and gazed far off into the distance.

Johan kept one eye on the road, the other on Eric. "*Ja* I can see that. Anything you want to talk about? You know Johan is a very good listener."

"You know exactly what it is Johan." Eric rubbed at his temples with one hand.

"She's leaving in a few days huh?"

"*Ja.*"

"Come, Johan's going to take you shooting."

"What, *now?*" Eric gawked at him.

Johan gawked back. "Yes now, of course now! Look at you, you need help *boet.*"

So much for the chat. Johan's solution to almost any turmoil of the soul was to place a few rounds of ammunition into the tin cans and glass bottles he'd set up as his private little shooting range behind the cabins.

The sun was setting, but there was enough light to last a half hour or so. Johan pulled up at his favourite spot, loaded Eric's rifle and handed it to him. He grabbed his own, hopped from the vehicle and lay side by side with Eric in the dirt. On the cold ground in the semi-darkness they pummelled tin cans with bullets. Eric did actually find it therapeutic, and by the time the sun set, they were laughing and fooling around again as usual.

***

Rachel's suitcase lay open on the tiled floor of her *rondavel*. How would she fit everything she'd accumulated over the months inside it? Her heart was heavy with the thought of leaving. Eric had called her since their kiss on Sunday night, but he hadn't come 'round, nor had he asked her out again. She could only think that he was avoiding her to try and make things easier on them both for her departure on Saturday. She knew her volunteer friends were planning a little farewell for Friday night, but she didn't know if Eric had been invited. Suzanne walked past her window and waved as she caught her eye.

"Come in Suz," she called as her friend neared the entrance. Suzanne came and sat down next to Rachel on her bed.

"So you're starting to pack I see. And how're you feeling about leaving us?"

Rachel found the older woman's eyes. "I'm gutted Suz, I'm not ready to leave."

"Well, we'll have you back in a heartbeat, you know that." Suzanne leaned forward onto her knees.

"I guess it's time to go back to a job that pays the bills." She laughed sadly.

"*Ja* that's right; you can't be a volunteer forever." Suzanne smiled sadly.

"In case I run out of time and don't get to say it Suz, thank you. Really, you've been so good to me."

Suzanne put her arms around the younger woman, gave her a squeeze, then pulled back. "Rach, my door is always open for you. If you ever need anything, remember I am here for you. You have a substitute mommy in South Africa, who loves you."

Rachel felt her eyes burning with tears and hugged Suzanne again. "I know. Thank you, I love you too."

The finality of goodbye was so hard, and Rachel knew the worst was still to come.

***

Even if it killed him, Eric had to see Rachel before she left, and time was running out. He kicked his boots off at the door and filled the kettle for a cup of strong coffee. Despite another full day of work on the reserve, he'd managed to organise her something special. He'd spoken to Uncle Kobus about using the game rangers' entertainment *lapa* to host a low key farewell party for Rachel on Friday night. Uncle Kobus still felt so terrible about what had happened the night of the shooting, that he'd readily agreed. He'd even offered for Rachel to stay over in one of the empty cabins that night. She needed to be at King Shaka airport early on Saturday morning, and this way Eric could drive her straight there. Eric had also organised with Suzanne to get all the volunteers there for the evening. Johan would collect them and take them home again after the party. He just needed to run it by Rachel now. He leaned against this kitchen counter, pulled his phone from his pocket and dialled her number.

"Hello, this is Rachel."

"Well hello beautiful." Eric smiled.

"To what do I owe this lovely surprise?" asked Rachel.

"I have a little idea I want to run by you."

"Okay then, let's hear it?"

"How about we have your farewell party here at the reserve? I've already cleared it with Uncle Kobus, and he's happy for us to use the *lapa* out back. There's an amazing view of the watering hole from there."

"Oh wow..."

"And I know you need to be at King Shaka really early on Saturday, so you could even sleep over in our guest cabin here after the party if you want, and then I could take you to the airport in the morning. Suzanne knows too, they're happy to move their party plans over here as well."

"It sounds perfect!" Rachel felt almost giddy.

"So you'd need to be all packed by Friday afternoon. Johan will come and collect all of you in the land cruiser, and take the other volunteers back home after the party.

"Eric, I'd love that!"

"Good! It's all settled then. And I'll see you soon."

Eric couldn't get the grin off his face. He ended the call and flicked the kettle on. He'd have one more evening with her. It would definitely make goodbye even more torturous, but what could he do? He was falling hard and he was powerless to stop himself now.

CHAPTER EIGHT

Eric tossed and turned. He picked up his pillow and fluffed it angrily, then plopped his head on it in yet another attempt at sleep. He was having second thoughts. It was the night before the party and he couldn't get Rachel out of his head. She was in his dreams when he did manage to sleep, and she was in his thoughts when he was awake. What had he been thinking letting himself get so close to her when she was leaving? He felt physically ill at the thought. This farewell party was a terrible idea. It was only going to bring them closer and make Saturday excruciating.

Eventually Eric checked the time. 5am. His head throbbed from the disjointed sleep. Giving up on sleep, he trudged through to his tiny kitchen and dug a couple of pain killers out the cupboard. He'd take an early morning run past the *lapa* to check that everything was ready for tonight. He headed back to his bedroom, pulled on shorts and *takkies*, locked up and left.

The fresh morning air felt good on his face and he upped his pace. After arriving at the *lapa*, he checked the *braais*, charcoal and tables were all ready. He found the beginning of the bush running trail nearby, and started up it. It felt good to push his body hard. Every step felt like it demanded his full effort, and took his mind off Rachel.

When he got to the flat section of grass along the plain, he sprinted as fast as he could. When he couldn't go a step further, he collapsed on his back on the dry grass and looked up into the morning winter sky, breathing hard. He could see the evaporation from his mouth with every laboured breath. The sun was rising in spite of the cold. It was going to be another beautiful winter's day in Africa, no matter how he felt on the inside. And no matter what he did, in twenty-four hours time, the woman he was starting to love would be gone.

***

Rachel had just managed to stuff the remainder of her things into her large flowery case. The quaint room was as bare now as when she'd arrived. She sat on the suitcase lid and struggled to get the zip all the way around. She was certainly taking more home than she'd brought. She pulled and pulled and eventually, she felt a tear start down her face. How could she leave now? She'd be leaving her heart here, and going home empty. It felt so wrong. But how could she stay for a man she'd known for only a few weeks? No one could fall in love in such a short time. It was just attraction she felt for the man. Her life was in Wales, her family was in Wales, her future was in Wales.

She'd enjoy tonight, and then she'd get over Eric as easily as she'd gotten over Tomos. Rachel took a quick look in the mirror and wiped her eyes. She locked up her *rondavel* and went to care for her babies for the last time.

***

Eric dropped the last group of visitors off at reception, and drove his Land Rover home. He would normally be exhausted after a full day of game drives, but tonight he was filled with nervous energy. After a long hot shower, he pulled on a pair of blue jeans and a checkered flannel shirt. He couldn't wait to be with her. Could she be the right woman for him? How would they ever know with her leaving? Eric pushed the thought deep inside. They had tonight, and he would make it count. His head warned him to guard his heart while he was with her now, that was the wise thing to do. But his heart longed more than anything to explore the depths of their chemistry.

He brushed his hair and teeth, and neatened up his stubble. He slid the key to the guest cabin in his pocket. It would be a difficult twenty-four hours, but he wasn't going to think past the next few now. If he left enough of an impression, who knew? Maybe the blonde beauty would be back.

***

Rachel was ready and waiting with her bags when Johan arrived to fetch them all for the party. She'd said goodbye to all the children, and had written a note to each of the volunteers. She took a final look around and hoped that she'd be back someday.

The mood among the volunteers on board the land cruiser was festive and fun. A few of the guys had brought drinks and were already handing them out to everyone. They all seemed ready for a night of raucous partying. Rachel wasn't quite in the same mood, but she hoped she would be able to enjoy the night nonetheless, and let her hair down a little. With that in mind, she accepted the cider that was offered to her. She needed something to help her relax a little.

When they arrived at the *lapa*, the fires were lit, and the music was pumping. The sun was sinking slowly over the waterhole in the distance, and a few animals gathered to drink in the relative safety of the low light. Rachel scanned the area for Eric. He was standing near the *braais* with Johan, turning meat, cider in hand. He looked her way and winked. Her heart squeezed. She needed to be near him. Especially tonight. She took a deep breath and walked over to the *braais*.

***

Rachel was a vision of loveliness walking toward him, the setting sun behind her. Her hair was down, and her eyes had a touch of vulnerability in them tonight. He'd never noticed it before. She put her drink down and joined them at the fire. "Hi! Can I help?"

"Oh no. No, no, no," said Eric, laughing and shaking his head. "Things might be different where you're from, but in South Africa, the men do the *braaing*. End of story." Eric smiled.

"It's tradition," offered Johan.

Rachel raised her one eyebrow at the oversized man.

"It just makes us men feel like we're good at something you see, like we're not totally useless to our womenfolk," Johan explained.

Rachel laughed then, and the men started giving her tips on how to *braai* the perfect piece of steak. "See the aim is to only turn it once, but you have to be very experienced to get the timing right for that," said Eric.

"And you should only salt the meat at the end, otherwise it dries out," said Johan.

"I don't know why you're bothering to teach me all this," Rachel teased, "as I'll never be allowed to use my newfound knowledge."

"Well… not in South Africa, but maybe you can teach the Welshmen how to *braai*." Johan laughed.

With that, Eric lost his appetite. The thought of Rachel with any other man turned his stomach. He finished his can of cider and grabbed another. He hoped that after everyone had gone home, he and Rachel could have some time alone together. He needed this party to end early. The earlier the better, unless they could slip away before then somehow.

The food was served and the group helped themselves to the variety of salads, rolls and meat on offer. While some were still eating, the music was turned up and the dancing started. This party was not going to end anytime soon. Eric felt his mood shift. He left his food and drank another cider instead. He scanned the crowd for Rachel and found her dancing in a group of people. He couldn't take his eyes off her, she was mesmerising. His frustration mounted, everyone needed to disappear. He needed to be close to her, alone with her. This was their last night together.

She caught his eye and came dancing over to where he sat on the edge of the *lapa* watching her. She sat down next to him. He put his arm around her waist and pulled her closer. It wasn't close enough.

***

"So, are you having a good time?" His voice was rough in her ear. "You look so beautiful."

Rachel smiled and leaned into him. He took her hand in his and rested it on his thigh.

"Thank you for organising this Eric, I'll never forget tonight." She looked down at their joined hands and rubbed her thumb against his.

Eric's smile held a deep longing. He looked defeated. "And I'll never forget *you*, Rachel. Tell me again why are you leaving?" He swallowed.

Rachel sighed. "Let's forget about tomorrow, Eric. We have now, we have this moment. Thinking about tomorrow's only going to ruin it."

"Wanna get out of here?" He looked up at her, his eyes filled with yearning.

She tilted her head. "You mean, leave my own farewell party early?"

He tucked a strand of her hair behind her ear. "They won't notice, they're having so much fun. Come, let's go. I need to be alone with you Rachel. I need you." His hand dropped back down onto his thigh.

She'd never seen Eric this down. He was giving her a glimpse of his soul, no holds barred.

"Let me just say a quick goodbye Eric. I'll tell them I need an early night. They won't mind."

Rachel slipped away and hugged her friends goodbye. Eric stood waiting, a bottle of red wine tucked under his arm. He reached for her hand as she approached, and entwined his fingers in hers. Rachel instantly felt the warmth spread throughout her body.

"Let's go down to your cabin. It's the one reserved for guests. There on the water… I have the key on me."

"It looks beautiful." Rachel retrieved her suitcases from the land cruiser and Eric helped her carry them down to the guest cabin. The front door of the wooden cabin had a patio which looked out over the water. On it was a small table and a two-seater padded wicker couch. It was an incredible spot. The night was clear and the stars so close, it felt as though you could reach out and touch them.

A shiver of excitement ran through Rachel as Eric unlocked the cabin. He rolled in her large suitcase, but didn't turn any of the lights on. He fetched two wine glasses from the small kitchen cupboard and brought them along with a corkscrew to the patio table. Rachel took a seat on one side of the couch and leaned back, admiring the view. The crickets and frogs chirped and sang as though there was no tomorrow. Rachel was going to miss so much about Africa. Eric passed her a glass of red wine and sat down on the couch next to her. After downing his glass, he poured another. He unlaced his leather shoes, took them off and stretched out his legs. Following his lead, Rachel did the same but pulled her legs up under her.

After a long while, Eric broke the silence. "Rachel, I... I know we haven't known each other very long. And maybe I wouldn't be saying this if you weren't leaving tomorrow… and it's probably not a wise thing to say now, but I've never felt this way about anyone before." Eric looked over at her in the semi-darkness, and she could see the depth of his feelings in his eyes. "I think I'm falling in love with you."

Rachel's heart felt tight, she could hardly breathe.

He looked down at the glass in his hand, then found her eyes once more. "I know that all we have is tonight, and I'm not asking for a long distance relationship, or that you uproot your life and move to Africa. I just… I don't know… I just wanted you to know." Eric leaned forward in his seat and put his head in his hands. He sat back up, refilled his wine glass, and leaned back. Rachel shifted and laid her head in his lap. He stroked her hair and drank his wine, pensive.

"Eric, there's something you should know too." Rachel spoke softy into the night as she lay there. "I've never felt this way either. And I don't know what to do with these feelings. I don't know how to say goodbye to you. I think I'm falling in love with you too, and it scares me. It scares me because I hardly even know you." Rachel turned onto her back and looked up into his face. Eric, with one hand on her hair and one on her chin, bent down and kissed her. Her pulse raced.

As she sat up, Eric lifted her onto his lap. She knew she should stop, but she couldn't. He felt so good, he smelled so good, and even though her brain told her this was a very bad idea, Rachel felt powerless to stop now. He kissed her lips, her face and her neck, his kisses growing in urgency. He had been drinking, he was probably drunk, or at least impaired in his decision making. She should end this. But she couldn't, and she didn't want to. She would get as close to him tonight as he let her. Tomorrow was coming, and they'd need these memories of their closeness to see them through. He lifted her and carried her inside to the bedroom.

***

Despite the warning voice in his head that shouted at Eric to stop what he was doing, he couldn't think of anything except how much he wanted Rachel. He needed to be closer and closer to her. He was in a hazy dream, and reality was far, far away. He never wanted the dream to end.

And on this night, Rachel's last night in Africa, Eric gave himself permission to explore the depths of all this dream had to offer.

CHAPTER NINE

Rachel's head throbbed. She pried her eyes open and squinted at the light seeping in through the flimsy curtains. She looked over at Eric, fast asleep on the white pillow next to her. Her chest tightened. All the beautiful memories came back and filled her with guilt and regret. His promise. She had dishonoured his promise, and her own. He'd been drunk and she should've stopped it. He'd been powerless. If she cared for him like she'd said she did, she wouldn't have let it happen. Shame filled her. Eric was meant to take her to the airport this morning, but Rachel couldn't bare the thought of facing him now. She'd make things easier on both of them. She'd write him a note and leave quietly. Suzanne would take her to the airport, she'd already offered.

  Rachel got dressed quietly and gathered her things outside the door. She quickly called Suzanne and asked for a lift. Then she tiptoed back into the bedroom to say goodbye to Eric. She longed to kiss him one last time, but didn't want to risk waking him. In the end she leaned down, kissed him on the head tenderly and left. Rachel had never felt such emptiness. She was leaving her heart behind in that cabin. She walked up to the entrance of the reserve with her bags to wait for Suzanne. Thankfully, she didn't have to wait long. Suzanne pulled up in her little maroon VW Beetle and helped Rachel to fit her suitcase in the boot.

  Once they were both strapped inside, Suzanne looked at her. "So, what happened? Why am I the one taking you this morning?"

Rachel did not want to go into all the details with Suzanne, or anyone for that matter, but she did owe her some sort of explanation. "Eric's still fast asleep Suz."

"What? He wouldn't wake up to take you?" The woman frowned in disbelief.

"He had a little too much to drink last night. I can't imagine he'd be in the best shape to drive this morning, so I left him to sleep."

"You didn't say goodbye?" Suzanne searched her eyes.

"It's better this way Suzanne. Easier on both of us." Rachel looked down at her hands.

"Okay well, if you're sure this is how you wanna leave things..."

No she wasn't. But what choice did she have? "Yeh it'll spare us the dramatic goodbye we've both been dreading."

And with that, Suzanne pulled onto the road and headed towards Durban and King Shaka airport. Rachel was acutely aware, minute by minute, of how the distance between her and Eric grew greater and greater. Would she ever see him again? After last night, would he *want* to see her again? The woman who he'd disgraced himself with… Rachel felt tears roll down her cheeks. Suzanne leaned over and handed her a tissue without saying a word. She spent the remainder of the journey quietly saying goodbye. To Africa, to the orphanage, and mostly, to a future with Eric.

***

Suzanne couldn't stay, so she said goodbye to Rachel in the drop off area of the airport, and left. Rachel took a deep breath and headed for the British Airways check-in counter. Before long she'd made it through security and boarded her flight home. Her eyes were still wet when she took her window seat and pulled the strap across her hips. She slipped her earphones in, closed her eyes, and tried to shut out the world and everything that reminded her of him.

Though she deeply regretted their night together, Rachel struggled to escape the memories of how he had been with her. He was tender and gentle. It was slow and intense, filled with longing. And no matter how hard she tried, Rachel knew she'd never be able to get the memories out her head, nor her heart. And did she even want to?

No. Despite the guilt, they were the most precious memories she had of him.

***

Someone was stabbing him in the head, over and over. He rubbed his forehead. What on earth was the matter with him? And who was making that dreadful siren noise?

Eric rolled over onto his stomach with a grunt and buried his face deep in his pillow. His phone alarm! He stretched out his arm and flapped his hand around on the bedside table. Finally he felt the offending object and turned it off. He rubbed his eyes and tried to open them. Where was he? The guest cabin? Had he spent the night in the guest cabin? With Rachel? Oh no, please God no! And where was she? Eric checked the time. 9:55am. Her flight left at 9:35am, she was gone. The reality hit him like a bullet to his gut. She hadn't woken him up... well perhaps she'd tried. With the state he was in last night, it would've taken nothing less than a natural disaster to bring him back to consciousness.

He sat up quickly and scanned the bedroom for a note... anything that would give him some indication of where he stood with her after... last night.

Last night... what actually happened? He remembered being with all the volunteers from the orphanage at the farewell party. He'd had way too much to drink, and so had Rachel. He'd never consumed that much alcohol in all his life. He'd had the odd glass of wine or a beer at a *braai*, but he'd always stopped after one. As a Christian, Eric had promised himself that he would never drink enough to get drunk. He knew his limit. He'd also seen his dad make a fool of himself one too many times. He refused to go down the same road. Though his dad was never abusive towards him or his mom, he had embarrassed their family time and time again. The drinking had eventually killed him. He'd died in a hit and run accident when Eric was seventeen. His blood alcohol level was 0.14. The accident saw his mom go into depression. They were both so lost.

It was then that Uncle Kobus had stepped in. He'd made all the difference in both Eric and his mom's lives. He'd taken them in, helped them financially and practically, and most importantly, he'd introduced them both to Jesus.

With Rachel leaving, he'd turned to alcohol to get him through. Maybe he was more like his dad than he realised. He had fallen so hard and so fast. He was an idiot. From the first time he'd laid eyes on her, caring for the children at the orphanage, it was like he could see into her soul. And he'd loved what he saw.

And there it was... on the dresser, a folded up piece of white paper. Eric stood and walked over with an impending sense of doom. The fact that she hadn't bothered to wake him up, to at least say goodbye, prepared him for what was probably written in her note. He held his breath as he unfolded the page.

Eric, please forgive me, I forgive you. After last night, if you care about me at all, please don't try to contact me.

Eric slumped down on the side of the bed and ran a hand through his unruly blonde hair. What on earth happened last night? What had he done that needed forgiveness? He remembered arriving at the cabin with Rachel, and they'd chatted outside on the patio. But after that... nothing. How did she even get to the airport this morning? What a mess, and now she was gone.

CHAPTER TEN

Rachel woke to the feeling of being nudged in the arm. She'd somehow managed to sleep through the entire flight, and she was grateful. Her headache was gone and her plane was now parked safely at Terminal 3, Heathrow Airport.

A quick look out the window and she knew she was home, grey clouds as usual. In a way, it was comforting, normal. Sunny South Africa felt a million miles away. Rachel's mom and dad would be waiting on the other side of the airport, ready to take her home to Swansea.

Although Rachel's parents were both English and grew up in Cheltenham, they'd moved to Wales when Rachel was fifteen. Her dad, a vicar, had been transferred to a small congregation on the beautiful Gower peninsula. Rachel had finished up her schooling there, and then went on to study accountancy. Once qualified, she worked for a local firm for a few years, and then decided she'd work from home as a self-employed accountant.

Rachel retrieved her carry-on bag and made it through passport control fairly quickly. After hauling her larger bag off the carousel, she made her way through customs and on to the exit, and there they were. Her dad, Peter, a big, burly man with a grey beard and her mom, Lyn, a petite, well-dressed brunette, both waving ecstatically, as though she'd been away for years. She'd missed them.

"I'm home!" Rachel felt relief as she hugged them both simultaneously. She needed the comfort their arms would bring.

"Welcome home sweetheart, we've missed you!" Rachel's mom stroked her hair. "We can't wait to hear all about your trip. Let's get your bags in the car."

***

Eric didn't have too much time to think before there was a sharp knock at the door. He stuffed the note in his wallet, and went to open it.

"Johan." Eric held the door open wide as his friend entered.

"*Howzit boet*, why are you in the guest cabin? I went looking for you at yours, and then, when I couldn't find you, thought I'd come down here." Johan looked at Eric with concern. "I'm worried about you. I've never *checked* you drink like that before."

"I've done something Johan; it's bad." Eric rubbed his forehead as he sat on the edge of the bed.

Johan frowned down at him. "I thought you were taking Rachel to the airport *boet*, why did I see her leave with Suzanne this morning?"

"Oh well that explains how she got to the airport." He swallowed. "Listen, something happened last night with Rachel, and I'm not sure what. She left a note basically saying 'Please forgive me, I forgive you, don't contact me'. Then she left this morning without even waking me up."

"*Boet* that sounds bad. Did you spend the night with her? Did you two…" Johan's eyes were wide, bulging in his direction.

"I can't remember." Eric shook his head and tried to think. "Oh no... wait... oh God forgive me." His heart sank as he remembered he and Rachel, together on the patio, kissing on the couch. His eyes burned. Had it gone too far? Oh no, he could never forgive himself. "*Bru* we kissed, I remember now, out there." Eric pointed to the window with the patio beyond. "Maybe things went too far *bru*, I don't know, what if we..." Eric didn't want to even think about it. "I made a promise, Johan." Eric rubbed his hands over his face. "I promised God, myself and the girl I marry that she would be the only one I'm with in that way Johan. What have I done? I hardly even know her! And was I gentle? Why did she say 'I forgive you.' I must've been so drunk to forget everything Johan, what if I hurt her? Johan, I'm not experienced in these things." Eric sank his head into his hands.

Johan came and sat down next to his friend. He took a deep breath and placed his hand on Eric's shoulder. "We don't know how far things went last night *boet*, but one thing I do know - I know *you*, and I know you'd never hurt a lady *boet*. Drunk or sober."

Eric turned to look at Johan, concern etched on his face. "I've never been drunk before Johan, who knows what I'm capable of? I've let myself down in a big way, and God. This is not the kind of man I want to be *bru*."

He had to know what had happened last night. Had they gone too far? And if he'd pressured her, or forced her in any way, he had to know. And in that instant, the decision was made. He'd go, he'd find her. He couldn't live with himself otherwise.

***

Rachel's mom and dad dropped her at her Caswell Bay seaside apartment. It was a tiny one-bedroom flat, but Rachel loved it. The view of the ocean filled the stretch of glass panes across the length of the room. A large part of Rachel's income went towards the rent, but for Rachel, it was worth the peace living near the ocean brought her.

Her dad wheeled her large suitcase into the bedroom, while her mom put the kettle on in the kitchenette for tea.

"Are you okay?" her mom asked quietly as Rachel joined her in the kitchen. "You've barely said a word since London."

"I'm okay mum, just tired."

Surprisingly, her mom seemed satisfied with that. Rachel hated keeping the truth from her, but in this situation, there was just no way her mom would understand, or be able to react with any sense of calm. As a solicitor, she would extract all the details in an intense cross examination, analyse every action and motive to death, and then demand an explanation from Eric himself as to why her daughter had returned home even more down than when she'd left. And it wasn't Eric's fault.

Rachel buried her thoughts and took the tea her mom offered. After just a few sips, her parents said their goodbyes and left her to unpack and rest.

Rachel's sleep was plagued by vivid dreams of the man she was trying to forget, or remember... she couldn't quite decide which, it was a conflict between her heart and brain. And in between the dreams of Eric, came thoughts of God. Would He forgive her? Could she even forgive herself? She had felt so close to Him at one stage of her life. Now He'd never felt further away. The combination of guilt and longing made her toss and turn through the night.

By the time morning came, she felt emotionally drained. How was it that she so clearly remembered every detail of their time together? She had been so far gone, yet she could still smell the scent of Eric's cologne and hear his voice with the accent she loved. She could picture every detail of his blue eyes gazing into hers as he so tenderly touched her face in the bedroom. Her face warmed at the thought. He had the wildness of Tomos, but the tenderness of her own father. What was he doing now?

She could not let herself go down this road, there was no way she could face him again. Rachel forced her tired body out of bed, pulled on a pair of running shorts, a tank top and trainers, and hit the beach. It was quiet this time of the morning. The cool air and exercise would clear her head and leave her feeling a little more like her old self. In control.

***

Uncle Kobus ushered Eric into his large office at the lodge's Welcome Centre. He took a quick drink from his coffee mug and sat down behind his dark wooden desk.

"Eric," he said with his Afrikaans accent, "I'm glad you came in to see me this morning, something's come up."

"Oh really *oom*, what is it?" Eric had come to ask his uncle for a few weeks off work. It wasn't looking promising.

"My boy, the Kruger National Park, they are having a nightmare there Eric." Uncle Kobus shook his head. "The rhino poaching has escalated, it's completely out of control. They've asked for our help. We can't let them down Eric. I know that conservation is very important to you, you've always said that. And now's your chance to really make a difference my boy. I'd like to send you and Johan up to help them."

Eric's heart sank. He knew how important this job would be. It would be his chance to make a significant contribution in the fight to save the White Rhino. But the timing was terrible. What could he say? There was no way he could refuse. His own personal issues would need to be put on hold. Just a few weeks, then he'd go. He'd find Rachel and make sure she was okay.

As soon as he got back to his cabin, Eric grabbed his laptop and carried it over to the kitchen table. He couldn't leave this for that long without at least contacting her. He tried Facebook… Rachel Wright… nope, nothing. He tried every social media platform he could think of. Nothing, she wasn't on any of them. Finally he remembered he had her UK number!

After seven rings, the phone went to voicemail, and her beautiful British accent filled his senses, "You have reached Rachel's phone, Rachel is probably out doing something really fun, leave me a message lovely person, thank you."

Eric froze for a few seconds, and the beep came and went. Say something! Quick, anything, but don't sound like an idiot. He rubbed at his temple. "Rachel, I know you said not to try to contact you, uh… this is Eric… I just had to know if you are okay. I can't remember much from the night of the party. I'm sorry I didn't get to take you to the airport. Call me please… on this number. We need to talk."

He was an idiot, he sounded like a blithering fool. He took a deep breath, it was out of his hands for now. Now he'd wait.

CHAPTER ELEVEN

Rachel usually loved Friday night family pizza night. It was generally a raucous evening of family board games along with a selection of her dad's adventurous pizzas. Everyone would be there. Tonight however, she just wasn't in the mood. She felt like curling up in her softest pyjamas and going straight to bed for the rest of the month. There was no way she could get out of it though. With missing weeks of work, Rachel was busier than ever. She'd had a pile of tax returns to work on, which meant she'd missed the last few Friday get-togethers. No excuse was going to cut it this Friday.

Rachel chose the most comfy jeans and jumper she owned, pulled a brush through her wavy hair and headed down to the car park. The tide was high and Caswell beach was breathtaking in the setting sun. Her thoughts turned to South Africa. It was never far from her mind. How she missed it. It was a different sort of beauty. It was rough and rugged, dangerous. It made you feel so alive. Alive and free.

Rachel couldn't keep the thoughts away as she drove over to her parents' house. Eric. She'd listened to his voice message over and over. She could recite it word for word. She could hear the vulnerability there, the concern and confusion. Could he really not remember what had happened between them? Perhaps if he did remember it all, he wouldn't be so quick to call her. Particularly after what he'd shared about the promise he'd made. He was so honest with her.

Shame filled her. Rachel had not returned his call. He'd since tried another three times to reach her. Each time she'd let it go to voicemail. He hadn't left another message. Perhaps it was finally dawning on him, she just couldn't face him. She needed to forget.

Sounds of laughter and teasing spilled from her parents' house as Rachel parked in the drive. Deborah would be here with her boyfriend, Gavin, and so would Blake, most likely on his own. Rachel had hardly seen her older sister and younger brother in the weeks she'd been home. It was going to be good to catch up. If only she could hold it together through the long-awaited family interrogation.

"Hey, get in here!" Deborah opened the front door wide and hugged her baby sister. Deb was full of life and warmth. Taller than Rachel, with dark silky hair, she was striking. Deb was the heart of any gathering, and people loved her. If she didn't have such an inclusive personality, it would've been easy for Rachel to find herself living in Deb's shadow. But Deborah had always made her feel loved and encouraged. She'd decided early on to pursue a medical degree, and now she was a junior doctor for the NHS. She worked crazy hours, but somehow, with a few exceptions, seemed to make it to the Friday family gathering.

Blake came up behind Deb and queued for a hug. Rachel's baby brother was confident and at home in his own skin. A pilot who also loved to dance and knew how to enjoy himself. Blake was single and to everyone's amusement, had never had a girlfriend. This fact made him the butt of his sisters' 'That's why you're still single' jokes.

It had almost become a family tradition, whenever Blake said or did anything remotely offensive, the words 'That's why you're still single' would immediately come pouring out of at least one family member.

It was good to be together. Rachel went through to the kitchen to find her dad taking the last homemade pizza out the oven. He laid it on the counter carefully and embraced his little girl. "So good to finally have everyone together again!" he said as he started slicing up the large pizzas.

"Ooooo…. so what's on the menu Dad? I've missed your cooking!" Rachel rubbed her hands together.

"I thought you'd never ask! We have chicken and apricot pizza, this one's spinach and salmon, and this one is my new speciality… I've named it Seafood Extraordinaire!"

Rachel looked down at the pizza nearest to her and her stomach turned. Prawns, mussels and some type of small fish she couldn't identify. She had to get out of there and fast.

"Looks great Dad!" She shot out as she moved quickly into the adjoining living area. Her mom was piling plates and cutlery onto the large family dining table.

"Hi mum." Rachel tried to look more upbeat than she felt and went over to hug her.

"Hi sweetheart, it's good to have you here at last! You look a little drained, are you feeling okay?"

Her mom didn't miss a thing, it was what made her such a successful lawyer.

"Yeh, I am a little tired mum, it's been a long week. I've finally caught up on everything though, so it's time to relax!" she answered with a sigh.

"I'll make you some coffee then Rach, there's a lot to catch up on! We can't have you dozing off on us! We all want to hear every detail about Africa! You've kept us waiting long enough!"

And with that, the plans for the evening had been decided. Rachel could no longer avoid the onslaught of questions. They were coming her way whether she liked it or not. She'd have to do some skilful ducking and diving to make it through the evening unscathed, with her secret intact.

Her dad brought trays of sliced pizza to the table and gathered the others around. Rachel was relieved that Gavin wasn't there. She had enough to deal with as it was with the four of them, without adding his brilliant brain into the mix.

After saying grace, everyone grabbed a plate and piled it high. When it came to Friday pizza nights, it was more like a feeding frenzy than a starchy sit-down meal.

"Sooooooo Rachel, do tell! We can't wait to hear all about your trip!" Deb made herself comfortable in the closest chair and tucked into her chicken and apricot pizza.

"I don't know where to start. It was amazing really. The orphanage, the weather, the scenery, the people. I loved it!" Rachel smiled and stuffed a large piece of pizza in her mouth.

"So tell us about the orphanage. Where did you stay? What were your duties like? Did you have any social time? Tell tell tell!" Deb leaned towards her.

"The orphanage had a row of *rondavels*, they're like round rustic type huts, where visiting volunteers could stay. It was just a bedroom and bathroom, but it was lovely. I made lots of friends from all over the world. My main duties were feeding and changing two of the babies every morning, twins, Vusi and Nandi. Then I'd arrange activities for the older children in the afternoon." She was doing well, so far so good.

"Twins, how cute! And did anything scary happen? Anything dangerous? Africa seems rather dangerous from the outside!" Deb seemed hungry for something more juicy. Rachel would have to be careful with her answers. So far she was the only one doing the asking, all the others were riveted though.

"Well, there was this gigantic snake that one of the children came across in the garden at the orphanage. A black mamba, deadly poisonous."

"Oh wow, that's crazy, with all the children right there, how frightening." Rachel's mom looked horrified.

"And then what happened? Did they shoot it?" Deb moved to the edge of her seat.

"Haha no. They called a local game ranger to capture it and release it into the wild." She could see him then, in her mind. Eric. His eyes, his sideways grin, their dance under the stars, his breath in her neck, how he held her hand on the game drive, their kiss in the car afterwards, his scent, their night together... Rachel quickly shoved another piece of pizza in her mouth.

"Eww… I hate snakes. I can't even stand the sight of them!" Deb shuddered.

"Did you see any other wildlife?" asked Rachel's mom.

"Yeh, lots! Incredible!" Rachel wasn't sure she should share about the game drive, in case one question led to another...

"So what did you see?" asked Deb.

"Buck, hyena, rhino and elephants and much more."

"Oh wow, you must've visited a reserve to see those?" Rachel's mom knew how to dig for answers.

"Um yes, I went on a game drive one evening." Rachel fixed her eyes on the remaining pizza on her plate.

"Oh, with the other volunteers? Did your manager organise it?" Her mom searched her profile.

Rachel turned to face her. "No, I went with a couple of the local game rangers." She bit her lip and looked away again.

"The same one who caught the snake by any chance?" her mom asked.

"Um yeh… as a matter of fact." This was not good. Not good at all.

Rachel's mom nodded and smiled. Rachel thought she'd better get the attention off of Eric. "And you wouldn't believe what happened, speaking of danger! We came across a group of poachers."

"What? Really?" Deb leaned towards her.

"The rangers chased them off the reserve." Rachel tried to minimise what had happened, hoping to change the topic altogether.

"What? Like a car chase through the bush? At night?" Deb was beside herself.

Rachel looked over at her. "I guess."

"How are you so calm? Did they have guns?" asked Deb.

"Uh yeh, you could say that."

"Did they use them?" Deb's brown eyes were as huge as Rachel had ever seen them.

"Yeh they did, they shot at us a couple of times. Blew out one of our tyres." The whole group gasped. At least the attention was off Eric for now.

"What? Rachel you could have been killed!" Her dad dropped his piece of pizza onto his plate.

"Yeh I guess so. It was quite scary at the time."

The family was quiet as Rachel continued eating her pizza.

"Well I'm so relieved you're okay Rach, thank you Jesus." Her mom eventually broke the silence.

"Amen to that," added her dad.

"Tell us about the people you met? Anyone interesting?" Blake sitting opposite her leaned forward in his chair and raised an eyebrow in her direction.

"Uh yeh, lots of people. I had a young German girl in the cabin to my right, and a retired American lady in the cabin to my left. The three of us often went into the city together, shopping and sightseeing, especially in the first few weeks. It was really fun."

Rachel looked down at the last piece of pizza on her plate and her stomach lurched hard. It was the Seafood Extraordinaire.

"Uh excuse me." Rachel forced out. She covered her mouth as she moved quickly for the bathroom while trying to downplay the extent of her nausea. Rachel just made it to the downstairs toilet in time to empty her stomach. She rinsed her mouth and splashed cool water on her face. That was weird. She had strong stomach and could normally eat anything. Perhaps she'd underestimated the stress she was under this evening. She was also exhausted, an early night was what she needed. At least now she had a good excuse to leave the gathering early.

"Are you okay? Sweetheart, I'm sorry, was my pizza too rich for you?" Her dad looked concerned.

"I'm not feeling so well Dad. I think I'll call it a night and get to bed, it's been a stressful week with work."

"Okay Rach, we understand. Please call if you need anything. Would you like Dad to run you home?"

"No I'll be fine thank you, enjoy the rest of your evening." Rachel waved and made her way out to her car. Though she felt slightly better, the thought of that fishy pizza still made her gag. Rachel climbed in the driver's seat and headed for what she thought she needed most, her bed.

CHAPTER TWELVE

Eric was on the verge of losing it. Rachel had not returned his calls and it had been weeks now. He sat in the warm December sun on the veranda step of his little *rondavel*. The only thing keeping him sane was trying to catch these poachers. As soon as he and Johan had arrived at Kruger, they'd been sent for training, debriefings and a refresher course on gun handling. Daily target practise followed.

Now they were in the thick of it. They were so close. They'd managed to collect vital details about this poaching group. They just needed them to slip up one more time. Ordinarily, this opportunity would've made Eric come alive. He loved the adventure, the adrenaline rush, and feeling like he was making a real difference. But he just couldn't get Rachel out of his mind. He wished she would just contact him, so he could apologise and they could both move on. He'd lost all hope that they could ever have a future together. Her silence had made that abundantly clear, but he still wanted closure. He wanted to know what they had done, what *he* had done.

He wanted the peace he used to have. He'd prayed and asked for God to forgive him, though he still wasn't sure for what exactly, but it couldn't hurt to pray for forgiveness in general. He was also pleading with God, that he'd regain his memory. It was becoming increasingly unlikely that he'd hear the truth from Rachel, unless of course, he went there himself. It was his original plan before he was sent to Kruger. He'd coaxed her home address out of Suzanne, and he could ask his mom to post his passport to him with overnight mail. He could technically go straight to the airport once the new recruitment of game rangers arrived in two days time. Kobus had given him and Johan two weeks off. It was the perfect time, and perhaps the only way to closure and peace.

***

Rachel walked through to the cosmetics section of Tesco, and then onto an aisle of vitamins and medicines. She was still not feeling herself. At all. The nausea had not stopped and neither had the fatigue. But worse than both of those was the paralysing fear that was growing inside her. It now felt like a monster she could not control. A monster she had to face.

She took a deep breath when she saw the home pregnancy tests lined up on the top shelf. Without comparing brands or prices, she grabbed the closest one and threw it into her trolley. It bounced off a bag of potatoes and landed in full view at the front. Rachel grabbed it and hid it under a large bag of crisps. Out of sight, out of mind. For the next few hours at least, she could pretend that she was still in control of her life, that the monster was just in her mind.

***

Rachel's eyes blurred over as she stared emotionless at the plus sign on the pregnancy test. She sat on the lid of the toilet seat and watched her tears drip from her chin onto her jeans. And there she stayed for what felt like hours. She was on a runaway train, going where she didn't want to go. She was helpless and completely out of control.

Her life had always been predictable, and she liked it that way. That's why she was so shaken when Tomos had left her, it wasn't part of the plan. In fact she was probably just as much affected by the fact that her plans had been derailed, as she was heartbroken over losing the then love of her life. But that little blip was nothing in comparison to the ground-shaking earthquake that was hitting her now.

A thousand thoughts shouted at her from all angles as the tears kept falling. The loudest was "You have to tell your parents. Everyone will know." And then, "You're going to be a single mom. This was not part of the plan, nothing will ever be the same again." And finally, "You're such a failure, you brought this upon yourself. You have no one else to blame."

As desperate as she was, she knew that abortion was not an option. With her strong commitment to God, Rachel would never even consider it. Even though He felt a million miles away right now, she didn't blame Him. She could understand that she was only getting what she deserved. And then there was Eric… should she tell him? He deserved to know he was going to be a father. But was it fair to turn his world upside down? If he knew, he'd never be able to live apart from his child. Either one of them would have to give up their current life and move country. Perhaps it was better that Eric never know.

***

Eric stood in a queue at Oliver Tambo Airport, Johannesburg, dressed for the North Pole. It was the middle of the South African summer, but Johan had insisted, *"Boet, you're going to land in the UK in the middle of winter, you're going to vrek from the cold. Take my advice, just take my jacket, boet."* He knew what Johan said was true, but the jacket was too big for him and could not fit in his suitcase. There was no time for clothes shopping in Johannesburg before he left, and so here he was. He was convinced the other passengers were laughing at him under their breaths. Not too much longer and he'd be in the plane, where he'd be able to take the blasted thing off. The discomfort was a good distraction, and before he knew it, he was seated comfortably coat-free in his aisle seat. He imagined Rachel wouldn't be thrilled to see him, but would she at least talk to him? He wasn't sure, but he had to try. This was his last resort.

***

Perhaps this wasn't the best idea, bringing Deb along clothes shopping with her. The tightness of her jeans was a continual reminder that she was running out of time to pretend this wasn't happening. It wouldn't be long before everyone knew. She was hoping to grab a few pairs of more roomy jeans, but it wasn't exactly easy with Deb there to 'help' her.

"What about these?" Deb teased, holding up a pair of skin tight jeggings. She knew Rachel hated jeggings.

"Those are actually perfect, I'll take them." Jeggings, that's genius. Why hadn't she thought of them herself? This wasn't going to be so hard after all.

"I think I'll take a few in different colours." Rachel grabbed one of each without letting Deb see that she'd chosen a size bigger than she usually wore. Deb raised an eyebrow as Rachel rushed through check out. She was happy to have them packed safely away in her carrier bag.

"Come let's do lunch, it's Saturday! We have lots of time and you still haven't told me everything about Africa. It's on me."

Rachel followed her sister from the shop. "Uh yeh, that sounds nice." As much as Rachel didn't want to be alone right now, she didn't relish the thought of having to lie to her sister. Perhaps Deb would be satisfied with vague answers and sideline stories. Anything but the main event.

They found a quaint pub near the mall that looked inviting. Deb chose a table for two near the front window. It felt good to get out of the chilly wind. Rachel unwound her scarf and placed it along with her woollen hat onto her lap.

"Fish and chips?" asked Deb, perusing a menu.

Fish. Rachel didn't think she'd ever be eating fish again. Ever. She picked up a menu and scanned it for something that didn't turn her stomach. "I'll just have the veggie soup of the day Deb, thank you."

"What? No fish and chips? It's your favourite! Something's wrong with you today Rach. Jeggings, soup…"

"What can I say?" Rachel laughed nervously. "Just when you thought you knew me!"

"And extra bread please, " Rachel called as Deb went to the bar to order. "I'm starving!" She was proud of how upbeat she sounded. She couldn't let Deb keep thinking that something was off with her.

When their food arrived, Rachel tried not to look at the battered fish on Deborah's plate. The smell was bad enough.

"So tell me, I've been dying to know! Did you meet anyone special in South Africa? I've heard the men are so manly! Meat-eaters! I've heard they even eat it raw! Wild and outdoorsy, just your type Rach… and mine! So did you?"

And there it was. Should she tell Deb about Eric, just a little? She didn't need to tell her everything. Perhaps it would be a little morsel to satisfy her sister's need for juicy information.

"Well, they don't eat it fresh, it's dried and spiced… biltong?"

"Oh right. Okay. Now tell me!" She scooted her chair in closer and leaned her elbows on the table.

Rachel found her sister's eyes. "Uh yeh actually, I did meet someone. We're just friends now though."

"Oh my goodness! Spill it now!"

"Well, remember the snake story?" Rachel twisted the paper serviette between her fingers.

"Yeh."

"The game ranger who came to capture the snake…"

"Him! The game ranger! The same one who took you on the game drive and got shot at with you? *Him?* Rachel that is the most romantic thing I've ever heard! What's his name? What does he look like?"

Rachel blushed as she pictured Eric in her mind. "His name is Eric. He's just under 6 feet I'd say, blonde wavy hair, blue eyes, stubble."

"Rachel how have you not told me this already?"

"Deb, we're just friends. There was a lot of chemistry, but we only met towards the end of my stay, so there wasn't much time to really get to know each other." Rachel looked down and spooned more soup into her mouth.

"But you're in touch on social media right? You're face-calling him at least, right?"

"Deb you know I hate social media, and besides, what's the point? I'm never going to see him again. It seems like a waste of time. We both just need to move on." Rachel brushed it off with a shrug.

"Fledgling love is never a waste of time, Rachel have I taught you nothing? What if he's the one and you've written him off?" Deborah was as animated as she got. She popped another forkful of fish into her mouth. Rachel was starting to wish she hadn't told her about him.

"Uh… I don't think so Deb. He's never going to leave South Africa, and well… how would I live without you lot? It would never work." Rachel took another spoonful of soup.

"Hmmm, I hadn't thought of that. Still, it's very romantic to imagine it... the English rose with the rough and tough South African wildlife man, living in the plains amongst the wild animals. African sunsets, thunderstorms, acacia trees... falling asleep to the sound of distant hyenas... well perhaps you wouldn't be sleeping..." Deb winked. "Does he play rugby?"

"No I don't think so. Please, let's just leave it Deb." Rachel looked pained and stood to her feet.

Deb sighed and pushed her chair back. "Well okay if you insist. Do you have his number for me then?"

"Deb!"

"Or his friend's number then? You said there were two of them with you on the game drive."

"Deborah!" Rachel scowled at her.

"I'm kidding, I'm just kidding!" She laughed. "I can just see Gavin's face as I break the news to him, 'Baby, I've got myself an African wildlife man, sorry it's not going to work out with you and me.'" She laughed.

Deb was playing out this joke way too far. It was part of her charm, but today Rachel could do without the charms of Deb.

"I've always wanted to go to Africa," Deb said dreamily. She took her sister's arm as they left the pub.

"Okay, okay, this has gone way too far. Let's get you home; you have a shift tonight."

"Fine. Boy are you a barrel of laughs today," Deb said jokingly defensive as they walked down the pavement towards the carpark.

Rachel released a breath, relieved their afternoon together was almost over. Soon enough Deb would know the whole truth, and then there'd be no more joking about Eric.

CHAPTER THIRTEEN

Eric shivered and pulled the hood of Johan's blue jacket up over his head. He could still feel the wind whipping past him as he neared the large coach. He handed the bus driver his ticket and climbed onboard with his backpack. Swansea, Rachel's home. He would be there this afternoon.

The flight had been uneventful. His mind had been consumed with thinking and re-thinking what he was going to say when he saw her. Then he'd play out the whole scene of how she'd respond to each of the various first liners he'd come up with. None of the played-out scenarios ended well in his head.

The grey day suited Eric's mood. He wasn't expecting much. In fact he'd be happy just with the truth. The bus ride was exhausting with many stops along the way, and Eric was tired of thinking. He knew he needed to freshen up before he saw her. Should he go to a hotel first and head over to her the next morning? After a proper night's sleep he might even be able to construct a coherent sentence. But that was never going to happen and he knew it. He couldn't wait a minute longer. He just had to see her, exhausted and smelly though he was.

After crossing over the Bristol Channel along the massive Severn Bridge, he was finally in Wales. The rain started to fall and the clouds took on a darker shade of grey. Rachel had mentioned that the weather in Wales was fairly dismal a large majority of the time. But when the sun came out, the Gower was beautiful enough to take your breath away with its award-winning beaches around every bend.

Eventually the bus driver took the exit which led to Swansea Bay. Eric had travelled before, so he was accustomed to the thrill of being in a new country. This trip however, was different from any other. This was no sight-seeing trip. This time, he was a man on a mission.

After arriving at the bus station, Eric caught a local bus which served Rachel's area. He was impressed that he'd figured out the bus routes so easily, but now that he was on his final bus, his nerves kicked in at full throttle. With one hand he gripped his backpack strap, the other held the top of the seat in front of him. He couldn't miss his stop. It would still be a little walk from there to Rachel's apartment block, and he was going to get soaked. At least the rain would wash off some of the sweat and he would smell a bit better.

As the driver pulled to the side of the road, Eric took a deep breath and stepped onto the pavement. He pulled out the hand-drawn map he'd copied from Google maps before he'd left. He tried to shield it from the rain with one hand as he headed down the steep hill towards Caswell beach. Would she be home? It was almost six thirty.

The closer Eric got to Rachel's apartment block, the faster his heart beat. Water dripped off his hair and every part of him. He tried to calm himself down with deep breathing, but it wasn't helping. And there it was, right in front of him.

He stood outside the main entrance for what seemed like hours, gathering his courage. Pulling the small towel he'd packed out of his carry-on bag, he tried to dry himself off. At least he would look slightly more presentable. He double-checked the paper. Number 36. Eric managed to grab the main door as someone was leaving, and made his way up to the top floor of the three story block. If he wasn't in such a state, he would've been amazed at the beautiful spot near the beach that Rachel called home. As it was though, all he could manage was simply putting one foot in front of the other. The truth that he dreaded and longed for was close at hand.

***

Rachel heard the knock on the door and frowned. Who could that be? She'd gotten home from lunch with Deb, pulled on a jumper, woolly socks and a pair of her comfy new jeggings. Now she sat on the sofa watching her new favourite series, Heartland, with a fluffy blanket and a bowl of salted popcorn; her current craving.

Rachel had been watching much more TV than usual. She'd being going from one series to another. Getting lost in the story of someone else's life helped her to forget her own. She'd also been eating way too much junk food. She knew she should be eating healthier, but just couldn't find the will power. She reluctantly left the comfort of her sofa and went for the door.

As she opened it, the colour drained from her face. Her deepest desire and her worst nightmare rolled into one. Her mouth turned dry. "Eric," she managed to mutter, "what are you..."

"Rachel, I'm sorry. I had to come. We need to talk." And with that she let go of the door handle and Eric entered her small apartment.

She shut the door and turned to face him. "This is not a good idea Eric, believe me." Rachel began to panic on the inside. He could not under any circumstances find out about the pregnancy.

"I just want the truth Rachel, please. And then I'll leave you alone."

Rachel took a deep breath and tried to think. But her thoughts froze and she just stood there. He was so handsome, and just an arm's length away. Rachel had to act normal.

First things first, coffee.

***

"Uh... would you like a coffee? Or a tea?" asked Rachel, as she moved shakily to her little kitchen area. She was different, and she was rattled. Why was she acting so nervous and flighty? But Eric took the offer of a drink as a good sign that things were going in the right direction. "Oh okay, sure. I'll have coffee. I could do with some caffeine."

"Milk? Sugar?"

"Uh, *ja* please, to both, two sugars. Thank you." This was weird. Awkward. Were they now going to sit down together for a drink like old friends? It appeared that they were. "Can I change somewhere? I'm soaked." He spoke to her back.

"Um… yes of course. The bathroom is that way." Without making eye contact, Rachel pointed to a short passage.

Eric took his carry-on bag and dried off in the quaint bathroom. When he returned, she was waiting, a mug of coffee in each hand. She handed him a steaming mug and gripped her own as though her life depended on it. She was beautiful. Beautiful, but different, not like the fun Rachel he'd been with at the party a couple months ago.

She led the way to her sitting area, cleared the blanket and popcorn away and took a seat. Eric followed and sat in a recliner nearby.

"You shouldn't have come." She cradled the mug in both hands and looked at him over the top of it.

"I had to." He held her eye, the smell of the coffee vaguely comforting.

"You should've just left it alone, given us both the space and time to move on."

He frowned. "Rachel, you know I can't do that. I need to know," he said softly.

Just as Eric thought he wasn't getting anywhere, Rachel said, "Okay then…" She looked him straight in the eye, exasperated. "We crossed the line Eric... all the way." She sighed. "Are you happier now that you know?" Still she studied him.

Eric sucked in a sharp breath and frowned back at her. He had so hoped that things had not gone further than the kissing he remembered on the patio. "Oh no Rachel! How did this happen? I don't even remember any of it." He sat on the edge of the recliner, his head in his hands.

***

"We were both drunk, Eric. You more so than me." She shrugged. "We were emotional, vulnerable... things got out of hand." Rachel downplayed it, but she could see the pain in his eyes, and the shame. He'd promised himself that he would wait until he was married. How could she derail his life with the full truth of her resulting pregnancy?

Rachel took a deep breath and closed her eyes. If he was struggling to grasp this bit of news, imagine his response to the whole truth. She couldn't tell him. He needed to leave, and soon! As she studied him sitting there with his head in his hands, her heart squeezed. He was probably praying and repenting right now as he sat there. He looked exhausted, broken. Did he even know where he was staying tonight? She didn't want to interrupt, but eventually she asked, "Have you got some place to stay tonight?"

"Can I just ask you one more question? Was I gentle, did I pressure you? I'm not very experienced in..." He looked pained.

Rachel swallowed. She shook her head slowly. "No you didn't pressure me, Eric." She smiled sadly.

Eric breathed in slowly, exhaled and nodded. "Uh… no I haven't found a place to stay yet. I'll just go to a bed and breakfast or something. It doesn't really matter."

"You don't have to leave tonight, you're exhausted. My sofa's all yours if you want it." She had to offer, though she doubted he'd take her up on it.

"No Rachel, you don't have to have me here any longer, I know it must be awkward for you. I'll leave now." He stood and pulled his backpack over his shoulder.

Rachel insisted. "Eric, it's fine, really. I can't just send you back out into this rain, you've travelled so far. I promise nothing more will happen between us." She stood and took the empty mug from him.

"Ah Rach, I know that. Are you sure you don't mind?" He'd called her 'Rach', she loved it when he shortened her name.

"It's the least I can do. We were friends before all this happened." She gave him a little smile.

"Yes we were, maybe we could still be friends? I'm here until Saturday. We could hang out if you want? No pressure. You could show me around maybe?" He looked hopeful.

Rachel smiled, but she knew that any friendship with Eric would need to be short lived. And once he was gone, that would have to be the end of their friendship, if you could call it that, or she'd risk him finding out about the pregnancy. Perhaps she'd allow herself this. She could let herself enjoy being near him for the last little while. She could do that… she could pause reality, and pretend the freight train headed her way didn't exist, just for a little while.

"Yeh sure, why not?"

CHAPTER FOURTEEN

Excitement and terror filled Rachel in equal measures as she opened her eyes and remembered the evening before. He was here, right in the next room!

She stretched underneath her down duvet, and placed a hand on her tummy. So relieved the morning sickness had tapered off a little, Rachel closed her eyes. She thought about her baby, Eric's baby. Each little detail was already determined. She still wasn't sure how she felt about him or her. Afraid and overwhelmed perhaps. Though she knew her baby was innocent in all this, she couldn't help but feel it was God's way of punishing her. Revealing her sin for the world to see, with lasting consequences.

Rachel climbed out of bed and walked over to the window. She pulled back the curtain and glanced out at the rainy day. Thick grey clouds lay over the ocean hiding the skyline completely. She pulled on a jumper, slowly opened her bedroom door and snuck out into the living area.

There he was, fast asleep on his stomach, his hands under his head. Tussled dark blonde hair fell over one eye. Rachel couldn't take her eyes off the beautiful form. He looked so peaceful. Perhaps he'd made right with God last night. His face twitched as his hair tickled it. She smiled. He was waking up.

Rachel tiptoed over to the kettle and refilled it. It was time to get moving if she was going to make it to church this morning. Her family would be expecting her. What about Eric? She hadn't thought this far, last night was an emotional whirlwind she hadn't even fully digested yet. He'd want to go with her, but then she'd be forced to introduce him to the whole family. A disastrous idea if ever there was one.

"Good morning." He rolled over and sat up on the edge of the sofa bed.

Rachel glanced at him over her shoulder. The blanket shifted to reveal his bare chest. "Hi. Coffee?" Rachel offered, quickly averting her gaze to the cupboard at her head.

"*Ja* please; make it strong." His voice was groggy and he had that just-woken-up gorgeousness about him.

"Did you sleep okay on that thing?" Rachel pulled two mugs from the cupboard and set them on the counter.

"Oh *ja*, I could've slept comfortably anywhere last night, I was so tired. Thank you for letting me stay. I'll have to find a place today." He dug in the bag at his feet and yanked out a white t-shirt.

"Well there are some holiday cabins just up the hill, but I'm not sure if you can rent one on a Sunday. Most places are closed here on Sundays." Rachel stirred the coffee granules into the boiling water and added milk from the fridge.

Eric pulled the t-shirt over his head and stood. "Oh right, well..."

"You can stay one more night Eric, really. It's fine with me." Rachel opened the fridge and returned the milk carton.

Eric sighed as he neared her. "Okay thank you, but first thing on Monday morning I'll go and get a place. Wouldn't want your neighbours to start thinking badly of you."

"Thank you for caring about my reputation, but they won't even notice, honestly."

"So are we going to church this morning?" Eric asked hopefully as he took the coffee Rachel held out to him.

"Uh yeh, my family will be expecting me for the morning service."

"Mind if I come?" He took a deep swig of the hot brew.

How could she say no? She couldn't very well tell him that she didn't want him to meet her family. "Yeh sure, we leave in thirty minutes though."

"Thirty minutes! Do you have an iron I could borrow?" Eric asked as he scratched through his carry-on bag.

Rachel smiled watching him panic over creased clothes. "Just hand them over and I'll iron them for you." Rachel stretched out her hand towards him.

He straightened, a fistful of clothes in hand. "Rachel you don't have to do that, I know how to iron."

"My iron is temperamental, seriously, I'll do it. Hand them over." Rachel held out her hand, palm up.

He passed her a crinkled button-up shirt and a pair of brown trousers. "Thank you! What can I do?"

"You… can take a shower!"

"That bad huh?" He grinned and sniffed at his armpit.

Rachel laughed and disappeared into her bedroom with the creased clothes. This was all so normal and uncomplicated this morning. She knew it wouldn't last though. It couldn't. It wasn't founded on the truth. If it was, there'd be no laughter, no light-hearted conversation, only guilt, shame and the weight of the consequences for their actions.

***

Eric followed Rachel into the old chapel through the side entrance. The air smelled musty, but the colours on the wall banners were vibrant, their messages full of life, hope and love. The congregation was already seated, listening as the organ music played.

Eric could feel every eye on him as he took an aisle seat next to Rachel on the third pew from the front. Was he imagining it, or could he actually hear whispering?

"He's quite a bit more handsome than Tomos, isn't he Anne?"

"Yes he is Margaret, looks like Vicar Peter did the right thing after all, sending her to Africa."

"Yes very true Anne, I'd say she's forgotten about Tomos alright!" They cackled.

Eric stiffened and tried his best not to look at the elderly ladies behind him. He felt his ears turn red, and glanced at Rachel. She looked over at him with a knowing smile, her cheeks pink.

The service began with Rachel's dad doing a reading from the Bible. It was quite different to what Eric was used to, but he enjoyed worshipping with other Christians. Being in God's house always felt like home to him.

After the service, Rachel's dad, stood at the door greeting all his parishioners. When he got to Rachel, he hugged her. "Good morning honey, and who's this?" he asked looking up at Eric.

"This is a friend from South Africa, dad, Eric Pieterson."

"Welcome Eric, pleased to meet you, I'm Peter. I'm sure my wife, Lyn, would like to meet you also." He shook Eric's hand, then gestured towards Rachel's mom, who was chatting to a few ladies just outside the door.

As soon as she heard her name, Rachel's mom turned towards him, hand outstretched. "Hello, I'm Lyn. Lovely to meet you." Lyn took Eric's hand and squeezed it politely. Rachel could see the look of surprise in her parents' eyes, but they held it together well. "You two must come around for dinner. I have a roast waiting at home."

"Uh… mum I don't think..." Rachel looked back and forth between Eric and her mom.

Lyn placed a hand on her daughter's shoulder. "No I insist Rachel, there's plenty of food, and we'd love to get to know your friend a bit better. I won't take no for an answer."

"Well I guess we'll see you there then." Rachel's voice sounded flat. Perhaps she was just as uncomfortable with the idea as he was.

"Thank you for the invitation Mrs Wright… uh… Lyn." Eric knew he sounded a little stiff. He wasn't sure how to behave in front of Rachel's parents after what he and Rachel had done. It seemed as though they didn't know. If they did, they certainly wouldn't be inviting him for roast dinner. He was a fraud. He would just have to make it through the meal with a smile on his face, for Rachel's sake.

***

"They don't know," Rachel glanced over at Eric in the passenger seat. She accelerated up the steep hill and turned right into a narrow lane.

"I figured, that's why they're being so nice to me."

"They wouldn't treat you badly if they knew..." Rachel pulled the car to the side and allowed the oncoming traffic to pass.

"But they wouldn't be inviting me for dinner either, right?"

"Hmmm not too sure, maybe not." She pulled back into the single-laned road. "I'm sorry." She sighed. "I should've known this was going to happen. And I need to warn you, my mum's a solicitor. She knows how to ask the right questions to make people squirm." Rachel indicated and turned down another road that looked way narrower than he'd be comfortable driving on.

"It's okay." Eric sighed. "I understand why you'd prefer to keep this a secret. I'll be careful."

"Thank you."

CHAPTER FIFTEEN

Eric knew the moment he set foot in Rachel's parents' home. This was a bad idea. Rachel walked him down the hallway and into the cosy dining area. The table was formally set for seven. That was all of them. Rachel's mum hauled dish after dish out of the oven.

"Hi mum."

"Oh hi sweetheart." The smart lady looked up briefly and smiled.

"Did *you* cook?" Rachel dropped her keys and handbag on the kitchen counter and leaned against it.

"Oh no, you're safe today! Deb's been at it this morning while we were at church."

"That's a relief!"

"Hey!" Lyn tried to look hurt as she slid a tray of roast potatoes onto the table.

It was no secret that Lyn could not cook. At all. She could talk someone around in circles, have them confessing that their own name was in fact not their own name by the time she was done, but she could not cook to save her life!

"Hi Mrs Wright." Eric knew he sounded nervous, but didn't know how to fix it.

"Oh please call me Lyn, Eric. Make yourself at home. Could I get you a hot drink? Or something cold?"

"Yes please Mrs, I mean Lyn." He laughed anxiously. "Uh… coffee would be great, thank you very much."

"What a lovely young man, wherever did you find him, Rachel?" her mom asked loud enough for all nearby to hear. Eric laughed even louder. The older lady took a mug from the cupboard and scooped in a spoonful of coffee.

"Eric's a game ranger, mum. He was the one who came to catch the snake I told you about?"

"Oh alright! I see. So what brings you to our neck of the woods then Eric?" Rachel's mom was going straight for the jugular. She poured the boiled kettle water over the granules and mixed in a dollop of fresh milk.

"I had some time off work, and well… Rachel's told me about how beautiful South Wales is, so I decided I'd come and see for myself," Eric said as he took the cup of coffee Lyn offered him. Eric hated dishonesty of any sort, but of course under the circumstances, he couldn't just come out with the real reason he'd come.

"And what do you think?" asked Lyn, her eyebrows raised, arms crossed over her chest.

"It is as she said, incredibly beautiful. Rachel's apartment on the beach, it's just the most amazing spot. I'm hoping to go surfing there at Caswell later in the week."

"Oh lovely, it will be freezing though. You'll need a winter wetsuit this time of year. How long are you staying for Eric?"

"'Til Saturday Mrs... Lyn. My plane leaves on Saturday evening from Heathrow." He took a deep sip of his coffee, not realising how hot it was. He swallowed the hot liquid in one gulp and hoped no one noticed the flash of pain that crossed his face. So far so good.

A tall dark-haired woman and two men came bounding through into the kitchen with enthusiastic greetings.

The woman stopped short when she saw Eric. "Oh hi, I don't believe we've met. I'm Rachel's more fun sister, Deb. And you are?" The woman studied him with interest and held out a slender hand.

Eric reached out and took the brunette's hand. "I'm Eric, a friend of Rachel's from South Africa."

"Oh... Eric," Deb said with a knowing lilt in her tone. "*The* Eric." Her eyes turned wide as she looked at Rachel, then back at him. "I've heard *all* about you."

"You have?" Eric balked.

"Oh yes… Rachel's told me *everything*." She smiled knowingly.

"She has?" Eric struggled to keep the panic out of his voice as his eyes darted to Rachel.

"Uh… yeh, I told Deb about how you caught the snake at the orphanage, how we chased the poachers with Johan, and how we became friends," interjected Rachel with a shrug.

"Oh!" Eric laughed and it sounded a little too much like relief.

"Well it's *lovely* to meet you, this is my boyfriend, Gavin." Deb gripped the taller man's arm and looked up at him. "Isn't he handsome, Eric?"

"Uh -"

"And *this…*" She pinched the shorter man on the cheek and gave it a shake, "is my baby brother, Blake. He's still single, but we're working on that, aren't we Rach?" Deb finished with a little pat on her brother's cheek and a laugh. She was on form tonight!

Eric slipped his hands into his pockets and rocked on his heels. "Hi Gavin, Blake, good to meet you both."

And with that Deb marched past Rachel, grabbed her by the wrist as she passed and led her into the utility room. The door shut behind them, filling the kitchen with an awkward silence.

***

"*What* is going on? Eric? What's he doing here?" she whispered excitedly, and a little too loud. Her brown eyes were huge and imploring.

"He came to see me, now keep it down!" Rachel's eyes flew to the door.

"What? All the way from South Africa? His accent is to die for. He's completely gorgeous!" she squealed. "Did you even know he was coming? I thought you were never going to see him again! Rachel what are you not telling me?" Deb took her sister by the shoulders and gave her a little shake.

"Deb, we're just friends, really. Please just leave it there." Rachel knew she was asking the impossible of her sister. Accepting this explanation from Rachel went against everything in her nature.

"Well he obviously wants to be *more* than that! Why else would he fly half way across the world? I bet he doesn't treat *all* his *friends* this way!" Her eyes bulged as she searched her sister's face for answers.

Should she just tell her about their drunken night together? It would appease her for a while. Now wasn't the time though. "Deb, if you promise to stop with the questions, and go out there and act normal, then I'll tell you everything once he's left for South Africa. I can't tell you about it now, it's not the right time."

Deb took a deep breath and frowned. "Okay. Okay I can do that." Deb pointed her finger at Rachel. "But I'm holding you to it, do you hear me? The moment that boy is on that bus, and I mean the *moment*, I want to know what's going on here." She wagged her finger between Rachel and the door.

"Okay fine. They're probably wondering why we're both in here with the light off."

Deb straightened up and ran a hand through her hair. "Yeh, okay, normal, I can do normal..."

***

Rachel and Deborah appeared in the open-plan dining area and Eric felt the relief down to his toes. Rachel's dad, Peter, had cornered him for a mini interrogation about his family and his life in South Africa. It seemed the older man was fascinated by both.

"Dad, give the man a break," said Deb. "I need your help carving the roast please." She waved him over to the kitchen.

Eric smiled nervously and rubbed his hands together. Just as he thought he was off the hook, Lyn joined him then and took over from where Peter left off. "So I overheard a little of your conversation with Peter. You studied in Pietermaritzburg, a Bachelor of Science is that right?"

"Uh… yes that's right, and then I went on to do honours and masters."

"Oh lovely, what are your main areas of interest?" She leaned in close, her eyes hungry for answers.

"I'm mainly interested in animal behaviour and conservation of endangered species." Eric crossed his arms. "For the last few weeks I've been assisting with the tracking of rhino poachers in the Kruger National Park." He took a tiny step back, but the dogged woman pressed in closer.

"Oh how interesting! And Rachel told us you were shot at recently! Wow, how frightening! I've just been reading about all the effort Prince Harry has been making to assist the parks. It must be extremely rewarding when you actually catch them."

"*Ja* we were hot on their trail in the Kruger when my friend and I were relieved by the other rangers who replaced us. Hopefully they've caught the guys by now."

Lyn nodded with interest. "Oh I see, and then you thought a trip to Wales would be a nice change of scenery."

"*Ja* something like that..." More nervous laugher spilled out.

"Eric would you like another coffee?" Rachel interrupted.

Eric shifted his gaze to the beautiful green eyes. Just the sight of her was enough to calm his frazzled nerves. "*Ja* please. Thank you Rach."

Lyn narrowed her eyes at him. "And how long have you known 'Rach' for Eric?"

"We uh… met a few weeks before she was due to fly home to Wales." Eric rubbed the back of his neck.

"Oh I see, so not much time then to get to know each other," she said sympathetically.

"Uh… no. I guess it was just enough for me to realise that I'd like a little more time... to get to know her." Eric smiled, his gaze gravitating back to the blonde beauty in the kitchen.

Lyn's eyes followed his gaze to Rachel, then fixed back on him. "So tell me, what is it you like about her Eric?"

Eric shifted his weight to his other leg and tucked his hands in his armpits.

Lyn looked as though she was just warming up. "If you know enough to want to know more, well then she's made an impression on you. What is it you like so much?" Lyn's eyes narrowed.

Eric didn't hesitate. "The way she loves people, Lyn. Her compassion and her gentle nature."

Lyn leaned in close and lowered her voice. "She's a special girl Eric, but you wouldn't have recognised her just a little while ago. She was broken over a man who cared more about himself than her.

You aren't planning on doing that to our girl are you Eric? Leaving her brokenhearted?" Lyn's eyes pinned him in place.

Eric swallowed. "No ma'am, uh... Mrs, Lyn. I'd never…"

"Good. Good chat then." Rachel's mom nodded, patted his arm and left the room.

Eric felt as though he'd just finished testifying on the witness stand. A bead of sweat trickled down his temple. He swiped at it with the back of his hand.

"Dinner time!" Peter called in his grandest voice. He set the platter of meat down in the centre of the table and waved the group closer. Lyn entered with two large trays of roast vegetables. The family made their way into the dining area and took their seats around the oval table. Eric took the final remaining chair next to Rachel. When her father started to say grace, he closed his eyes and took a calming breath, a minute free from questions and prying eyes.

Dinner time consisted of hearty laughter and much banter. Blake was sharing his most recent embarrassing moment, and the girls followed the story with their 'and that's why you're still single!' jibe. Lyn had relaxed to the extent that it was hard to imagine their earlier conversation had even taken place. And after a little while, Eric felt himself start to relax too. He wasn't used to big family get-togethers. With his dad's alcohol problem, his mom had avoided them at all costs. Eric understood why, she didn't want to give him an occasion to get drunk. He couldn't help imagining though what it would be like to get together with his own family like this one day. A few grown-up children and their spouses, even grandchildren maybe.

And who would be there alongside him, Rachel? Laughing, loving, being the heart of their family. He smiled to himself. It wasn't all that hard to imagine.

CHAPTER SIXTEEN

It was a beautiful Sunday night, dark and cold, but crystal clear. The ocean glistened in the light of the moon as it hung low over the water. And Eric did something he'd wanted to do ever since he'd arrived. He hired a winter wetsuit and a surf board at Caswell beach.

"You're crazy," Rachel sang the words as she watched him pull the wetsuit over his shorts. She hugged herself as a chilly breeze rose up over the inky water. Eric zipped up the suit, gave her a cheeky wink and ran for the water, surfboard under one arm. "You're a crazy African! You've never even felt water this cold!" she called after him.

"Yep, that's me! I'm a crazy, wild African!" he yelled back as he hoisted himself into the freezing water, hair flying.

He needed this release after an emotionally draining weekend. When Eric saw the size of the waves, he knew he couldn't pass up this opportunity. They weren't big by African standards, but they were big enough to surf tonight, and that's all that mattered.

***

Rachel followed after him and found a rock to sit on. She cradled his things in her lap and watched him paddle and surf the waves. It was hard not to dream of them together. Very hard. He was everything she wanted in a man and in a husband. She kept having to remind herself of the reasons why it was just a fantasy. Reminding herself brought her back to reality and she felt a tear slide down her face. Just then, Eric smiled and waved at her. She grinned and waved back, all the while remembering just how temporary this happiness was.

He bounded up out of the water and ran towards her, shaking his hair like a dog after a bath. Water sprayed all over Rachel and she squealed. "Noooooo!"

Eric put a hand on either side of where she sat on the rock, and leaned in close. There was teasing in his eyes. "Oh you think that was bad hey? How about a nice hug..."

"No, don't you even think about -" She pointed a warning finger at the dripping man.

"Come here girl!" Eric reached for her.

Rachel managed to escape him with ducking and diving and grabbed his towel as a shield. "Don't you dare Eric! Don't you dare come any closer! I'm warning you!"

"But Rachel, I thought we were friends..." He spread his arms wide and edged towards her again, laughing. She threw the towel over his head, turned around, and ran for home.

"Rachel you can't outrun me," he shouted and yanked the towel off. "Seriously? She's seriously going to try to outrun me?" he said, more to himself than Rachel who was now half way to her apartment. "Here I come, you'd better run!"

Rachel could hear the footsteps right behind her now. Eric circled her waist from behind, and pulled her towards him. They both lost their balance and landed in a heap on the sand.

And suddenly she was in his arms. He let her go quickly, but didn't get up. Neither did she. The mood shifted. His arm was under her neck, her body pressed against his chest and she could feel his warm breath on her face. She looked down, avoiding his gaze.

Eric lifted her chin with his thumb and looked into her eyes. "You need to know something Rachel," he said as he lightly touched her hair.

"What's that?" she asked softly.

He whispered back, a glint in his blue eyes, "I'm a very fast runner." He teased. "You can't outrun me, I ran for my province. I will catch you, every time."

Rachel laughed and shoved him away as she stood. He took her hand as they walked the little way back to her apartment.

CHAPTER SEVENTEEN

Monday morning and it was raining again. Eric walked over to the glass balcony door and pulled back the floral curtains covering it. The beach was wet and empty. He smiled to himself thinking about the night before. It was just as well that he kept up his fitness or he wouldn't have been able to walk this morning after that sprint on the beach. He'd wanted to kiss her so badly, but he wasn't sure how that would've gone down. She was definitely keeping him at arm's length a whole lot more now.

"Good morning!" came a feminine voice from behind him.

He smiled at her over his shoulder. "Good morning to you!"

She was irresistible in a soft cream knitted top and dark blue jeggings. Her hair was down, just the way he liked it. She ambled over to the kitchenette and filled the kettle.

Eric suddenly realised he was still half naked. He found a t-shirt on the top of his bag and pulled it over his head. He was rapidly running out of clean clothes, particularly warm ones. Wales was colder than he imagined it would be. He was so grateful for Johan's big blue coat.

"Rach, I don't want to get in your way, if you have work to do or whatever, I understand. I'm going to take a walk to those holiday cabins and see if I can rent one until Saturday. After that, if you could just point me in the direction of a shop where I could get a few more warm tops? I can catch the bus. I didn't bring nearly enough and this African boy is not made for Welsh winters."

Rachel turned and leaned up against the kitchen counter. "Eric, I'll take you. We can go past the cabins now on our way, and then to the mall."

"Rach are you sure? I really don't want to interfere with your work." Eric collected a few stray items of clothing and shoved them into his backpack.

"Trust me it's fine." She smiled as she stirred his coffee and then her tea.

As she handed him his coffee, their hands touched. A jolt ran up his arm. This was not good. He would have to guard his heart with her, especially with her keeping her distance the way she was. He had to continually remind himself that he was leaving on Saturday.

They ate a quick breakfast of cheese and toast and headed off. Stopping at the holiday cabins along the way, Eric managed to rent himself one right in the woods, but near the beach.

The mall was lovely and quiet on a Monday morning.

"Surf shops please!" said Eric with a grin.

Rachel feigned shock. "What? No way!"

"Okay, okay. I'm predictable I know. Just lead me to a good one."

Eric liked to keep things simple. So when he found clothes that he liked, he stuck to them. Life was too short to get bogged down with trying to keep up with the latest fashions. Rachel led him to a large one near the entrance. Eric strode over to a rail of jumpers on sale. He found his size in a few different styles and flung them over his arm. Done.

"What, no trying on? No indecisive back and forth about which ones to get?" She tilted her head, a smile playing on her lips.

Eric shook his head. "No Rach, when I know what I want, why waste time? Life is too short to bother with things that don't matter. Come, let's go."

Rachel followed Eric over to the check-out and he paid for his jumpers. The moment he walked out the door, he grabbed a red one out the bag, yanked off the tags and pulled it on. Eric was pleased with himself. "See, no mess, no fuss, perfect fit."

Rachel laughed. "I wish it was that easy for me! Looks good."

"You think?" He looked down at the Salt Rock jumper and checked the length of the sleeves.

"Yeh, you always look good to me."

Eric's heart warmed and took her hand, threading his fingers between hers. "So what's for lunch? My treat! What can we have that's really Welsh?"

"Oooo I know just the thing, come with me!" She pulled him along by the hand. "Prepare to be amazed!" she said with a naughty twinkle in her eye.

***

Eric stared at the tub of black slime and tiny sea creatures. He frowned. "Rach, are you having me on?"

Rachel had taken Eric to the indoor market near the mall. It was packed with vendors selling all sorts of food, clothing and local fare. "No, I'm being serious Eric. This is a Welsh delicacy. It's cockles and lava bread."

"Well then where's yours?"

"Well I'm not Welsh, and I've tasted them before," she shot back.

"What is it?" Eric looked from the tub up into the dancing eyes before him.

"Well you know what cockles are?" Rachel pointed out the hideous bottom feeders.

Eric scrunched his nose up. "Little sea creatures that come out of shells?"

"Yeh, and lava bread is seaweed." She shrugged.

Eric's eyes bulged in horror and Rachel couldn't stop the snicker that followed.

"Just try it you big baby." She perched a hand on her hip and waited.

Eric closed his eyes and raised the spoon to his mouth. It was like eating algae and small garden snails. A mixture of cold slime and gritty flesh. It was vile, possibly the worst thing he'd ever tasted. But as vile as it was, he couldn't let Rachel win. It took all of his will power... "Mmmmmm this is delicious!" He hooted. "He he he! Oh wow!" he cooed, mouth full of black slime, and spooned more into his mouth. "What have I been missing all my life!" Another spoonful went in until he'd scraped out the entire tub.

"I'm so pleased you enjoyed it so much Eric! I'll get you another tub!" Rachel sprang up to the counter.

Eric tugged at her shoulder. "No really Rach, you don't have to…"

"No I insist!" She looked back at him. "It's not every day you get to eat a Welsh delicacy! Could we have another tub please, large this time." Rachel handed over a five pound note.

"Aaaaw thanks Rach, you shouldn't have." Eric launched his best grin as he took the large tub and plastic spoon.

"Go on, I'm sure you're still hungry." She watched in anticipation.

"I uh… I don't want to waste it Rach, I'll… keep it for later…" He patted the lid of the tub a few times.

Rachel smiled, she'd won and she knew it. They walked around the market and did a little shopping. Eric found a necklace for his mom and a huge "I love Wales" T-shirt for Johan. On the back it said, 'Fancy a *cwtch*?', meaning 'Fancy a cuddle?'. It was perfect.

They stopped in at the grocery shop en route to the car and Eric bought enough food to fill his mini fridge at the cabin.

Eric looked over at her as they arrived back at her car and packed their parcels into the boot. She looked tired. Eric climbed into the passenger seat and turned to her. "How about we have a lazy evening, get some take out and watch a movie at my cabin? Unless of course you need to go home to work or rest, I'll understand."

"Yeh, that sounds like a great idea." She said as she started the engine. "Who's choosing?"

"Choosing what, the movie? Or the take out?" asked Eric with a sideways smile.

"Both." Rachel watched her rearview mirror as she reversed out of the tiny parking space.

"You can choose the movie, I'll choose the take out!" Eric wanted to make sure they were taking home something other than another Welsh delicacy.

Rachel laughed. "Oh so you won't be having your cockles and lava bread for dinner then?"

"Saving it, for later." He rubbed his stomach. "Much, much later."

***

Rachel smiled. She loved being with him. This is how it was over the few weeks they'd had together in South Africa. They were so good together. She remembered every detail.

"So I think I'm going to go with KFC if that's okay? Is there one near here?" He drummed his fingers on his thigh.

"No problem, let's go through the drive-through." Chicken, she just might be able to stomach.

Before long they had their order on Eric's lap and were headed to his cabin. The wooden rentals were just fifty metres or so from the beach. It was very quiet during the winter months, and it seemed like Eric had the entire place to himself. Rachel pulled her car up at number 15, which backed onto the woods. It was a beautiful spot. Though it was only around five in the afternoon, the sun was already starting to go down and darkness was settling around them. Eric got his bags out the boot of the car, unlocked the door, and followed in behind Rachel.

"Very nice, but cold!" he said as he placed the bags down on the kitchen counter.

Large windows overlooked the woods on one side of the cabin. A roomy sofa, tv, and coffee table took up most of the living area.

"Rach, can you put the heating on please? And show me how?"

"Yeh, course." Rachel found the boiler and turned on the central heating.

"So I think we've got Netflix or something on this tv..." Eric found the remote and turned it on.

"And I've found some coffee sachets!" Rachel busied herself making two cups, while Eric tried to figure out the Netflix.

"So what genre are we going for Rach?"

Rachel thought for a second. She couldn't choose anything remotely sad, she'd been so much more emotional with the pregnancy. "Let's go for an action movie or something."

***

Eric could hardly believe his luck. Could the girl be any more perfect? "Right!" he said quickly before she changed her mind. "Bourne Identity?"

"Yeh okay, let's do it."

Rachel placed the coffee mugs on coasters on the table and brought a couple of plates through for the chicken. She was ravenous. Once their plates were full, they got comfortable on the soft sofa and started the movie. Eric couldn't believe how quickly Rachel ploughed through her food. After wiping her fingers on a paper towel, she took a cushion and lay on the opposite side of the sofa with her feet on the floor.

Fifteen minutes into the movie and Rachel was fast asleep. Eric looked over at her and smiled. He fetched a spare blanket from the bedroom and covered her with it. Then he lifted up her feet, removed her leather boots, and placed her feet on his lap. This was the life.

Once the first movie ended it was still quite early. Rachel showed no signs of waking up, so Eric moved on to the next Bourne movie. By the end of that one though, he was tired and ready for bed. He smiled down at the sleeping beauty on his couch. He didn't have the heart to wake her and have her drive home now. She looked so peaceful, and didn't flinch when he touched her hair and ran his thumb down her cheek.

CHAPTER EIGHTEEN

"Eric I'm sorry. I was so, so tired last night!" Rachel was sitting on the sofa pulling on her boots as Eric walked through the living area, fully dressed for the day minus his shoes.

"Good morning sleepy head." He tousled her hair as he walked past towards the kettle. "I'd like to think that it was you who was really tired, and not me who was really boring!" He laughed as he flicked the kettle on. "Coffee?"

"Uh… no thanks. Well I *am* starting to get a bit tired of you." She teased.

Eric gawked at her over his shoulder.

"I'm just kidding, kidding!" joked Rachel as she zipped up her boot.

Eric shook. "How do I put up with you?" he muttered to himself as he poured boiling water into his mug. "Trying to poison me with lava bread, falling asleep on me, insults…"

Rachel laughed as she stood and straightened her jersey. She took her woollen coat off the hook behind the door and pulled it on. "So it's Tuesday morning, and I'm going to have to put in a bit of work this morning Eric. Maybe we can meet at the beachside café for lunch at around one?" Rachel did up the buttons and flung her scarf around her neck.

He turned to her, coffee mug in hand. "Sounds good."

She ran her hands through her tangled hair and gathered up her purse and keys.

"I'll see you later." She smiled as she opened the front door.

"Bye Rach. See you soon."

Rachel was no sooner out the door when she was wishing she was back there with him. The cold wind whipped her hair off her shoulders. Rachel wrapped her scarf tighter around her neck as she walked. Saturday morning was going to be hard. She was dreading it.

Once back in her apartment Rachel took a hot shower and settled at the desk near her bedroom window. She loved doing accounts. It was the one place in her life where things still made sense. It was logical and no emotion was involved. A few hours of work felt like a welcome rest from her out-of-control life.

Before she knew it, it was twelve thirty. Rachel brushed her hair and put on some make-up. Once happy with her reflection, she pulled on her leather boots and coat, locked up, and started the walk across the bay to the café. The tide was quite high, and she just managed to make it through on the sand before the water started touching the rocks. The tidal range was extreme, and walkers who had been cut off by the quickly rising water often needed to be air rescued. It was deceptively dangerous. A thick mist had settled over the beach and Rachel could just make out the café in the distance.

***

Eric pushed open the glass door of the café and made a beeline for the corner table near the open fire. He was cold and hungry after spending the morning walking along the cliffs. He'd packed his bible and a flask of hot coffee for the morning. When he'd found a bench with a beautiful view, he'd sat and connected with God. He'd needed the time to think and pray, especially with what had happened with Rachel in South Africa, but also now, when he felt that he was more in love with her than ever. In some ways he wished he could remember that night, then he could feel that conviction and repent. It was weird repenting for something he had no memory of, but he'd done it anyway. He hated feeling far from God, and when he did, he knew it was because of his own actions. God had not left him, and would not leave him, ever.

Johan had first invited Eric to church when he had just started working at the lodge. Johan was also new to the area and looking for a church to attend. He asked if Eric would go with him to try out a church he'd found online. It was the same church that Uncle Kobus went to. It was a large, vibrant church, and Eric was overwhelmed at first. But Johan kept inviting him, and Eric kept going along with him. Then one Sunday evening, everything Uncle Kobus had been saying about Jesus became a reality to him. Eric could feel Jesus drawing him and calling him. He felt His love and something deep inside him changed. It wasn't an experience he could put into words, but from then on, Eric believed. He was baptised the next week, and had walked closely with God ever since that day fifteen years ago.

And now, here he was in a café on a Welsh beach waiting for the girl he was in love with to arrive for lunch. Despite his failings, he couldn't help but feel blessed. Saturday was coming though, and that meant goodbye. Still, he'd make the most of every moment he had with her.

***

Rachel felt the warmth of the café against her ice-cold cheeks. She unwrapped her scarf and scanned the small diner. She loved this café, with its large spread of windows just metres from the beach. She found Eric sitting at a table near the front window, the roaring log fire just behind him. What could be more romantic? He was wearing one of his new jumpers, and had hung his huge blue coat over the back of his seat. He caught her eye and smiled. Her heart squeezed as she neared him and took the seat he offered her. She shrugged off her coat and hung it on the back of her chair.

"You look beautiful." He crossed his arms on the table and studied her.

"You're not half bad yourself," she answered cheekily, leaned over and pulled a '50% off' sticker from his new jumper.

Eric chuckled. "Haha, nice. So, did you get some work done?"

Rachel folded the sticker in half and found his blue eyes. "Yeh, I'm on top of things. What've you been up to?"

"I've been walking your amazing cliffs along the coast." Eric gestured out the window to the left where a footpath snaked around the edge of the mountain.

"Aaah that explains it…" She grinned.

"Explains what exactly?" He frowned.

"Your pink ears, nose and cheeks of course!"

He laughed. "Okay so I'm not exactly cut out for a Welsh winter. Next time I'll be more prepared."

Next time. Would there be a next time? If she didn't want Eric to know about the baby, then there could be no next time. Was she doing the right thing by not telling him? How could it ever work out? No, these few days were all she'd allow herself. Then she'd have to move on, and so would he.

"So what's good to eat around here?" he asked, pulling a menu from the stand on the middle of the table.

"Just about anything, but on this chilly day, I'm going to go for lasagne."

"Right, okay! Two lasagnes coming up." Eric went over to the counter to order the food while Rachel glanced out the window at the roaring waves. The tide was now just a few metres from the café. The mist had thickened and hung like a cloud over the grey water.

Eric returned and broke into her thoughts. He lay his hand, palm up, on the table and waited for her to take it. When she did, he closed his fingers around hers and looked at her intently. "Rach, I spent some time praying this morning and just thinking. Do you think you could clear up a few things for me about that night? You don't have to… if you feel too uncomfortable." He shifted in his seat.

The vulnerability in his eyes made her insides ache. "What do you need to know?" she asked softly.

"Well... how did it happen?"

It was Rachel's turn to feel embarrassed. She looked down for a second, and then met his eyes. "Well... we were chatting on the patio couch and drinking a bottle of wine."

"*Ja*, I remember that bit." He rubbed his forehead with his free hand, eyes still fixed on hers.

"And then we started kissing. You... started kissing me..." She swallowed. The memories were as vivid as if it were last night.

He rubbed the back of his neck. "*Ja* I remember that. Go on, please."

"And then you picked me up and carried me to the bedroom, where there was more kissing and then one thing led to another..."

They sat without speaking. Eric closed his eyes and rested his head on one hand. He looked at her then, his eyes filled with regret. "Rach, please forgive me. I can't tell you how much I wish that we could start over." He swallowed.

Oh how she wished the same thing. She'd never wanted something so badly in all her life. "Me too," she said softly, "and I do forgive you. Besides it was both of us, not just you. I'm sorry too Eric. Your promise..."

He nodded sadly. "Rach, I just can't tell you how relieved I am."

"About what?" She frowned and shifted forward in her seat.

He sighed. "That you're not pregnant. Imagine what that would've meant. I mean, did we even use protection?"

Rachel's mouth turned dry. "No, we didn't Eric."

"Can you imagine? I don't even want to think about how our lives would've had to change. I am *so* not ready to be a father that's for sure. We can be so thankful." He squeezed her hand.

Rachel just looked at him and nodded. And there it was. The reason she could never tell him the full truth. He didn't deserve to have his life turned upside down, and from his own lips, he wasn't ready to be a father. As painful as it was to hear, she needed to hear it. She needed to constantly remind herself of all the reasons why this could never work.

Their food arrived then and Rachel was relieved to have a distraction. Eric looked ravenous as he added salt and tucked into his steamy lasagne. Rachel loved watching him eat. He was so... not British.

"What?" He frowned at the amused expression on her face.

"You… you're just..." She shook her head, a smile tugging on her lips.

"Just what?" He shoved another forkful of lasagne into his mouth and chewed.

"Just so… so African." She laughed as he picked at the side salad with his hands.

"What's that supposed to mean? I'm a bit rural or something?"

"Yeh that's exactly it!" She nodded. "You've hit the nail on the head!"

"This is just me enjoying my food, eating with my hands, this is nothing my girl."

His girl, Rachel's heart tightened. "Oh there's more is there?" Her green eyes danced.

"Oh there's much, much more. You don't know the half of it!" He teased and took another huge mouthful of lasagne.

CHAPTER NINETEEN

The next few days flew by like a whirlwind. Rachel had to work most of Wednesday, and so Eric caught a bus to explore the Gower coastline. The following day, Rachel had a doctor's appointment in the morning. That evening Eric walked over to her apartment to invite her for a walk on the cliffs. She hadn't contacted him after her doctor's appointment as planned, and he hoped that whatever it was, was not serious. He approached her apartment door and knocked.

No response. He knocked again, slightly louder this time.

Finally Rachel peeped around the door with one towel wrapped around her body, another around her head. Eric could hardly breathe at the sight.

"Eric, sorry I just got out the shower. Come in, I'll just be one..." Rachel disappeared into her bedroom.

"Uh... sorry for the intrusion, I didn't realise..." Eric swallowed and closed the door. He couldn't help but think that if they were married he'd be seeing her like this almost daily. They'd be sharing all the intimacies of each other's lives. Despite the warning voice in his head, he yearned for that type of closeness with Rachel.

He looked around and walked over to the kettle to make coffee. "Rach," he called out into the empty living room. "Can I make you a cup of tea or coffee?"

"Tea please!"

Eric found two mugs drying at the sink and put coffee into one, a tea bag into the other. She came walking out dressed in jeggings and a hoodie, drying her damp hair over her shoulder with a towel. He could smell her shampoo from the other side of the room. She was irresistible.

"So how'd it go at the doctors?" he asked cautiously as she neared.

"All good, I'm very healthy!" She smiled as he stirred the tea and removed the bag.

He studied her briefly. "Okay, so just a check up then?"

"Yeh, just a check up." She tossed the towel over the back of the sofa and took the cup of tea he held out. "So what do you want to do tonight?"

Eric sighed and turned to face her. "Well… we are running out of time here Rach…" He grew serious and took a step closer. Reaching for the cup in her hand, he placed it on the kitchen counter behind her. Then he entwined both his hands with hers, palm to palm, and looked at her intently. "Please tell me you have nothing on from now until I leave."

Rachel smiled sadly. "Nothing except a family fun night on Friday."

Eric looked pained and raised an eyebrow. "Oh boy, is it compulsory?"

"Yeh, I'm afraid it absolutely is."

"Hmmm... we could feign illness, a stomach bug would do nicely."

Rachel giggled. "They're not *that* bad, come on now."

"Who, your parents?" He gawked. "We are talking about Peter and Lyn are we not? They are *worse* than bad! Rachel I lost about 10kgs on Sunday!"

Rachel laughed at the memory of that bead of sweat trickling down his temple. "It won't be as intense this time, they've already asked all their pressing questions. All that's left is to enjoy your company!" She smiled, her head tilted.

"Pfffft! I don't buy that for a second. Your mom was just getting warmed up!"

"I'm sorry Eric... I know it was a tricky evening." She squeezed his hands.

"No worries, Rach. You're worth it." He rested his forehead against hers and felt his heart start to pound in his chest. Rachel looked down and then back up into his blue eyes. Her lips parted. He wanted to kiss her, badly. But what good would that do? It would only make Saturday harder. As it was, he didn't know how he would be able to say goodbye to her. With every day it became increasingly clear, the more time he spent around the beautiful blonde, the more he knew without a doubt, that his heart, was hers.

***

Rachel woke up on Friday morning with a heavy heart. She dragged her body out of bed and towards the kettle. Just one more day and he'd be gone. Then she'd have to face her new reality. They'd planned to meet at the beachside café, and spend the day alone on the cliffs together. But when Rachel looked out the window and saw the heavy rain, she knew their plans were going to have to change. She heard a knock on the door and knew it was him. Her pulse hammered as she moved to open it.

"Hello gorgeous." He walked in soaking wet and irresistible. His blue coat which had done well up until now to keep him fairly dry, was drenched right through.

She laughed at his nonchalance. "Eric, wow. Don't you look...uh…" She hurried to the bathroom for a towel.

"Wet, well *ja,* I'd say." He called after her, "Wales gives a new definition to the terms 'drenched', 'soggy', 'soaked' and 'washed out'." He grinned and a drop of water dripped from his chin and onto the laminate floor. "It doesn't look like our cliff walk is going to happen today, sorry Rach," he said as Rachel handed him a towel.

"Well I've got an idea, but I'm not sure you'd be up for it." She raised her eyebrow in challenge.

He rubbed his face and hair hard with the white towel, then emerged from behind it, hair at attention. "Lay it on me!"

She giggled. "That's an interesting look on you." Rachel reached out and ran her fingers through his damp hair, trying to style it. It was just as soft as she remembered. "How about we go go-karting?" Her eyes glinted.

Eric handed the towel back to her with a glint of his own in his blue eyes. "You're on beautiful!" He pointed a finger at her. "Speed is my thing!"

***

Eric looked around, impressed by the size of the indoor arena. This was an elaborate set up. He followed Rachel to the back of the queue, itching to get on the track.

"So, are you feeling lucky, punk?" Rachel had a rosy glow on her cheeks and a cheeky look in her eye.

"Oh very!" Eric nodded, just as confident. "In fact, I'm so sure I'll win, that to up the stakes, I think we should make a little wager." Eric wasn't so sure how wise this was, but he couldn't help himself.

"Let's hear it!" Rachel crossed her arms, sounding very sure of herself. Perhaps he *should* be worried. She had likely driven this course many times and seemed convinced she had the upper hand with her home advantage.

"The winner gets a kiss from the loser. Simple as that." He shrugged. How could he lose? Either outcome would end with him getting a kiss from the beautiful blonde.

"Hmmm..." Rachel said thoughtfully. "Any fine print?"

"Terms and conditions… well let's see..." He rubbed his stubbled chin thoughtfully. "The winner should receive his or her prize before tomorrow morning. Anything you want to add Rachel?"

"Nope that sounds good. Get that pucker ready!"

They reached the front of the line, bought their tickets, and put their helmets on. Eric could not afford to lose; there was more than pride on the line.

He climbed into his little kart alongside Rachel's and revved the engine. Rachel looked over at him from her kart and glared. Then she mouthed the words, "Bring it on!" and floored her accelerator.

Eric knew he'd met his match when all he could see was the dust rising from the back of Rachel's go-kart. He wasted no time, he flattened his accelerator pedal and sped after her. Rachel took her turns tight and fast, it was clear she'd raced this track many times. At every turn Eric tried to pass her on the inside but she was just too fast. Eventually it was the final stretch and the beautiful blonde just took it.

Eric removed his helmet and grinned at her. "Well, well, well, a girl who can race. Impressive."

Rachel removed hers and just smiled.

"Best of three?" Eric suggested cheekily, an eyebrow raised.

"Why not? Let's do it." Rachel was more confident than ever.

After learning the track on the first race, Eric made a much quicker start on the next round and managed to get ahead of Rachel. She was right on his tail until the finish.

"Alright then," Rachel said as she climbed out her kart. "It's game on! The big finale!"

They had a quick drink at the vending machine and were once again in their go-karts at the starting line. This time they were neck and neck at every turn. Eric felt the adrenaline pulse through him, he was determined to win this wager. He managed to get the upper hand on the final turn and edged ahead right at the finish. He was smiling even before he had his helmet off his head. He stood triumphant and called to her, helmet in hand, "Where's my kiss?"

Rachel smiled. "I have until tomorrow morning to give it to you. I might just have to wait until you're sleeping," she said as she climbed out her kart.

"What? That's not -"

"It's perfectly in line with the terms and conditions. A little kiss on the cheek shouldn't wake you."

Eric's face fell, his jaw dropped.

She ambled over to him, a hand on her hip. "Your terms and conditions were absolutely useless. I'm a lawyer's daughter. How easily you forget." She patted his cheek.

"Cruel, heartless woman! How can you deprive a man of his well-deserved prize based on some minuscule fine print loophole? Disgusting!"

She raised both eyebrows cheekily. "Watch me!" Rachel turned and sauntered away.

"Rachel!" he called after her.

She turned back and threw him a quick wink over her shoulder. "Just kidding." She laughed as he caught up with her.

"Okay, whenever you're ready then. Let's have it." He stood facing her, his heart in his throat. He swallowed.

Rachel placed a hand on his chest. "Later okay? Not here."

He raised an eyebrow. "Okay, but I can promise you now beautiful, that I will be collecting my prize."

CHAPTER TWENTY

The mood was festive as they drove to Rachel's parents' home for pizza night. Eric turned on the radio and they both sang along and acted silly all the way there.

As they entered the house, the smell of melted cheese filled the hallway.

"I'd forgotten how hungry I was!" Eric said to Rachel as they made a beeline for the kitchen.

Rachel turned back to catch his eye. "Eric, you haven't seen pizza like this before. You might just lose that appetite altogether! Consider yourself warned!"

"Rachel and Eric! Hello and come on in!" Rachel's father was in his element, 'I love Wales' apron tied around his thickset waist.

"Hello Peter. It's good to see you again."

"And what have you been cooking up tonight, dad?" Rachel gave Eric a grin.

"Well, I've got blue cheese and cinnamon pizza over there, red pepper and carrot pizza over here… and in the oven, the showstopper, hummus and leek!"

"Mmmmm, sounds… adventurous."

"You only live once, honey!"

And with that in walked Deb and Gavin with Blake in toe. After all the greetings, hugs and high-fives, everyone grabbed a plate and started on the pizzas. Eric was surprised that no one seemed to mind the strange pizza toppings. He decided to do likewise, grabbed a plate and filled it. After the unusual meal, the family gathered around the table for an evening of Pictionary. Rachel's mom arrived home late from work and joined in the fun.

As the evening went on, Eric was acutely aware that his time with Rachel was running out. He'd hoped they'd be able to sneak away early for a romantic dinner, but it seemed that wasn't going to happen without some sort of miracle. When Rachel got up to get a drink from the kitchen, Eric excused himself also.

Leaning against the kitchen counter, he sighed. "Rach..." His voice was rough.

"Yes I know..." Rachel filled a glass with water from the tap.

"Can we slip away?" he asked quietly.

She nodded and led the way back to the dining room. "So, I've got to get Eric home early, he has a long trip ahead of him," she announced.

"Good bye all!" Eric raised his hand in a small wave. "Thanks very much for a great evening guys."

He watched Deb give Rachel a knowing wink. Perhaps she did know more than she was letting on. Once they'd said their goodbyes, they headed back to Eric's cabin.

***

It was another cold, clear night and Eric turned up the heat as soon as they arrived at the wooden cabin. As Rachel put the kettle on,

Eric came up behind her. "So, it looks like the perfect moment for me to collect my prize." He grinned hopefully.

"Nice try smooth guy, but I get to decide when." Rachel continued making coffee.

Eric brushed her loose hair to one side and ran his fingers down the side of her neck. Rachel breathed in and gritted her teeth. He wasn't going to make this easy. "Not fair, you're not playing fair..."

"What? By doing this?" He kissed her neck. His lips soft as a petal against her skin.

Rachel closed her eyes and felt the sensation down to her toes. "Your prize is for *me* to give, not for *you* to take." Rachel turned around to face him, the side of her mouth curving upward.

"Hmmm... well okay then..." Eric tucked a strand of her hair behind her ear. "But I don't know how much more patience I can exercise here Rach. I'm a patient guy, but..."

"You'll live!" She grinned as she handed him a cup of coffee.

"Oooo Rachel Wright, you know just how to tear a man's heart out!" Eric feigned anguish, but in actual fact, the anguish was starting to feel very real. The clock was ticking on their time together, and he was not nearly ready to say goodbye.

***

Rachel laughed as she got comfortable on the sofa. Eric sat down next to her and stretched his legs out on the coffee table, mug in hand. "So, tonight was fun. Your family didn't decide to off me, which was a plus." He smiled at her.

"Haha! And… we could've won if you'd known what a parsnip was!" She poked at his shoulder.

"How can I draw something I've never even heard of? Parsnip? We don't get those in South Africa! I've never seen one in all my life!"

Rachel laughed at how defensive he was being. Eric hated losing, and when he was to blame, well, even more so then.

"Rural African! Doesn't even know what a parsnip is… tut tut…" Rachel teased, shaking her head.

"Rachel, it's like me asking you to draw a… a *beshu*."

She thought for a moment. "Yeh, I could draw that no problem."

"Okay then, prove it." Eric jumped up and searched around for a pen and paper. He handed her a till slip and a pen from out the kitchen drawer. "Let's see your best *beshu* then Rach."

Rachel tried to hide her smile as she drew the perfect traditional animal skin rear apron, worn by young Zulu men.

"What? You *know* what a *beshu* is?" Eric gawked, holding the slip close for inspection.

"You bet, I've just been to Africa! And there's lots about me you don't know Eric," she teased.

"Okay, like what?" he asked as he settled back next to her on the leather couch.

"Wouldn't you like to know!" Rachel crossed her arms, a teasing lilt in her voice.

"Come on Rach, let's hear it..." He squeezed her knee.

Rachel couldn't help the disappointment that filled her when he moved his hand away again. "Well… I can surf."

"You? Surf? Really?"

"Why are you so surprised? That's rude!"

Eric laughed. "Oh sorry, *ja* I can totally see that. Are you any good?" He looked at her hesitantly.

"I'm okay." She smiled.

"Hmmm… I'm impressed. We'll have to surf together sometime then. What else don't I know about you?" Eric pulled her hand onto his thigh and played with her fingers.

"I hate social media," she said, her eyes fixed on their hands.

"Right okay, that explains why you're not on there."

"Oh did you do a little search for me?" She looked at him, amused.

"You bet!" Eric laughed. "Tell me more..."

"I've had a few boyfriends, but only one serious one."

"Tomos, your ex-fiancé right?"

"Yeh."

"So, what happened Rach?"

Rachel sighed deeply. "He changed his mind. Decided he didn't want to marry me after all." She found his eyes. "Or anyone for that matter. He said marriage just wasn't for him."

Eric nodded. "I see, that must've been quite rough for you Rach." He squeezed her hand.

"Yeh, it was for a little while there. But not anymore. Now I feel like I dodged a bullet!"

Eric laughed. "I hope you don't say that about me someday… to some other man."

"Eric I don't think you realise."

"Realise what?" Eric frowned.

"What I feel for you is very different to what I felt for Tomos."

Eric studied her. "How so?"

She averted her eyes. "We probably shouldn't go there Eric. You're leaving tomorrow and that'll be the end of it."

"Tell me Rachel."

"There's no point Eric." Rachel pulled her hand away from his and crossed her arms.

Eric took a deep, frustrated breath. "Well then, come back with me Rach. Come back with me and then there *will* be a point. Then we'll have a future."

"I can't do that Eric." She turned to face him.

His shoulders sagged. "Don't we owe it to ourselves to see where this goes Rachel?"

"Eric, you're asking me to give up my home and my family, everything I know. I haven't even known you for more than a few months."

Eric sat still and resigned. Finally he nodded. "Okay Rach, I understand."

"I wish things were different Eric."

He exhaled. "*Ja* me too. I love you. For what it's worth." He shrugged in resignation.

The tears spilled onto Rachel's cheeks and she lay her head on his lap. Eric could feel his own welling up and he swallowed. He put his hand on her head and stroked her hair. And that's how they stayed.

Eventually Eric could hear Rachel's breathing deepen and he knew she was asleep. He'd arranged for a taxi to take him to the bus stop tomorrow morning, mainly to spare them both a traumatic goodbye in full view of the public.

Eric gently lifted her head, placed a cushion under it, and covered her with a blanket.

For a long while, Eric just sat there on the edge of the coffee table, watching her sleep. Then he stood and went to his bedroom to pack the few things he'd brought.

***

Rachel stirred. Where was she? Eric's cabin. The previous night's conversation landed like a boulder in her soul. It was over. Her and Eric, their time was up, and now it was time for goodbye.

She checked her phone. 5:15am. He'd still be asleep, she should probably just sneak out now. It would make things easier for them both. But she had to see him, just one more time.

Rachel tiptoed into his bedroom. He was sound asleep on the far end of the double bed. She walked around quietly and looked at him. Tears welled up and spilled over onto her cheeks. She stepped closer. She could see the rise and fall of his chest. Another step and she could smell his cologne. One more step and he was inches from her. She leaned down and kissed his cheek. He didn't stir. She grazed his cheek with hers, and then, with her lips just centimetres from his, she kissed his mouth. When Eric responded, Rachel couldn't pull away. He wrapped his arms around her neck and pulled her closer.

"Come with me Rach… please come back with me," he whispered roughly in her ear.

"I'm sorry. Goodbye Eric. I love you." And with that she pulled away from him and hurried from the room.

CHAPTER TWENTY-ONE

Rachel ran. She let the tears fall without restraint as her legs carried her as fast as they could over the sand. She wrapped her coat around her as the wind whipped hard on every side. She'd never felt such a deep despair, not even after Tomos left her. She was being ripped in two, with one half of her leaving for good.

Once back in her apartment, she shut the curtains, climbed into bed and sobbed. She hoped she was making the right decision. Surely it could never work with one of them giving up everything to be with the other.

After she'd cried until there was nothing left, Rachel poured herself a bubble bath and sank deep into the warmth that covered her. She placed her hand over her baby, Eric's baby, and closed her eyes. She felt comforted in one way, that she'd always have a piece of him with her.

When the clock passed the time that Eric was meant to leave, Rachel felt the tears well up again with a vengeance. He was gone.

Rachel wrapped herself in her bathrobe and put the kettle on. Just then there was a knock at the door.

"Rach? Are you home? It's me, Deb. Open up! We have some unfinished business." Deb sounded so upbeat, that it took all of Rachel's strength to let her in.

"Finally! Hey, are you okay?" Deb frowned when she caught sight of Rachel's tear-stained face.

"Um… no. No I'm not," Rachel answered quietly.

"Oh Rach, of course, he's just left. I'm so sorry." Deb came over then and embraced her younger sister. Rachel was tired of crying, but Deb's embrace drew more tears from her already swollen eyes.

"I'm here because you promised to tell me everything once he'd left. Is now a good time? Maybe it will help to get it all out."

"I'm pregnant Deb." Rachel spoke into her sister's shoulder.

"You're what? Pregnant?" Deb's eyes flew open and she jerked her sister back. "Who did this to you? I wanna know now!"

"Deb, the baby is Eric's." Her heart ached just saying his name out loud.

"But how did this happen?" Deb was still frowning.

"Deb..."

"Yes I mean I know *how*, but how did you *let* it happen?"

Rachel sighed from deep inside her. "On our last night together in South Africa, we got drunk together. That mixed with our chemistry and emotions running high… this was the result."

"Oh wow! Wow..." Deb eyes grew even larger. She blinked a few times, stepped backwards and sat on the armrest of the couch. "Do mum and dad know?"

"No, you're the first person I'm telling."

"So, did Eric come to see you about the baby? Is that why he was here?"

"No, Eric knows nothing about the baby. He doesn't even remember our night together. He came here because he needed answers about what happened on that night. I gave them to him, and now he's gone."

"He knows nothing about the baby?" Deb's eyes never left hers.

"No."

"Rach *why* not? Are you *crazy*? You could have an amazing, supportive man at your side through all this."

"Deb, it's not that simple! I couldn't ask him to give up his life in South Africa. He was born to do what he's doing there. If he knew about the baby, the guilt of not living near us would drive him crazy or alternatively, he'd give it all up, move here and end up resenting me."

"But Rachel, that's *not* your choice to make! That's *his* choice. He needs to know he's going to be a father."

"Deb, I don't wanna talk about this now, please."

Deb looked pained. "Sit Rach, I'll finish up making the tea." Deb stood and moved towards the kettle. "When are you going to tell mum and dad?"

"Tomorrow after church. It's going to break their hearts." Rachel plopped down onto the couch.

"They'll be shocked at first, maybe disappointed, but they'll come around."

"I know. Still, I'm dreading it." Rachel held her head in her hands.

"Want me to come with you?" she asked, placing a mug of tea in front of Rachel on the coffee table.

"Yes, please Deb."

Deb leaned over and squeezed her hand. "So, tell me how it feels to be pregnant? How far are you?"

It was good to finally tell someone the truth. Rach and Deb spent the rest of the day and evening chatting and dreaming about what the baby would look like and what sort of mother Rachel would be. By the end of the evening, Rachel felt confident that with the love of her family, she could get through this. With the four of them by her side, she could survive anything.

***

Eric's legs felt like lead as each step took him further and further from Rachel. He'd boarded his flight and landed at King Shaka Airport the next morning. The thick humidity was suffocating, so he slipped into the men's room to change into a t-shirt and shorts. Johan would be waiting at arrivals and Eric looked forward to seeing his friend. Perhaps he would have some wisdom for how to deal with the situation he found himself in now.

As Eric walked through the doors he spotted his friend instantly, head and shoulders above everyone else in the vicinity. Still, Johan waved his arm and grinned. "*Boet!* It's good to have you home my *china!*" Johan said loudly and slapped Eric on the back. Then he took one of the bags from Eric.

Eric smiled. "Great to see you *bru*. Thanks for fetching me. Where're you parked?"

"Not far. Come, let's go."

The sun was setting over the hills as they drove, and the familiarity soothed Eric's soul. He shared with Johan what had happened between him and Rachel during their night together, as well as all the details of the past week. It felt good to empty himself of all the emotion inside of him. His mind wondered to Rachel. What was she doing now? Had she found the gift that he'd hidden in her apartment? Perhaps a gift wasn't a good idea, considering the way things had ended. At the time though, it felt like a romantic thing to do. He'd found the necklace in a curio shop during his time at the Kruger National Park. It was perfect for her, she was going to love it.

***

The Sunday morning service was over far too quickly. Rachel knew that she could no longer hide her pregnancy from her family. Today was the day to tell them everything. Deb had met her at church and sat with her through the service, quietly offering her support for what lay ahead.

When Rachel and Deb arrived at their parents' home, Rachel couldn't stop the tremble in her body. She glanced at herself in her rearview mirror and took a deep breath, steeling herself. As she left her car, Deb appeared and took her hand. Together they walked into the house.

The smell of roast chicken greeted them and they could hear their parents chatting with Blake in the kitchen.

"Hello you two!" Rachel's mom welcomed them in the hallway and offered them both a drink.

"No thanks mum, not for me," said Rachel.

Her mom studied her, and then moved her scrutiny over to Deborah. "Is everything okay girls? Something seems a little off with you both?"

Rachel's mom was like a bloodhound, and Rachel was actually surprised that she'd managed to keep this from her for so long. She decided she'd rather wait 'til after lunch to tell them, and so she brushed off her mom's question. "Yeh fine mum, we're both just a little tired after our late night of girl bonding last night."

"Yeh okay, let me make you some coffee then."

"Sounds good!"

After the meal, while the family was still seated at the dining room table, Rachel leaned forward in her chair, her heart pounding. She cleared her throat and tried to keep the tremor from her voice. "There's something I need to tell you all." She took a deep breath. Her family looked at her with worried expressions.

"When I was in South Africa, I met someone."

Her mom grinned. "I knew you and Eric had something going on…"

"Uh… mum, just let Rachel finish," Deb said quietly, taking her sister's hand.

"Yes Eric." Rachel swallowed. "Well Eric is more than a friend, shall we say."

"He's your boyfriend?" asked Blake. "Rach, why's that a big deal? He's great."

"No, he's not my boyfriend." Rachel was struggling, and took another deep breath before she said, "He's the father... of my... unborn baby."

The room went dead quiet. Nobody moved. They all stared at Rachel in disbelief.

Rachel needed to fill the silence. She rambled on, "We really liked each other, a lot, and on my last night in South Africa, we were both emotional, and we got a bit drunk, well… very drunk you could say, and then one thing led to another, and now... here we are." Rachel took in a sharp breath and looked around the quiet room.

Deb smiled. "Well, I'm going to be an aunty, how exciting!"

No one else spoke and Rachel looked from one face to the other. She'd never seen her mom lost for words before.

Eventually, Peter spoke up, "Okay Rachel," his voice was scratchy and broken, "we just need a little time. Thank you for telling us."

"When is the baby due?" her mom asked, barely louder than a whisper.

"June 6th."

"So you're..." Her mom found her daughter's eyes.

"13 weeks tomorrow."

"And Eric? How does he feel about all this?" The subdued woman threaded her hands together on the table in front of her.

"Eric doesn't know mum. He doesn't even remember what happened between us."

Lyn's eyes grew large. "Sweetheart, you have to tell him. You tell him as soon as possible."

"He should do the honourable thing, Rachel," said Peter.

"Dad, I'm not expecting Eric to move to Wales. He belongs in South Africa. I can't tell him, it would ruin his life."

Rachel's family agreed with Deb, that Eric deserved to know, but Rachel remained adamant that she was doing the right thing for her and for Eric.

CHAPTER TWENTY-TWO

Eric lugged his backpack onto his sunny bed and collapsed alongside it. He stretched out and drew in a deep breath of warm African air.

A gentle knock sounded at the door. He knew exactly whose knock it was. "Come on in, mom." Eric jumped off his bed and went to greet her in the kitchen.

"Welcome home my boy, I've missed you." Janice embraced him warmly.

"I got you a little something." Eric returned to his bedroom and dug around in his backpack. Finding the little black box, he strode back to the kitchen. "This is for you."

"Awww... you didn't need to get me something." Janice opened the box to reveal a beautiful gold chain. "Eric, I love it!"

"Here let me help you put it on."

Janice turned and lifted her long blonde locks while Eric did the clasp. She dropped her hair and turned around to show him. As she touched the necklace, Eric noticed something he'd never seen before. His mom had removed her wedding ring, the ring she'd been wearing night and day for well over thirty years. What could this mean? He didn't want to ask her, he'd wait for her to tell him when she was ready. He couldn't help but wonder though, was his mom finally moving on? Eric sincerely hoped so. They were long overdue for a catch-up. Eric put the kettle on and told her all about his feelings for Rachel. It was time.

***

Rachel had just started on her accounts for the day when her phone rang. It was the ringtone she used for her mom, and she was a little apprehensive to answer. After telling her family everything yesterday, Rachel felt tender. They didn't exactly embrace the situation, not that Rachel had expected them to, but she'd hoped for a bit more warmth. Instead, they'd asked for time to digest the news.

"Hello mum." Rachel leaned back in her chair and gazed out at the calm, silvery ocean.

"Hi honey. How are you feeling?"

"I'm okay thanks mum."

"Rach, I need to talk to you. It's probably nothing, but there's something I need to share with you… under the current circumstances."

"Okay mum, I have time now, what is it?"

"Oh I can't do it over the phone darling. How about we meet at the beachside café for a coffee in an hour."

"Okay sure mum, I'll meet you there."

By the time Rachel arrived, her mum was waiting at a table with a cup of tea. Rachel ordered an orange juice and joined her mum at the table near the window.

"Hi honey." Her mom placed her tea cup down on the table.

"Hi mum."

They sat in silence for a short while before Rachel spoke, "Look mum, I just wanted to clear the air. I know you must be wondering how I let this happen, and how I could've been so stupid. It's not really consistent with the behaviour of a church-going 31 year old vicar's daughter."

"Sweetheart, that's not what I'm thinking at all. But, I do have some questions."

"Please just ask them mum, whatever they are. I need the air cleared between us now."

Lyn threaded her fingers together on the table. "Okay, well… do you love him?"

"Do I love Eric?" Her heart felt torn open by the question. "Yes, but I've only known him a few months, mum."

"I know you said he could never leave Africa, but have you considered moving to be with him? And in time, you could be a family." Rachel had thought about it, and had come to the same conclusion every time. She needed her parents, her siblings. She loved her life in Wales. She couldn't imagine living away from home permanently. "Mum, I can't just leave. This is my home! Where my family is." She felt like a stuck record on this point. No one was getting the message. "Next question please."

"Well no more questions for now, but I need to tell you something Rach. Now that you're pregnant, you need to know. Before I was born, my mum, your Nan, gave birth to a baby son. He unfortunately was born with a rare disease and didn't make it to six months old."

"Mum, I'm so sorry." Rachel frowned.

"The disease is genetic Rach, your baby will need to be tested. Just as a precaution, it's very rare." Lyn handed Rachel a slip of paper with the details written down.

"It's called Severe Combined Immunodeficiency Syndrome. Just get the baby tested Rach, but I'm sure it will be fine. I had all three of you tested. You all tested negative, but you could be a carrier."

"Okay mum, I will make a doctor's appointment." Rachel tucked the paper into her purse.

"I'd love to go with you to your next scan if I may Rach?" The corner of her mom's mouth lifted.

"Of course, I'd love to have you there mum."

Lyn reached for her bag at her feet. "Okay well, I'd better get going. Please let me know if there's anything you need. Anything at all."

"Thanks mum."

***

Getting back into the routine of work was good for Eric. Though Rachel was still on his mind continually, working and being with people gave him less time to think, and got him through the day faster.

He arrived at the reception early for his first drive of the day, only to find the desk unmanned. He headed back into the staff-only area and found Uncle Kobus and his mom in the back room, mulling over some papers together.

"Good morning!" Eric surprised them from behind.

"Morning Eric." His mom turned to greet him with a smile.

"My boy! Welcome home! We've missed you. I hope your trip went well." Uncle Kobus embraced him, slapping his back as he did so. "Hope you didn't freeze over there in England!"

"Wales *oom*. *Ja*, it was very cold, but so beautiful. It's good to be back at work though. I can't be away from the bush for too long *oom*."

"*Ja*, of course, I understand." The Afrikaner squeezed his nephew's shoulder. "And it's another busy day Eric. We have every game drive fully booked again today."

"That's great! I'm going to fetch the land cruiser." He pulled the keys off the hook near the door. "Have a good day, both of you."

As Eric left, he couldn't help but wonder if perhaps his mom and Uncle Kobus were becoming more than just good friends. They'd known each other for ages - firstly as in-laws, while Kobus' brother, Eric's dad, was alive, and then as close friends since then.

But today, something felt different. Eric couldn't put his finger on it, but he hoped he was right. Was *he* the reason she'd removed her wedding ring? They both deserved a second chance, and he knew they could make each other happy. He only wished they hadn't waited so long.

***

Rachel was running late for her doctor's appointment. She'd planned to do a little shopping before, and had struggled to find parking. Eventually she'd found a space, but it had set her back at least ten minutes. It was pouring with rain, which didn't help either.

She rushed into the surgery and up to the counter. Thankfully she was led straight into an examining room.

"Good morning Rachel." The doctor was an older, fatherly type, and Rachel felt at ease with him instantly. She'd seen him a few times in the past for minor illnesses, and was pleased to have him for today's appointment. She removed her wet coat and sat in the chair in front of him.

"Morning doctor."

"What can I help you with today?" The man pulled out a yellow file and opened it.

"Well I'm three months pregnant, and we have a genetic condition in our family."

"Oh I see. Well congratulations on your pregnancy. Can you tell me more about the condition?"

Rachel realised then with sadness, that he was the first person to congratulate her, a near stranger. "Um yes…" Rachel retrieved the slip of paper her mom had given her. "It's called Severe Combined Immunodeficiency Syndrome. My uncle had it. He died as a baby." Rachel had been trying not to think about that fact, but saying it out loud brought a new fear into her heart. She knew the risk was small, but still, perhaps it was much larger because the disease was in the family. She couldn't help but imagine how much better she'd feel if Eric was sitting next to her right now.

"Okay, what I'll do Rachel, is schedule an amniocentesis. There is a very slight risk with the procedure, but under the circumstances, it is highly recommended that we rule out SCIS. And if your baby is positive, then the earlier we detect it, the better. I'm going to refer you to a consultant, who will take over your care from now on. His name is Doctor Simmons, and you'll need to see him at Singleton hospital."

Rachel took a deep breath. Maybe this was a whole lot more serious than she'd realised. "Thank you Doctor." Rachel felt light-headed as she left the surgery. So much so, that she sat in her car for a few moments to compose herself.

The rain hammered down on the windshield. What if her precious baby had this awful syndrome? Rachel knew she'd need to be fully prepared, just in case. She covered her stomach with both hands. "Please God, please protect my baby. He or she doesn't deserve this," she whispered.

CHAPTER TWENTY-THREE

Something was definitely going on, and Eric was going to get to the bottom of it. Preferably, without upsetting his mom or Uncle Kobus in the process. He was laying out fresh hay and water for the rhinos as Uncle Kobus approached. He hauled a large bale up into the trough and turned to greet his uncle. "Hello *oom*."

"Eric, how's everything going over here my boy?"

"They are doing really well *oom*. Sophie is finally eating the quantity she should be taking, and Oubaas is loving the pellets."

"Good, good. You are doing an excellent job caring for them Eric. But I didn't come over here to check on you, I uh… wanted to have a talk with you." Uncle Kobus fished a hanky from his pocket and wiped it across his brow.

Eric frowned. He'd never seen his uncle so pale. "*Ja oom*, anytime." Eric used his hand to shield his eyes from the low afternoon sun.

"Okay, well… it's about your mom." He swallowed and dug his hands into the pockets of his khaki shorts.

"Is everything okay *oom*?" Eric wondered if he should make this easy on him, Uncle Kobus looked ready to pass out.

The older man cleared his throat. "I know that you've been, and are, a very good son to her Eric. And I know that you have been through a lot together, some very hard times." Uncle Kobus moved to the wooden fence and gripped it with both hands.

"*Ja oom*." Eric joined him at the fence and leaned up with his side against it.

"I never thought I could love a woman again my boy, after your aunt passed away. But your mom has become more and more precious to me over the years. And it seems that the Lord is blessing me once again…" The anxious man looked him in the eye. Was that a hint of vulnerability there? "Eric, I want to ask your permission to ask your mom to marry me."

Eric balked, his eyes wide. "Oh wow, *oom*. I wasn't expecting that. Marriage I mean…"

"*Ja*, I'm sure you must be quite surprised, but I've had feelings for your beautiful *ma* for quite a long time now."

"*Oom*, I am very happy for you both, I just have one question."

"*Ja*, of course. Ask whatever you need to know my boy."

Eric shifted his weight to his other leg. "Does my mom feel the same way? Is she ready for a marriage proposal?"

Uncle Kobus sighed. "My boy, we are about to find out." He rubbed the back of his neck, then scratched at the side of his face.

Eric smiled seeing him this rattled. "Okay *oom*, I'm sure you know what you're doing. Let me know if you need help setting up a romantic mood for the big question."

Uncle Kobus' face fell. "Seriously, my boy? Must I now set up a romantic evening or something? I was just going to go over there and ask her. That's what I did the first time round with Lindie, and we were married three months later."

Eric's jaw dropped. "*Oom,* you might need some serious romance for this one. You can't go in cold *oom*."

The older man frowned, then sighed. "Okay, I'm listening." He crossed his arms over his chest and leaned his ear towards Eric.

"If you want to romance a lady, you need preparation. Take her on a night drive, pack a picnic, have it under the stars. Then speak about your future, and how she belongs in it."

"Okay that is very good advice my boy. I will organise it."

Eric patted him on the back and laughed. "Can I call you 'dad' then?"

Eric was just kidding, but Uncle Kobus answered seriously. "*Ja* of course, my boy. I've always seen you as a son anyway." He smiled and strode off towards the reception.

***

Rachel had a growing ball of nerves inside her stomach. The amniocentesis had been scheduled for this afternoon, and her mom was on her way to fetch her.

She turned up the Christmas music, and put on the kettle for a quick cup of tea to calm her nerves. Finding a mug in the cupboard, she set it on the counter and placed a teabag inside it. Then she noticed that the mug wasn't empty. She fished out the bag and saw a black jewellery box lying underneath it.

Rachel frowned as she tipped the velvet box into her palm. It creaked as she opened it. Her heart caught at the sight of the most delicate gold chain. But it was the pendant attached that touched her. It was in the shape of South Africa, and inscribed on it, in beautiful calligraphy-styled writing were the words, *'South African Love'*. How true those words were! Rachel stroked the pendant with one finger, and let herself remember. Eric, dressed in his khakis driving his Land Rover. Eric, trying to impress her with his meat *braaing* and ridiculous barn dancing. Eric, showing her the wonder of African wildlife. For Rachel, South Africa was synonymous with Eric. Eric lived and breathed Africa. So when Rachel read the inscription, all she saw was, *'Eric, my South African Love'*. And she knew it would always be true.

***

"And that's it Rachel, all done." The young doctor stuck a plaster over the area and pulled her t-shirt back down.

"That's it?" Rachel couldn't keep the relief from her voice.

"Yes. You're going to want to take it easy for the rest of the day." She smiled. "No heavy lifting or flying. If you experience any severe cramping, leaking of amniotic fluid, spotting or fever, come straight back in."

"Okay. Thank you. Mom, are you okay?" Rachel looked up at the pale woman next to her.

She took a few slow breaths, then asked "Is shopping too strenuous for her right now doctor?"

"Just don't overdo it, make sure she takes frequent rests." The doctor helped Rachel up and she swung her feet to the floor.

"What do you say sweetheart? Baby shopping time?" She wriggled her eyebrows just the way Deb so often did.

"Absolutely!"

Her mom knew exactly what she needed; time to let loose, to get excited about becoming a mother, and to dream about the future. It was what they both needed.

"My first grandchild is going to be well kitted out! We'll have to get a little gift for him or her for under the tree too! Let's go!" Lyn placed her arm around her daughter's shoulders and ushered her to her car.

Rachel had never had a more special afternoon with her mom. They went from baby shop to baby shop, browsing and buying. Imagining the outfits they'd bought being filled by a real little person. They stopped for a coffee and cake, and chatted for ages about when Rachel and her siblings were young, and all they got up to while they were living in England.

When the conversation sobered, Rachel leaned forward on the table, "How am I going to do this mum? How am I going to be a single mother?"

Lyn took her hands. "Rachel, you are going to make an amazing mother. I know it. And you might be single, but you'll never be alone. Anything you need, I am here for you, we all are. This baby is all of ours, our flesh and blood. We'll take care of the both of you."

Rachel nodded. She'd managed to avoid talking about the procedure, or the chance that something could be very wrong with the baby... just to pretend for one afternoon, that all was well. To pretend that she was filled with hope and joy for the future, and not the fear she truly felt.

***

Eric unbuttoned his sweaty khaki shirt and threw it into his plastic wash basket. He yanked open his wardrobe and grabbed a t-shirt and shorts from the top of the pile. Where were they now... his mom and Uncle Kobus?

Tonight was the night. His uncle had left with his mom half an hour ago for their romantic game drive. In hindsight, Eric should've insisted on a chaperone! He chuckled at the thought.

He stretched out his tired muscles, and prepared for his run through the bush. His body felt a little stiff at first, but it wasn't long and Eric was racing through the plains, in his element. He pushed his body hard up the hill, until he was completely out of breath. He slumped over, leaned against a thorn tree, and sucked in deep, long breaths.

Far in the distance, with the setting sun ahead of them, he could just make out Uncle Kobus' Land Rover trudging through the dense bush. He knew what he needed to do. Pray. Eric didn't know how his mom would respond to Uncle Kobus, but by the end of the evening, whatever her answer, their relationship would be forever changed.

Eric prayed for God's will for them, and that they would both find the happiness they so deserved.

***

Deb took Rachel's hand as they sat together in the consultant's office. The fact that they'd called Rachel in for a chat, suggested that the result of the amniocentesis was not good. Good results were given over the phone.

Rachel could feel her palm sweating on the arm of the faux leather chair. Her hand then went instinctively to the pendant on her necklace. Whenever she thought of Eric, her hand went there. Eric's baby… she knew there was something wrong. After the test, Rachel had done as much research on the syndrome as she could. She needed to be prepared just in case.

The consultant came in with a thick file and introduced herself. Taking the seat opposite them, she leaned over her desk and looked at Rachel intently.

"Rachel, I'm afraid it's not good news." Rachel couldn't stop the moisture flooding her eyes. "The result is positive for SCIS, I'm so sorry. Now if left untreated, your baby will have a severely compromised immune system and ultimately won't survive past the first two years. In the past doctors have attempted to help affected children by placing them in oxygen-filled tents, in order to keep germs out. Thankfully, today we have a much more successful treatment. You and your partner will need to have your bone marrow tested. If either of you is a match, we can do the transplant and your baby will have an excellent chance at a perfectly healthy life."

"What if there is no match?" Rachel asked in a small voice.

"We'll cross that bridge when we come to it, there are alternative treatments. But we'll exhaust this one first. How soon could you both be tested?"

Rachel froze. Deb came to her rescue. "The baby's father lives in South Africa. If we could maybe test Rachel first, and only if she's not a match, perhaps move on to test him? Would that be possible?"

"Yes certainly. Would you be available to do the test now Rachel? Or would you prefer some time to get your head around things?"

"I'd like to do the test now." Rachel was pale and still.

"Are you sure Rach?" asked Deb. "Don't you want some time to absorb all this?" Deb squeezed her hand in concern.

Rachel turned to her sister, a tear trailing down her cheek. "No Deb, I just want to know if I can help my baby."

"Okay Rachel, I'll organise it now for you at the day ward."

***

Rachel hardly felt the stinging and pulling as the local anaesthetic was inserted and then the larger syringe needle. All she could think about was saving her baby. She prayed continually in her heart that she would be a perfect match. And when the test got more uncomfortable, Rachel prayed harder. Were her prayers making it past the ceiling? It didn't feel like it.

Deb looked down at her with concern and rubbed her hand. "It's almost over now Rach."

"All done," said the doctor as he placed a plaster over the area. "But you'll need to stay in bed for a couple of hours so we can keep an eye on you. Well done Rachel."

When the doctor left, the tears started to fall again. She had reached her limit of being strong.

"You're so brave Rach, well done." Deb stroked her hair.

"I'm not brave Deb, I'm so, so scared."

Deb helped her up and to the edge of the bed. "And you're facing your fear, head on, that's being brave."

Rachel swung her feet over the side. "What if I'm not a match Deb? I'll have to tell Eric everything."

"Yes Rach, you need to be prepared for that." Deborah handed her sister a long-sleeved top and a pair of jeggings.

"I know." Rachel shuddered as she took them.

"I just need to call mum and dad and tell them you're okay. They're driving me crazy with their texts." Deb pulled her phone out of her white lab coat pocket and pressed on the touchscreen.

"She's okay... yeh, it's all over." Deb stepped out the room, and Rachel was alone.

And being alone fitted her mood perfectly. It was exactly how she felt on the inside. She turned her face into her pillow and sobbed.

CHAPTER TWENTY-FOUR

Eric was not known to be nosey or interfering, but when it came to his mom, with all she'd been through, he was a little protective.

So when she and Uncle Kobus had still not returned from their evening drive, Eric was about to round up a search party. Every five minutes he'd walk over to his cabin window and check whether his mom's house lights were on. Her Christmas tree was twinkling in the window, but the house was otherwise dark and still.

Eventually he heard and then saw Uncle Kobus' Land Rover heading up to her house. The engine cut out, but neither of them climbed out. Eric felt a little guilty for watching them, and tried to busy himself preparing for bed. But his bedtime routine wasn't exactly very time consuming, and within a few minutes he gravitated back to his kitchen window.

The driver's door opened, and out stepped Uncle Kobus in his khakis. Eric chastised himself for not giving the man any outfit advice. He walked around the car and opened the passenger door. Out stepped his mom. She looked beautiful in a summer dress he'd never seen before, her blonde hair flowing down around her shoulders. Uncle Kobus walked her to her door, gave her a kiss on the cheek, and left.

Eric felt disappointed. A chaste kiss on the cheek could mean anything. He sighed, closed the curtain and retired to bed. He'd have to wait until morning. He hoped with all his heart that his mom had said 'yes'. It was past time for her to find happiness again.

Eric's thoughts then turned to Rachel, as they always did when he turned out the light at night. What was she doing? How was she feeling? Did she find his gift? Should he try to contact her? How long had it been since he'd been with her? And finally, would he ever see her again?

With every day that passed, it seemed less and less likely. He didn't want to burden anyone with the truth of what he was going through, and he managed to hide it very well with the day's distractions. But at night?

At night Rachel was as real to him as she had been in the flesh. She was living in vibrant colour. Every memory was as vivid as the day it happened. Having Rachel so alive in his mind was pure joy, and pure torture.

***

"I'm very sorry to have to tell you this…" Rachel felt numb. The mobile phone fell from her hand and landed at her feet on the carpet. She wasn't a match. And it was highly unlikely that anyone in her family would be either. Shakily, she retrieved the phone and turned it off. Her hand went to her pendant and she rubbed the inscription with her thumb. There was no way to get around it, she was going to need Eric. She was going to have to tell him everything and let the chips fall where they may.

Rachel considered phoning him, but this conversation was not one for over the phone. It needed to happen face to face. She'd have a front row seat, watching his expression switch from shock to anger to shock again, and then sadness and confusion. He was going to be so upset that she'd kept this from him.

Rachel phoned her family and told them the news. She booked her flight online for just before Christmas, and organised for her dad to take her to Heathrow. She poured herself a warm bubble bath, climbed in, and held her little baby in her hands. If ever she needed to feel God near her, it was now.

***

"Come on! How on earth? Is this even possible?" Eric muttered, trying a different angle. He had been tasked with putting up the Christmas tree at the reception. Unfortunately, Johan was away and the other rangers had game drives and various decent excuses as to why they weren't able to help him. He'd managed to drag the tree through the double door entrance, and was now trying to get it upright in its stand.

"Who in their right mind would choose such a ginormous tree?" He spoke to himself in utter disbelief. Boxes of lights and decorations strewn around, waiting for him to sort and place.

Uncle Kobus trudged in through the main entrance. He approached Eric, placing his hand on Eric's shoulder. "She said 'no', my boy."

Eric looked back at him. "What? Really?"

"She said she's not ready to marry me." The older man shrugged.

"*Oom*, I'm so sorry." Eric lost his grip on the tree and the monstrosity came hurling down to the ground.

Uncle Kobus didn't seem to notice or care. "*Ja*, that's the way it goes sometimes hey. Who knows, maybe she will change her mind one day. She took her wedding ring off a few weeks ago. I thought that meant something. Maybe it does, maybe she just needs more time."

"I really hope so *oom*. Really," Eric answered sincerely.

"*Ag…ja.*" Uncle Kobus slapped him on the back and headed towards the back room. Eric felt a new heaviness weigh down on him.

A fine Christmas this was turning out to be. He wasn't looking forward to it in the least. He would put up the tree, hopefully, string the lights and place the ornaments, but he wouldn't be celebrating. Because as it was, Eric was just trying to hang in there, one day at a time. And with each day, hoping that with every tomorrow he'd remember a little less about Rachel.

***

"You need a new *chick* to distract you, *boet*." Johan was seriously starting to irritate Eric. They'd been tasked with checking that the boundary was secure, and while Johan drove, Eric made notes of any potential weaknesses.

"Listen *bru*, just leave it, please. I don't want any other girl."

"And *that's* your problem, right there *china*. You don't *want* to move on. You *need* to, but you don't *want* to. And there's a string of girls at church who wish you would notice them."

"*Bru*, I'm fine just the way I am."

"You?" Johan shook his head. "*Boet*, you are *not* fine, and you haven't been fine for a long time. You think no one's noticed, but Johan has. You've lost weight, you've got bags under your eyes, who knows if you're getting any decent sleep, and your smile."

"What about my smile?" Eric frowned.

"*Boet*, it doesn't go all the way to your eyes like it used to."

"*Eish*, the all-seeing eye of Johan." Eric shook his head.

Was it really that bad? He had felt that his clothes were a bit looser, but he didn't think it was enough for anyone else to notice. He wasn't getting the solid sleep that he was used to, and it was true that his heart had never felt so heavy. Would it be so bad just to meet up with a girl from church?

Suddenly Johan braked and pulled up the handbrake. "Look." He pointed to a small hole in the fence. "Looks like they came in on foot this time *boet*."

"But how'd they cut through the electric fence?" Eric climbed out the vehicle for a closer look. He found a torn piece of grey fabric snagged on the wire, examined it, and tucked it in his pocket. At least two sets of footprints could be seen leading from tyre marks on the other side of the fence.

"These guys know what they are doing *boet*. They probably wanted to scope out the best way to get to the rhinos. They are planning something now." Johan nodded gravely.

"Definitely looks that way. Let's get this fence wired up temporarily while we're here."

Once back on the road, Eric radioed Uncle Kobus with the news.

"Okay, my boy. I think I'm gonna have to employ a security team now. Over."

"That's probably a good idea *oom*. These guys are determined. Over."

The incident at the fence didn't do much to help Eric's mood. As they continued along the border road, he thought back to his earlier conversation with Johan. It took all his strength to ask Johan about the girls who'd noticed him at church. "Okay, so tell me Johan. If I did decide to try and move on, who should I take for coffee then? Which girl do you recommend?"

"My *boet*, Stacey is a very nice girl. And she always asks about you when you aren't at church."

"Stacey de Jäger?"

"*Ja boet*, she's not bad on the eyes either." Johan nodded approvingly.

Eric shook his head. He was starting to feel desperate for some mental and emotional relief from his thoughts of Rachel, but was this the best way? He'd be using Stacey. Who'd want to be the rebound girl? "Johan, I can't. I can't use Stacey to get over Rachel. It wouldn't be right."

"You wouldn't be *using* her *boet*, it's just a cup of coffee man."

Eric sighed. It wouldn't be right or fair on Stacey. He needed to get over Rachel on his own, he just had to figure out how. They'd had no contact since he'd left Wales, thankfully. He'd never be able to move on if he was still hearing her voice in his ear, her accent, her laugh. Any word from her would set him back weeks of progress. As it was he heard and saw her in his dreams.

For now, he'd just take things one day at a time. Just get through each day... one foot in front of the other.

CHAPTER TWENTY-FIVE

Emotionless, Rachel boarded her plane and found her window seat. She hadn't packed very much, as she didn't plan on staying long. She doubted Eric would want her to hang around after she told him the news. She'd organised for Suzanne to fetch her from the airport. They'd had a two hour Skype call the night before, and Rachel had told her everything. Suzanne had offered for Rachel to stay as a guest at the orphanage while she was in town.

The weather was bleak and drizzly, perfect for her mood. Rachel pulled off her soft coat and used it as a blanket. She removed her shoes, and put her earphones in. Closing her eyes, she listened to worship music. It was the only thing lately that soothed her soul. She was desperate to reconnect with God, to have that closeness she used to feel. She needed Him now more than ever before. *'For I am the Lord, who takes hold of your right hand a*nd *says, do not fear, I will help you.'*

As the scripture drifted through Rachel's mind, it took root in her soul. She felt a deep peace settle in her heart. And as the plane took off, Rachel fell into a restful, dreamless sleep.

***

Rachel felt the wheels of the plane touch down firmly on the runway. She pulled her earphones from her ears and looked out at the sunny landscape of KwaZulu-Natal, Eric's home province.

King Shaka Airport was festive, with Christmas music, brightly coloured decorations and flashing Christmas trees. Despite the difficult road ahead, the thought of being back in Africa and seeing Eric sent an undeniable thrill through her.

Rachel collected her small suitcase and went through to arrivals. Suzanne was waiting there with a smile and a bunch of yellow roses. "Welcome back, Rach." She took her in her arms and embraced her warmly. "And these are for you, congratulations on your baby." The older woman smiled.

When Rachel saw the flowers and felt the love radiating from Suzanne, she couldn't hold back the tears.

"It's okay Rach, it's okay. Everything's going to be okay, you'll see," Suzanne said as she hugged her again and rubbed her back.

Eventually, Suzanne pulled back and handed Rachel a tissue from her pocket. "It's good to have you back... I've missed you. You're looking so well too." Suzanne smiled through her wet eyes.

Rachel smiled back and nodded, but couldn't say anything. She quietly thanked God that she had this loving, strong woman to lean on while she was here. What would she have done without her? Suzanne put her arm around Rachel's waist and led her to her car.

***

"So, I've got your old room all ready for you." Suzanne looked over at her as she drove.

"Thank you Suzanne, really. Thank you. I can't tell you what this means to me."

"You don't have to. I said I'd always be here for you, and I meant it." Suzanne reached over and squeezed Rachel's hand.

"I love it, by the way." Suzanne looked over at Rachel.

"What's that?" Rachel asked.

"Your necklace. It's every bit as beautiful as you described."

Rachel fingered the pendant. Eric. He was about to have his whole world shaken up. She'd played it out in her mind, what she'd say, and every possible response from him she could think of. She hadn't let him know she was coming. She didn't want him to get excited and assume it was because she wanted to be with him. She'd just show up at his cabin, like he showed up at her apartment.

Rachel felt her love for him well up inside of her. She prayed that God would prepare him for the news, and hold him close while he came to terms with it.

***

With the mood on the reserve more somber than usual, especially for the festive season, Uncle Kobus asked Eric to help him throw a Christmas Eve party. All the staff who weren't going home for Christmas, along with close friends of the family were all invited. They'd been stringing lights and arranging tables and chairs for most of the afternoon down at the *lapa*. Eric had removed the infinity swimming pool net and cleared all the leaves off the top of the water.

The pool had never looked more inviting as it glistened in the starlight. He hoped that the festive atmosphere would ease the strain between his mom and Uncle Kobus.

Since the night of the botched proposal, things had been tense between them, and Eric had noticed that his mom's wedding ring was firmly back on her ring finger. Uncle Kobus had confided that he too hoped that this party would lighten the atmosphere. They needed to have some relaxed fun together tonight.

As the sun began to set, the fires were lit and the guests started arriving. Though Eric was thankful for the distraction, he hoped that Johan hadn't invited the group of church girls he'd been threatening to bring along. Eric wasn't in the mood for socialising with people he hardly knew.

His mom's front door opened and out she came. She was wearing a summer dress again, and carried a beach towel under her arm. The warm breeze blew her hair back, and she looked ten years younger than her 52 years. He saw Uncle Kobus frown, take a deep, calming breath and busy himself with the fires.

Eric couldn't help but feel like Rachel should be with him at the party, that a piece of himself was missing. Instead she was thousands of miles away, where she thought she belonged.

He turned the Christmas music up loud and started *braaing* the meat with his uncle. The distraction worked for a little while as Eric lost himself in the festivities. It was just what he needed.

***

Rachel hadn't expected such an overwhelming welcome from the children at the orphanage. They waited for her in the Christmassy living area of the main house, and called to her with their excited little voices, "Aunty Rachel, Aunty Rachel..." They hugged her and brought her pictures and cards they had made her. Rachel wiped at a tear as she looked over at Suzanne and smiled. The older lady walked towards her and put her arm around Rachel's waist. She spoke quietly to her. "Listen Rach, I've been invited to a Christmas Eve party over at the reserve tonight. I wasn't sure how soon you were hoping to see Eric..."

Rachel's heart rate shot up. She edged backwards towards the couch, and sat down slowly with Vusi in her lap. She looked up at Suzanne. "Okay well, perhaps you could take him a note for me. It might be better than surprising him out of the blue."

Suzanne placed her hand on Rachel's shoulder. "Okay I'll get you some paper and a pen. Why don't you go and get settled in your *rondavel*, and I'll bring it out to you there?"

Rachel nodded. Suzanne disappeared down the hallway and Thandeka started preparing the children for bath time.

It felt surreal to be back in this place that she loved so much. She hadn't realised how much she'd missed it, and in such a short time too. The heat would take some getting used to though. Rachel had never experienced such hot weather at Christmas time.

As she neared her *rondavel*, it was impossible to stop the memories. The thought that Eric was just a few miles away made her giddy. How she wished she'd come under different circumstances.

Rachel sank into the bed and unzipped her small suitcase, Suzanne arrived with a pen, notepad and a vase for her flowers. "I'll leave you now so you can think about what you want to say. I'll fetch the note just before I leave in about twenty minutes or so."

She looked up at her with gratitude. "Okay, thank you Suzanne. For everything."

Rachel turned the ceiling fan on and felt the relief of the breeze drifting down into the room. She sat back down on the edge of her bed and collected the notepad and pen. She stared blankly at the empty page. Finally she thought she'd keep it simple, and wrote:

Dear Eric,

I need to see you and I apologise for the short notice. I'm at the orphanage. Text me a time we can meet, I'm using my old mobile number.

Rachel

Rachel debated whether or not she should say 'love, Rachel.' But in the end she just left it as it was. She didn't want him to be misled and think she was there to pursue their relationship.

Suzanne arrived at the door and Rachel handed her the folded up note.

"Try not to worry Rach," she said as she took it, "it'll all work out, you'll see. Eric is a very good man."

Rachel swallowed back the tears that threatened. "I know he is. Hopefully he can forgive me for keeping this from him."

As Suzanne headed off to the party, Rachel took a shower and got changed into her pyjamas. It wasn't quite time for bed yet, but after her journey and a very emotional few weeks, she was exhausted. Her bed called to her, and there was nothing quite like falling asleep to the sounds of the African bush.

CHAPTER TWENTY-SIX

Eric noticed with dismay that his mom and Uncle Kobus had been sitting on opposite sides of the *lapa* the whole evening. Both of them currently appeared to be engaged in meaningful conversations, but Eric had his doubts. It seemed they were trying a bit too hard to keep themselves distracted.

Eric, on the other hand, was doing his level best to try and enjoy the party. They'd started the evening's entertainment off with a secret Santa amongst the staff. It turned out to be enormous fun, with a wild variety of weird and wonderful gifts emerging from the woodwork. Eric had received a t-shirt from Sipho, one of the newer rangers on staff, with 'Single and ready to mingle' printed on the front. He'd laughed and put it on just for fun.

Most of the crowd were in the swimming pool now, splashing around and having a good time. Suzanne wasn't quite herself tonight. She was usually very chatty, and they always connected well. But this evening she'd hardly said a word to him. She definitely had something on her mind.

He glanced over at her, she was watching him. She quickly looked down and started digging in her handbag. Not finding what she was after, she checked her pockets. She pulled something out and strode over to him. "Eric, this is for you. Read it in private." She slipped a note into his hand and headed towards where her Beetle was parked.

Eric frowned and looked down at the folded paper. He moved over to a quieter spot where the light was better, and unfolded the note.

Dear Eric,

I need to see you and I apologise for the short notice. I'm at the orphanage. Text me a time we can meet, I'm using my old mobile number.

Rachel

Eric's heart took off at a hundred miles an hour. Rachel was here? Just a few miles away? And she was asking for him? Eric didn't need to think about it. He ran for his Land Rover, dug the keys out his pocket and made a beeline for the orphanage. He did his best to focus on the poorly-lit road, but he could think of nothing else except holding Rachel close.

After what felt like hours, he pulled up outside the orphanage in a cloud of dust. All was still as the children were in bed for the night. Where would she be? Her old *rondavel* most likely. He'd head there first.

***

A loud thumping sound broke into Rachel's semi-conscious state. What was that?

She rubbed her eyes. Where was she? The last twenty-four hours came flooding back in an instant. South Africa, near Eric. Someone was knocking on her door! It sounded urgent. She climbed out of bed half asleep and opened the door a crack.

Rachel's breath caught in her throat. Eric. She yanked the chain off and opened the door wide. He swooped in, took her face in his hands and covered it with urgent kisses. His lips found her mouth and he kissed her passionately.

Rachel turned away. "Eric..." Her voice trembled and her eyes filled with tears. She squeezed them shut, she couldn't look at him. "No."

His hands dropped to his sides. Slowly she looked up into the eyes she loved and could see the hurt and confusion there. "We need to talk, Eric."

He blinked a few times. "Rachel, I don't understand, I... thought..."

"I know, and I'm sorry, but I haven't come so that we can be together."

Eric looked so vulnerable standing there in his 'Single and ready to mingle' t-shirt. How she wished things were different.

"Then why... why are you here?" he asked quietly as he slipped his hands into his shorts' pockets, the tension thick in is voice.

Rachel swallowed. She dragged her eyes up to his. "Eric, I have... kept something from you, but I can't any longer... because... I need your help."

Rachel ached with the tender look he gave her. He ran his thumb across her cheek. "You know I'd do anything for you."

"Does that include forgiving me?" Her shoulders sagged as she searched his face.

He frowned. "Rachel, what's going on?" Eric turned and closed the door behind him, diminishing what little light there was in the room further.

Alone in the darkness, Rachel looked down. "Eric, I... don't know how to tell you this..." She lifted her wet eyes to his.

He took her by the shoulders and gave her a slight shake. "Just tell me."

"I'm pregnant Eric."

***

The bottom of his world fell out, and he was falling along with it… turning, swirling, round and round he went. "You're what?" He blinked.

"Nearly four months now. The baby's yours. You're going to be a father in June."

The tears streamed down Rachel's cheeks as the reality hit him. He was going to be a father? But this wasn't right. They weren't even married, how could he be a father before he was a husband?

How could this happen? Was God punishing him for what they'd done? Revealing his sin like this so that all the world would know? It was one time! One moment of weakness!

Dizzy, Eric stumbled for the edge of Rachel's bed. He sat and leaned forward on his knees, head in his hands, struggling to draw breath.

"There's more Eric, whenever you're ready." Rachel twisted her hands together.

Eric looked up at her, eyes wide. "There's more? Please... don't tell me it's twins."

Rachel moved to sit near him. "The baby... the baby is not well. That's why I'm here, Eric. The baby needs a bone marrow transplant. I'm not a match. You are the baby's best chance at survival."

God *was* punishing him. Exposing his sin with a terminally ill child no less! Eric's mind couldn't take this, it wasn't real. Surely he was dreaming. Just a few minutes ago he was partying with his friends, now he was going to be a father to a very sick child?

He had to leave, he had to get out of there, and fast. "Rachel, this is all too much." He rose, not looking at her. "I need to think."

Eric strode past her and left without another word.

***

The roar of the Land Rover's engine quietened as Rachel closed her door and locked it. "Oh God, please get him home safely," she whispered. "Don't let him do anything stupid."

She curled up in her bed and sobbed. It was out of her hands now. She had to trust that God would protect him, and that Eric would forgive her for keeping this from him.

The sobs wracked her body until finally she fell into a deep, troubled sleep. Dreams of Eric plagued her through the night as she tossed and turned. No matter what she tried, she couldn't escape the images of him in her mind. The shock, the confusion, the vulnerability on his face, tore at her heart. She knew that he would do the right thing and offer the bone marrow, but would their relationship ever be the same again? Rachel very much doubted it. That would take much more than a simple apology, that would take a miracle.

***

Eric raced up to his cabin door and parked his Land Rover. He flung the door wide, climbed out and started running. Sparing no thought for the fact that it was dark and dangerous to run in the bush at this time of night; he just ran, as fast and as far as he could.

He headed for the hill, pushing his body on the gruelling uphill climb. But he didn't stop where he usually stopped, he kept climbing higher and higher over the rocks, until he was at the very top.

There he fell to his knees on the dry grass, and then flat on his back. Nausea hit him, and he knew he was going to be sick. He got to his knees just in time to empty his stomach of all he'd eaten at the party. He felt anger building up inside him. It was unwelcome and unfamiliar. He looked up to the stars. The heavens looked peaceful, and in order, each star under God's control. Yet his life was in such turmoil, such disarray, so out-of-control.

"Don't You care about me?" Eric stood, shouting angrily into the night sky. "You don't care about me at all! I do *one* thing! *One* thing wrong, and You are *so* quick to punish me! Where's the grace? Where's the mercy, where? Where are they God?" Eric was growing hoarse, but still, he continued, "Where's the love?" His voice broke. "Don't you love me anymore?" He collapsed back onto his knees and sobbed.

Once all the tears were spent, he slept there in the grass until the rising sun woke him the next morning.

CHAPTER TWENTY-SEVEN

Rachel awoke to the sound of scurrying feet and tapping on her door. The children's voices called to her, "Aunty Rachel, Aunty Rachel. We're waiting for you, it's Christmas! It's Christmas!"

Rachel smiled in spite of her inner turmoil. She padded over to the door and pulled it open. A group of excited little faces greeted her, eyes aglow.

"It's Christmas! You all look so excited! Okay, just let me get dressed. I'm coming!"

The children ran back to the house and Rachel closed the door. She hadn't even spared a thought about Christmas. She had no presents to offer the children, nor the staff. All she had was a huge bag of Haribo sweets she'd brought as an afterthought for them.

She pulled on a pair of stretchy tights and a top and checked her reflection. She was going to need some make-up to cover up the rough night she'd had. What sort of night had Eric had? She couldn't imagine that it had been anything but tough, very tough.

Tears stung at her eyes as she dug for her concealer and eye make-up. Once happy with her reflection, Rachel locked up and put on her best festive face. She wouldn't be the one to spoil Christmas for these precious children. Regardless of how she felt inside, she'd go and have fun with them, all the fun they wanted.

***

The morning sun beat down on Eric and he stirred. His body ached from the uncomfortable position he'd slept in on the ground. And considering how hard he'd pushed himself last night, it was no wonder he could hardly move this morning.

He didn't need a moment to remember how he got there, or what he was doing up there, the truth of his new reality had never left his mind. Eric rubbed his eyes, and tried to sit up. Stretching out each limb, he rose stiffly, and stretched them again. Then he walked over to an overhanging rock and sat on the end of it. Not even the beauty of the Savanna could soothe his soul today.

Was Rachel ever going to tell him? How had she kept this from him? She must've known the whole time he was with her in Wales, and she'd said nothing. The doctor's appointment made sense now too. Why didn't she want him to know he was going to be a father? If the baby was healthy, would he ever have found out about him or her?

His emotions were overwhelming, his thoughts, conflicting... towards God, towards Rachel, towards himself. He closed his eyes and rubbed his temples hard. He couldn't be around anyone anytime soon. He needed to be alone, to process. Then he remembered, it was Christmas morning. He sighed deeply. His mom would be expecting him to spend the day with her. He couldn't bear the idea of her spending Christmas on her own, worried about where he'd disappeared to. And so, Eric gave himself another hour, then he slowly started making his way back down to the reserve, and back to his new reality.

***

"Oh wow Vusi, look at that! An aeroplane!" Rachel smiled and did the hand motion. "Vroooom!"

In spite of everything, she couldn't help being affected by the joy of the children as they opened their presents. Local shops and friends of the orphanage had brought donations of toys, books and clothes which Suzanne and Thandeka had lovingly wrapped and assigned to each child.

The main house was beautifully decorated in the traditional Christmas colours, and a huge tree filled the corner of the spacious living area where they now sat. Little boys buzzed past her with aeroplanes, as the little girls dressed their brand new baby dolls. She had never seen such happiness. Thandeka and Suzanne watched the children with tender smiles on their faces. Rachel felt truly blessed to have witnessed this precious time.

She went around and added a small bag of sweets to each child's pile of presents, and watched as their smiles grew even bigger. She hoped with all her heart, that next Christmas would be a happy one for her too.

There was so much uncertainty. If Eric wasn't a match, perhaps the baby wouldn't even survive to see his or her first Christmas. Rachel didn't want to think about it, not ever, and especially not now in the midst of all this joy.

***

Eric reached his hand beyond the shower curtain and yanked the closest towel from its hook. He rubbed his hair vigorously, then wrapped the towel around his waist. He felt a remaining blade of grass in his hair and tugged it out. The steaming water had eased his sore muscles somewhat, but hadn't done much to ease the pain inside him. He trudged to his bedroom in search of anything that was clean and ironed. To his relief, Mariette had returned a large pile of laundered clothes the day before.

He chose a pair of shorts and a t-shirt from the top of the pile. They weren't really into dressing up smart for Christmas. Most Christmas days they'd spend in the swimming pool anyhow due to the heat. He dressed quickly then returned to the bathroom to brush his teeth. He caught a glimpse of himself in the mirror. He didn't look any different to the day before, but he was. Everything had changed. He was going to be a father. Ready or not.

He sucked in a deep breath and prepared himself for some quality time with his mom. She deserved his full attention. As he reached the kitchen, he grabbed her gift from the table and strode towards her thatched-roof house.

The lights on Janice's Christmas tree were sparkling, and Eric could hear Bony M playing even before she opened the front door. They'd spent every Christmas together. Since his dad had died, it was mostly just the two of them, though Janice would sometimes invite Uncle Kobus over for Christmas Eve dinner. Janice opened the door before Eric had a chance to knock.

"My boy, come on in. Merry Christmas!" She hugged him firmly.

"Merry Christmas Mom!" said Eric as he stepped inside the hallway and closed the door behind himself.

The tantalising aroma of garlicky, roasting meat made his mouth water. He hadn't had breakfast yet. "Wow, something smells good," he hinted. He placed her gift under the tree in the lounge, and followed the smell towards the kitchen at the back of the house. The oven made the room even hotter, and the ceiling fan did little to cool it, even with the back doors wide open.

"Roast lamb." Janice rubbed her hands together.

"Oooo my favourite! Is there anything ready to eat yet mom?" Eric scanned the kitchen counters.

"What? Haven't you had breakfast?" His mom gawked at him.

"No I haven't, can I have a piece of toast or something? Please?" He shot her a cheeky smile.

"Sit at the counter. I'll make you a couple pieces. Cheese?"

"Perfect, thanks mom."

Janice took two slices of wholewheat bread and placed them in her double toaster. "So I didn't see you after the party last night, did you go to bed early?" She turned to face him, leaning against the counter.

Eric didn't want to lie to his mom, but he just wasn't ready to tell her yet. He felt his palms start to sweat. He ran them down his thighs. "Can I explain a bit later maybe? If you don't mind mom?"

"Oh, okay." His mom furrowed her brow. She reached into the cupboard at her head for a plate and took his toast out the toaster.

"*You* looked beautiful last night, is there something you're not telling me?" He raised his eyebrow at the flustered woman.

A knock sounded at the door.

"Should I get it?" Eric shifted on his bar stool.

"No, no, stay where you are and have your breakfast, I'll get it." Janice slid his plate of toast onto the table where he sat and disappeared down the passage.

Eric grinned at the sound of Uncle Kobus' voice at the door. The man was not giving up easily. It was only a brief exchange and Janice came through with two small wrapped boxes. She placed them on the kitchen counter nonchalantly.

"Oh, was that Uncle Kobus' voice I heard at the door?" Eric smiled knowingly.

A red hue travelled up his mom's neck and onto her pretty face. "*Ja*, he uh… he brought us Christmas presents." Janice turned her back on the gift and busied herself making coffee.

"Well aren't you going to open yours?"

"Uh… In a bit, I just need a cup of coffee, then we'll sit by the tree and open our gifts." Janice grabbed the kettle and marched over to the sink.

Eric knew it was just a matter of time before he had to tell his mom everything. He wasn't ready to say the words out loud just yet though. Telling her would make it real, very real. How would she take the news? She'd be disappointed in him.

Janice's gaze drifted out the window. She wasn't quite herself today. It was most likely because of Uncle Kobus, and of course, her unopened gift on the counter. Perhaps later, they'd both be more ready for a difficult conversation.

"Come, let's go and sit in the lounge." She took their coffee through to the living area, walking straight past the small wrapped boxes on the kitchen counter. Eric put his empty plate in the sink, grabbed the gifts and followed her. She wasn't going to be let off the hook that easily.

They got comfortable in front of the tree and exchanged presents. Janice received a beautiful turquoise silk scarf, her favourite perfume and a new hair straightener. She was so pleased, she put the scarf on instantly and sprayed herself with the perfume. Eric unwrapped his little pile to find an electric toothbrush, a t-shirt, a smarter button-up flannel shirt and of course, the tradition of new socks and underwear which Janice would buy every year. He chuckled as he pulled a silver watch out the small box from his uncle. A subtle hint maybe?

"It looks like Uncle Kobus hasn't forgotten the time I arrived late for work!"

Janice laughed with him.

"Thanks mom, they're all perfect."

"I love mine too, thank you!"

"Yours aren't finished yet." His gaze travelled to the box under the tree. "There's one more for you under there."

A blush returned to his mom's cheeks. "Uh… *ja* okay." Janice reached down to retrieve it and quickly unwrapped the present. When she found a maroon box with jewellery shop branding on it, she hesitated and looked over at Eric.

"Open it mom," he encouraged gently.

Janice hesitantly opened the box. She gasped. "Oh my!" Her eyes grew large as she slammed the box shut.

Eric leaned over. "Can I see mom?" He held out his hand.

Janice placed the box in his palm, her hand shaky.

Eric pried the lid open to reveal a pair of sparkly diamond earrings. "Wow! That is one amazing gift mom." His uncle was making a statement with this present.

"I know, it's too much," she clipped the words out. "I'll tell him to return them."

Eric sat still for a little while, hoping she'd say more. When she didn't he placed the velvet box on the seat between them and found her eyes. "Mom, I know what happened."

"What do you mean?" Her gaze flittered his way anxiously.

Eric sighed. "I mean, I know he asked you to marry him, and that you turned him down."

"You do?" Janice jerked her head back.

Eric lifted his face to hers. "He came and asked my permission to marry you mom."

"He did?" Janice chewed on a fingernail.

"And after how tense things have been between you two over this last little while, I think the whole reserve knows that something is going on."

Janice pulled her hand from her mouth and exhaled deeply. "Eric, I wanted to tell you. I'm sorry. I've been so confused."

He covered her hand with his. "I understand mom, I'm not upset with you. I'm just trying to figure out why you turned him down?"

"It's not that I don't care about him Eric, I do. I just… I don't know… I don't see him in that way. He's more like a protective brother-in-law."

"Okay, I understand. As long as you're not running. If it's fear that's keeping you from being with him, then that needs to go." He searched her pale face.

She lifted her eyes to his. "I'm confused Eric. I need time, much more time. And when he gives me gifts like this, I feel so overwhelmed."

"It's okay mom, I think that's normal under the circumstances. What did you get him?"

"A pair of *braai* tongs!" she spat out, her lips pinched together. Was she holding back a smile? And then the laughter started. She laughed and laughed, and Eric laughed with her. Their cackling built and built until they were holding their bellies, red faced, and could hardly breathe. They wiped their tears and looked at each other with smiles that filled up their faces and lit up their eyes. Somehow in that moment, they both knew that they'd needed that.

"Come let's go for a walk on the hill," Eric suggested and pulled his mom up from the couch.

"I'll get my *takkies*, give me one minute."

CHAPTER TWENTY-EIGHT

Eric could see the festive commotion from where he and his mom walked up the side of the hill. The orphanage children had been invited for ice-creams and a swim as a Christmas Day treat. He scanned the area for a glimpse of Rachel. Was she there?

The children lined up near Thandeka. She pasted each one with sunscreen while Suzanne blew up a small mountain of arm bands. No sign of Rachel. He sighed and collected his thoughts. Surely now was as good a time as any to tell his mom what was going on. He slowed his pace.

"Mom, there's something I need to tell you."

"Okay?" She frowned, looking back at him.

"It uh… has to do with why I needed to leave the party early last night." He felt the sweat build up in his palms once more.

"Okay, should I be sitting down for this news?" She studied his face.

Eric laughed nervously and rubbed the back of his neck. "Um… maybe you should be, actually." He bit his bottom lip.

"Really?" Janice balked, her eyes wide.

Eric swallowed. He stuffed his hands into his shorts' pockets. "Last night at the party, Suzanne came over and gave me a note. A note from Rachel."

Janice's frowned deepened. "From *Rachel?*"

"She's here mom, she's over at the orphanage." He gestured with a flick of his head.

"She's back? To see you? But that's grea-"

"It's not what you think." He closed his eyes and shook his head.

Janice crossed her arms. "Okay, care to explain?"

Eric stared down at his feet and sucked in a deep breath. "Mom... we uh... the night before she left, at the farewell party... we were both drinking a fair bit, and well, emotions were running high..." He lifted his eyes to hers. "I don't know if you remember how distressed I was 'round about then?"

"Okay. I think I need to sit down 'round about now." Janice laughed anxiously. She looked around and found a nearby rock she could sit on, concern etched onto her face.

Eric turned towards her, his chest tight. "We went down to the guest cabin to be alone and well, things went a bit too far." He tried to swallow but his mouth was dry. "Actually, way too far. I don't even remember it all mom, but I woke up in the guest cabin bed the next morning." Eric slumped down next to his mom and put his head in his hands.

"And that's why you had to go to Wales so urgently?" she asked in a small voice.

Eric didn't lift his head. "*Ja*. I wanted to find out what exactly happened between us."

"Okay…" Her voice floated away on the warm breeze.

His stomach knotted. "She's pregnant mom, almost four months." He raised his head in time to see the pain in his mother's eyes. "Congratulations mom, you're going to be a grandmother." He smiled sadly. "It's not how I'd pictured having my first child, but there it is."

Eric's eyes grew wet as he looked into the face of the first woman he'd loved. "I've let you down mom. I've let everyone down, Uncle Kobus, Rachel, myself, God." He shook his head. "Maybe I am just like dad after all."

Janice sat still for a little while looking into the distance. Then she put her arm around his waist and squeezed him tightly, her tears falling silently onto her lap. Then she sniffed and said, "Congratulations, my boy, you're going to be a father." Janice lay her head on his shoulder as Eric wiped his eyes on his t-shirt sleeve.

"I'm sorry mom," his voice cracked.

"Please don't say that Eric. Don't you say that. You are the pride of my life. The greatest gift God ever gave me. Nothing, nothing could make me ashamed of you."

Eric's tears started up anew as his mother held him. "There's more mom."

"It's twins?" Janice's eyes flew his way.

"No, just one baby, as far as I know. But the baby… the baby needs a bone marrow transplant mom, or it won't survive. Rachel came here to ask me to get tested, hoping I'd be a match to save the baby."

Janice nodded silently. Was this all a bit too much for her? "Oh, okay." She sighed deeply as she digested the new information. "She didn't come for you then?"

"No. Not for me." Eric picked at a blade of dry grass.

She turned to him. "So you need to be tested then?"

"*Ja*. I think I'll go as soon as I can, probably just after Boxing Day." Eric flicked the grass into the bush.

"It must've been very hard for Rachel to come here and ask you."

Eric leaned back on his hands. "Do you think so? I can't believe she kept the pregnancy from me."

Janice spoke over her shoulder. "She probably had her reasons my boy. Just hear her out before you judge her."

"Mom, I can't think of one reason that would be good enough to deprive me of my child. If the baby was healthy, I may never have even known I had a child. I don't even want to think about that." Eric straightened, dusting the small stones from his palms.

"I understand why you're upset Eric, but don't be foolish here. I know you love her. From what you've told me…"

"*Ja*." He nodded.

"Well, this just may be your chance to be together. Don't let your pride keep you from your heart's desire."

"It's not pride mom, it's trust. How can I trust her after this? We were together for a week in Wales, and she said nothing! If she could keep such a big secret from me, how will I be able to trust her again?"

Janice put her hand on his knee. "Just hear her out. Trust the Lord, and hear her out."

Eric nodded, but he still wasn't sure. There was no reason that would justify her not telling him such life-changing news. No reason at all that he could think of.

As they strolled back down the hill, Eric couldn't keep his eyes off the group at the swimming pool. Suzanne was sitting on the pool step with the children now, but still no sign of Rachel.

"Mom, I'm just going to say hi to Suzanne. I'll see you later?"

Janice smiled and nodded.

Eric turned down the steeper path that led down to the infinity pool. Suzanne spotted him the moment he emerged from the longer grass. "Look what the cat dragged in!" She was on form today.

"Hey. Looks like you're having fun." Eric untied his laces and pulled off his running shoes. He dipped his feet into the cool water and sat on the step beside her. "How is she?" he asked quietly.

"She's okay. We had a lovely morning of present opening, which was a good distraction, but of course, I can see the worry is always just beneath the surface. Congratulations, by the way." She nudged him in the arm.

"Thank you. I'm still in shock though. I've only just told my mom. No one else knows yet."

"Ooooo good luck telling your uncle!" Suzanne's eyes bulged.

Eric flinched visibly at the thought. Perhaps his mom could break it to him, very gently.

"She's leaving soon though, I don't know if you know that. She'll be gone in a few days."

Suzanne turned to the children. "No Lungelo! Don't splash her! Last warning and then you're out!"

"So soon..." Eric frowned, deep in thought. "Look I'd better go. Thank you Suz." Eric stood and stepped out the pool.

"For what?" She frowned up at him.

"For taking such good care of her... and my baby. Thank you."

***

"She's what?" Johan yelled, flinging his mini fridge door shut as he gawked at his friend.

"She's pregnant *bru*." Eric turned and leaned back against the kitchen counter.

The large man straightened, his mouth gaping. "She's pregnant! *Boet*, I thought you were joking." He slammed the milk down on the table. "One time, and she's pregnant?" Johan shook his head in wonder. "That would be quite impressive under different circumstances *boet*." He slapped his bear hand on Eric's shoulder a few times.

"Johan, please, this is serious man." Eric scowled at him.

"Sorry *ja*, you're right. Sorry." Johan pulled out a seat at the kitchen table. "Want me to take you shooting?"

"Johan, please man…" Eric shook his head. He wished he'd caught his friend in a different mood. He wondered if now was the right time to tell him the rest. Perhaps the rest would do the trick and sober him up a bit.

Eric plonked in a chair opposite him and held his brown eyes. "The baby is not well *bru*. It's very serious, potentially."

Johan's eyebrows furrowed together. "Oh no, really *boet*? That sounds hectic man. What is it?"

Eric sighed. "It's an immune syndrome. The baby will have a severely compromised immune system, unless he or she has a bone marrow transplant as soon as possible."

"Hectic *boet*. Shame man." Johan leaned forward, planting his elbows on the table between them.

Eric rubbed his forehead. "So I need you to take me to the hospital please, tomorrow morning. I need a bone marrow test, and I can't drive for a while after."

"*Eina*, I heard those are really painful. Like the hugest needle you've ever *checked*." As if his choice of words wasn't enough, the large man demonstrated the size of the needle with his hands.

"*Ja*, you might have to hold my hand *bru*." The corner of Eric's mouth curled up.

"No problem, as long as I don't have to look at that thing. I don't do needles *boet*. Man I can't believe you're going to be a dad!" He grinned at his friend. "And Johan will be there for you every step of the way. Especially if you make Johan the godfather." He winked and Eric laughed.

CHAPTER TWENTY-NINE

Eric took a shuddery breath and knocked on Uncle Kobus' front door. It was the evening of Boxing Day, and Eric didn't want to leave it any longer. He'd hate for his uncle to find out via the grape vine. He had been preparing himself with dread for most of the day, and now the time had come.

"Come on in, my boy, perfect timing." Uncle Kobus held the door wide open and ushered him through to the living room. "I'm just watching the Blue Bulls thump the Sharks. Take a seat."

Uncle Kobus handed him a bowl of *biltong*. Without moving his eyes from the television, he sat back down in his favourite seat. If there was one thing Uncle Kobus loved as much as *biltong* and *braais*, it was rugby. Particularly when Eric's team, the Sharks were getting beaten by his team, the Blue Bulls. Not much could make the man happier than that.

Eric sighed internally and took a seat. This was bad timing. "I'd forgotten this game was today." Eric had had way too much on his mind lately to think about rugby.

"It's nearly all over, and then we can talk. 34-20 to the Bulls." He chuckled.

Sitting around waiting did not help Eric's nerves. His appetite gone, he placed the bowl of *biltong* onto the coffee table.

With every minute that passed by, he could feel the perspiration build up under his t-shirt. When the final whistle eventually sounded, his stomach was in knots.

"*Ja nee*, I love a good game of rugby. And the Bulls were on form today my boy. Pity about the Sharks." He laughed softly, and turned off the television with the remote. "So what can I do for you Eric?" The older man leaned forward, elbows on knees.

"*Oom*, this isn't a social call, I need to speak to you. And you're not going to like what I have to say." Eric swallowed and scooted forward to the edge of the couch.

Uncle Kobus raised both hands. "Okay, look, my boy, if it's about your mother, I -"

"No *oom*, this has nothing to do with her." Eric rubbed his eyebrow.

"Oh, I see..." Uncle Kobus frowned, his interest piqued.

Eric sighed. "Um… this is hard… okay..." he said to himself as he pinched the bridge of his nose. "Do you remember Rachel?" He looked over at his uncle.

"*Ja*, the girl you took on the game drive, I remember her." He nodded, rubbing his chin with his hand.

"*Ja*. Well, she and I, we got quite close before she left for Wales." Eric scratched the side of his face.

Uncle Kobus narrowed his eyes. "Just *how* close are we talking about here my boy?"

"Uh..." Eric felt his face go hot under his uncle's scrutiny. "Very… very close *oom*."

Uncle Kobus' deep frown, deepened further. "What did you... did you sleep with her? Eric? Did you sleep with her?"

Eric swallowed. "I'd been drinking *oom*. I can't remember the details, but... she's pregnant *oom*. Rachel is pregnant."

Uncle Kobus' breathing changed as his nostrils flared. His frown was fixed in place, his fingers white as he clenched his knees. And then a deep sadness washed over his face.

He slowly stood and trudged from the room. His response was worse than any telling off Eric could imagine. He felt the weight of his uncle's disappointment deep in his soul. Shame filled him once more, and his shoulders stooped. His uncle must be thinking he was just like his father with alcohol, but worse.

He sank his head into his hands, and prayed. He prayed that God would take his shame, and that one day he would make Uncle Kobus proud of him again.

***

Eric fixed his eyes on the wooden door beyond his car windscreen. He wasn't ready to see her, but he needed the medical information and files to give to his doctor for this morning's test. He hadn't slept well, his conversation with Uncle Kobus weighed heavily on his mind. But even more than that, what if he wasn't a match for the baby? Would God shame him with the consequences of his actions and then take the baby too?

He massaged his temples, rubbing his hand back and forth over his brow. He couldn't allow himself the joy of imagining himself as a dad just yet. He'd get through this test first, and guard his heart until he knew it was safe enough to dream.

Eric took a deep breath and climbed out his Land Rover. As he reached her door he steeled himself for the sight of her. After three quick knocks, the door opened and there she was, dressed in her summer pyjamas, hair like a flowing river around her shoulders, eyes filled with something he couldn't fathom.

Without his permission, his eyes fluttered down to her middle. Eric's breath caught in his throat. Her pyjama top was stretched over the small bump of her belly. His heart squeezed inside his chest. He lifted his gaze back to hers. "Uh… morning." He cleared his throat, all business. "I'm headed for my test this morning. I was wondering if you have files or medical records I can give my doctors?"

"Yes of course." Rachel disappeared into the *rondavel* and brought out a thick yellow file. "This is all the information I have. It has everything your doctor will need to know."

It was peace. That was the emotion in her eyes. They were filled with assurance and calm, everything he wasn't feeling right now.

"Okay, thanks." Eric took the file and placed it under his arm.

"Do you want me to come with you?" she called as he turned to leave. "It's not very pleasant."

Eric frowned. "Uh… that's okay, Johan is taking me. It only takes a few hours."

Rachel's shoulders dropped. Did she really want to come along? "But you can if you want, I guess."

A glint appeared in her eyes. "Can you wait ten minutes while I get dressed?"

"I'll be in the car." Eric felt the strain between them as though it was a real, living thing, but he was powerless to destroy it. Perhaps once he had heard her out, like his mom suggested, things would be better between them.

He climbed into the driver's seat and put the radio on. It wasn't long and Rachel appeared. She looked beautiful in a yellow summer dress. He could just make out her little bump, and once again it caught him off guard. Seeing the beautiful evidence of the love between them growing within her made him desperate to start the dreaming he was trying so hard to avoid.

***

Eric tugged his car door closed as Rachel neared the Land Rover. She had never seen him look so exhausted. She climbed into the passenger seat and pulled her seatbelt across her baby bump. Eric kept the radio playing, and the music managed to occupy the awkward silence.

Once back at the reserve, Johan took over the driving and they headed for the freeway.

"It's good to see you again, Rachel." Johan looked back at her briefly over his shoulder.

"Thank you Johan. I've missed this place. It's good to be back." Rachel meant every word as she gazed out the window over the grassy plains.

"And of course, congratulations," he added and cleared his throat.

"Thank you." Rachel was relieved to have Johan around to break a bit of the tension. Eric sat unmoving in the front passenger seat. What was going through his mind?

Johan glanced over at his friend. "So *boet*, you've got Rachel with you, so I'm just gonna drop you at the hospital. I'll get some stuff done in town and then just call me when you're ready to be fetched."

"Okay thanks *bru*."

Rachel and Eric exited the car and headed for the reception. The reception area was modern and classy, unlike anything she had seen in the UK. "Wow. Eric, this hospital looks…"

"Expensive. *Ja*, it's private, that's why so many South Africans have a medical aid. You won't believe these prices."

After a brief conversation at the main desk, they took a seat in the plush waiting area.

"Mr Pieterson?" A young doctor in heels and a lab coat came through.

Eric stood and wiped his palms down his thighs, Rachel beside him.

"Follow me please."

Once seated in the doctor's office, Eric handed her the yellow file. She placed it down and linked her fingers together on top of it. "Okay so today we are going to do a bone marrow biopsy on you, Mr Pieterson. We are hoping that you will be a full match for your unborn child. As you know, your baby needs a transplant, the sooner the better, in order to give him his best chance at a healthy immune system."

"Him?" Eric scooted forward in his seat.

"Oh dear, I'm so sorry I thought you knew?" she smiled cautiously. "This syndrome is far more common in boys than girls, as it's linked to the x-chromosome. For a female, the other x-chromosome would most likely mask the syndrome. Gender was determined during the amniocentesis. I apologise, it's in your notes, so I thought you'd been told."

"It's a boy." Rachel looked over at Eric with moist eyes and saw the shine in his as he blinked.

"Okay, so how soon do we get started?" he asked.

"Right now, follow me please. Rachel you are welcome to come through. He might need a hand to hold." The doctor smiled and led them through to a procedure room nearby. Eric changed into a blue hospital gown behind a screen and came through looking a little anxious. The doctor gave him a light sedative as he lay on the bed, and positioned him to reveal the hip where the marrow would be extracted from. Rachel stood near his head. She wasn't sure if he'd welcome her holding his hand, but she was desperate to.

As the doctor inserted the first needle, Eric flinched a little and Rachel instinctively grabbed his hand and held on tight. He squeezed back and closed his eyes as the larger needle was inserted. The procedure was over soon after that and Eric was moved to a recovery area.

"You okay?" Rachel asked as the nurse left them.

"*Ja*, I'm fine. A bit thirsty though." He adjusted his pillow to lift his head higher.

"Would you like a coffee or a soft drink?"

"Uh… *ja* please, whatever you can find Rachel. The cafeteria is near the main reception where we came in."

"Okay, I won't be long."

Rachel returned with two coffees, a bottle of water and a couple of chocolate muffins.

"Thought you might be hungry too."

"I'm always hungry. Thank you." Eric moved to sit slightly higher in the bed and took the bottle of water. After swigging back half of it, he started on his coffee and muffin. Then he shifted his head back down onto his pillow and drifted off into a deep sleep. Rachel wasn't surprised to hear gentle snoring a short while later. His exhaustion was so apparent that morning, and now the sedative was helping him get the rest he needed.

Watching Eric sleep did strange things to her heart. She knew she shouldn't take advantage of the situation, but she needed to be near him, especially now with so much uncertainty. She moved closer and touched his hair, winding a lose curl around her finger.

Then she bent down and kissed his forehead, his skin smooth and warm against her lips. His eyelids fluttered and he frowned.

"Oh I'm sorry," Rachel took a step back.

Eric, with eyes still closed, laid his hand out at the edge of the bed. Her heart melted. She drew near and placed her hand in his.

"Don't leave me Rachel, please don't leave me," he mumbled.

***

When Eric finally awoke, Rachel had lunch and a glass of orange juice waiting.

"Thank you. How long did I sleep for?" He rubbed his eyes, his voice groggy.

"A couple hours. You needed it. I had no idea you could snore like that," she teased.

"What?" He balked. "I don't snore."

"You don't eh?" Rachel hauled her phone out her bag and played him the recording she'd made. The hideous sound vibrated through the small room.

"Pffft! That could be anyone! Besides isn't that a violation of privacy or something. Taking advantage of a tired, drugged-up man, shame on you Rachel." Eric shook his head and clicked his tongue the way the Africans do, in mock anger.

"How do you do that?" Rachel frowned.

"What?"

"That clicking."

Eric grinned. "Africans are born knowing how to do that my girl. Not something that can be taught I'm afraid. We'll know you're becoming African when you start clicking your tongue like one," he joked as he took a large bite off the corner of his sandwich. Rachel laughed. She'd missed him. And she'd missed this easiness between them.

"So… it's a boy." Eric smiled slowly up at her as he chewed.

"Yeh, little Eric junior." Rachel laughed and held her stomach.

"We'll have to find him a good South African name," Eric joked.

"Hmmm... we'll have to see about that!"

CHAPTER THIRTY

"'Johan' is a very nice name for a baby. And that's especially true if I'm gonna be the godfather." Johan said as he turned off the engine.

Eric rolled his eyes. "Oh here we go again."

"I'm telling you Rachel, I don't know anyone called 'Johan' who's not totally awesome." He looked at her over his shoulder. Rachel laughed and pushed the back passenger door open.

"Oh give it a rest!" Eric huffed and climbed out the car.

Johan had arrived at the hospital room as the discussion of names was starting, and now they'd arrived back home, and still he couldn't stop talking about it.

Johan shut his car door and turned to Rachel. "So let's get the patient into his cabin, and then I can take you home Rachel."

Eric looked over at her. Did their time together have to end so soon? As it was, she was scheduled to fly home in five days. They still had so much to talk about. Rachel caught his eye. Was she thinking the same thing? "Uh... Johan just wait... Rachel do you want to stay a while?"

"Uh... yeh. Why not?" Rachel flung her handbag strap over her shoulder.

"*Bru*, would you mind taking her a bit later? Maybe we could all go to church together tonight?" Eric searched her face.

"Yeh, that sounds good." She nodded.

Johan jingled his keys. "Okay *boet*, I'm leaving at six sharp for the meeting. And you two must promise to behave yourselves!" His brown eyes bulged back and forth between the two of them. "If something's gonna happen here now, it's gonna be Johan's fault."

"Just go!" They laughed as Johan headed for his cabin.

***

"Feel like a walk?" Eric asked as he led the way into his tiny kitchen.

"As long as you promise to take it easy." Rachel lay her handbag on his kitchen table and looked around his modest living area.

"Done." He grinned and strode to the fridge.

Eric filled his backpack with snacks, drinks and a blanket and swung it over his shoulder. "Let's go, I'm going to show you my favourite spot."

"Okay!"

Eric took her hand as they walked towards his running trail up the hill. He chose the route that was longer, but less steep, and kept the pace slow.

"So, I guess we have a lot to talk about. Sorry for leaving you hanging for a few days there." He caught her eye briefly.

"It's okay. I had a lot more time to process it all than you did."

"So what happens now?" Eric let go of her hand and took the lead as the path narrowed.

"We wait for the test results, and pray you're a match. If you are then the baby will have the surgery."

"Before birth?"

"Well, we could wait until after, but there are risks associated with both options. The operation itself is a bit more tricky in utero as you can imagine, but then the baby will have no chance of being exposed to germs. If we have the operation after birth, well then there's a chance the baby could catch something before the operation."

"I see." Eric looked back at her. "So what do you think?"

"I think I'd prefer to do it as soon as possible really."

"You'd have it done in Wales then?" They reached a steep rock. Eric climbed up and turned back to offer her his hand.

"Yes through the NHS." She took his hand and he pulled her up beside him. He didn't let go.

"What if you could have it done here? At a private hospital?"

Rachel gazed back the way they'd come. "Eric, I just don't have that kind of money."

"Would you like me to try and register you on my medical aid? That way it would be covered by them."

Rachel thought for a long time. She felt the strength in his hand. He made her feel safe. She needed him with her, she couldn't go through this without him.

"Okay."

He squeezed her hand. "Let me see what I can do."

***

When they reached a grassy plain halfway up the hill, Eric laid the blanket underneath his favourite acacia tree. It was a hot day and Eric loved the feeling of lying in the cool, breezy shade. He reclined next to Rachel propped up on his elbow. Chewing on a long blade of grass, he watched her thoughtfully. "Can I ask you a question?"

"You can ask me anything." She turned towards him and held his eye.

"Why didn't you tell me you were pregnant? I was with you all that time in Wales, and you said nothing. Why?" He searched her face in the speckled light.

She shifted onto her elbow. "Because I knew you'd do the right thing Eric." Rachel played with a piece of grass between her fingers. "I knew you'd offer to give up your life here, the life you're called to, and move across the world. You'd lose everything you'd worked so hard for. It's who you are, it's your identity. The UK is nothing like Africa, Eric. Do I want to be a single parent? No, but I can't bear to see you make such a sacrifice."

"You're right." He flicked the blade of grass far into the bush. "I would've offered to move to be with you."

"I know," she said softly.

"I would've been willing to give up everything, not just because it's the right thing to do Rachel, but because... I love you. I'd give it all up in a heartbeat, still." He held his breath.

She found his eyes. "And I, well I can't let you do that. Because... I love you too."

Eric's chest tightened as he looked deeply into her green eyes. He leaned in close, cupped her cheek with his hand and kissed her, long and slow. He closed his eyes and rubbed his forehead against hers. "Can I feel him?" Eric asked quietly.

"Who?"

"The baby, can I feel him? Would you mind?"

"He's not strong enough yet that you could feel his movements, but yeh, of course you can." Rachel took his hand and placed it over her little bump.

Eric's face lit up. "I can't believe there's a tiny person in there," he said with wonder.

"And not just any person, he's yours," she said.

"How did your family take the news Rach?" he asked, removing his hand.

"I think they took it quite well really. It was tense at first, but mum took me baby shopping just before I left. That was a good sign. And yours?"

"My mom was great... is great. I think she'd love to spend some time with you at some stage. Uncle Kobus, well... he didn't take it too well. He got up and left before I could tell him about the baby's condition. So I'm not even sure he knows the whole story yet. Maybe my mom will tell him, hopefully soon."

Rachel frowned. "I'm sorry Eric."

"No, don't be. I kind of expected it. He's a straight and narrow kind of guy. I know he'll come around though. He just needs some time."

"Is there something going on between those two?" Rachel raised an eyebrow.

Eric laughed. "He wishes! *Ja*, he asked my mom to marry him a little while ago. But she's not ready. I'm hoping she'll come around. He's a really good man. They've both been through so much, they deserve to be happy."

Rachel shifted onto her back and gazed up into the tree branches with a contented sigh. Eric lay close to her on his side. He covered her bump with his hand again. Within minutes Rachel was asleep.

As Eric lay there, feeling the warmth of her body next to his, despite all the uncertainty about the future, he felt peace. He knew now, deep in his soul, that God wasn't out to punish him, He loved him. Yes there were consequences for his actions, but that was just life, not God's vengeance. With Rachel and his unborn baby within an arm's length away, how could he be anything but blessed.

***

Rachel roused to the sound of rhythmic snoring. How could the man be sleeping again? The thought that they'd fallen asleep together warmed her heart. She'd never felt closer to him. She rolled over onto her side and studied his profile. It was late afternoon and the air had cooled somewhat.

Eric turned towards her as he opened his eyes lazily. "Well hello there."

She smiled and he pulled her near. He wrapped his arm around her waist and held her close. She could feel her little bump pressing against his waist. He stroked her face with his thumb and looked deeply into her eyes. Rachel leaned in and kissed him slowly. His lips were soft and warm. He moved his hand behind her head and into her hair. The mood shifted as Eric deepened the kiss. Rachel knew she had to pull away before it became too difficult to stop. "Eric," she said breathlessly, leaning her forehead against his.

"I know..." he whispered and closed his eyes, his breathing hard and fast. He shifted his weight onto his elbow. "We'd better go. Johan's going to send out a search party soon."

They packed up their belongings and meandered back down the hill, hand-in-hand.

Once back at Eric's cabin, Rachel freshened up in the bathroom and fixed her make-up. Eric pulled on a fresh t-shirt and together they met Johan at his Land Rover.

"So what's your church like?" Rachel asked as she climbed into Johan's Land Rover.

"It's big... and loud and passionate." Eric raised both eyebrows at her over his shoulder.

"Okay, so I should be able to hide in the crowd then?" She squeezed her hands between her knees.

The men chuckled. "Uh... no. Everyone will want to meet you," said Johan as he changed gear.

"O... kay," she said slowly.

"Rach, we'll just say you're a friend visiting from Wales. That's all they need to know. For now anyway." Eric smiled at her.

Rachel nodded in relief.

When they arrived in the expansive parking lot and Johan struggled to find a parking space, Rachel realised they hadn't exaggerated about the size of the church.

"Okay, so it's a bit bigger than I thought," she said looking out the window with trepidation.

"I won't let you out of my sight, I promise," Eric said over his shoulder and caught her eye.

They entered the heaving building and managed to find three seats towards the middle of the left side. They sat for a few minutes and listened to the music as they waited for the meeting to start. The lights were dimmed where they sat, and Rachel could feel the growing anticipation of the crowd around her. They expected to meet with God tonight.

Rachel felt overwhelmed and challenged at the thought. The background music stopped as the band walked onto the stage. This made quite a change from the organ music Rachel was used to in her father's church. But as the band started to play, Rachel felt the hunger in her spirit growing more and more intense. She glanced over at Eric just in time to see him lift his hands. He closed his eyes and sang with conviction. Rachel felt conviction just watching him. She hadn't realised the depth of his relationship with God until tonight. She closed her eyes and let the worship wash over her soul. And in her heart, she prayed simply. "Father, forgive me. I've strayed so far from You. I'm choosing tonight to draw close to You again. And I know that You will draw close to me too."

By the end of the worship, Rachel felt completely relaxed. A large older man came to the pulpit then and opened his bible with a smile that stretched across his weathered cheeks. He spoke with deep passion on the father heart of God. Rachel listened to the message intently, soaking up every precious word. She was so pleased she'd come. She'd needed this.

As the meeting came to an end, Eric faced her, eyebrows raised. "Ready to meet some people?"

"Yeh sure. Why not?"

As Eric introduced her to his vast crowd of friends, she realised just how well respected and loved he was, and her opinion of him soared.

Johan was in the thick of it, mingling and socialising. "I'm just going to talk to the band. I'll meet you in the foyer in about ten minutes, okay?" Johan strolled over to a little redhead near the keyboard. Eric smiled knowingly and shook his head. He leaned towards Rachel. "Ready to leave?"

"Yeh okay, shall we wait outside for Johan?"

"Let's go."

It was far easier said than done. Every metre or so, Eric would be stopped by someone or other for a chat.

Eventually they made it out into the warm night and found a bench to sit on.

"So what did you think?" He covered her hand with his and pulled it onto his thigh.

"Wow, it was... incredible actually. I was a little nervous at first, but I loved it. The worship, the message, all of it."

"Not too overwhelming?" He searched her expression.

"A little. I've just never seen so many people so passionate about Jesus."

Eric smiled. "*Ja* it's contagious around here."

"I can imagine!"

Johan sauntered over then and they headed for the car, exhausted. They dropped Rachel off at the orphanage and headed home. With a full heart, Rachel was asleep as soon as her head hit the pillow.

CHAPTER THIRTY-ONE

"No, she's not my wife... She's not a family member either... Yes she's four months pregnant... What? Why not? What, are you serious? There's nothing you can do? What am I supposed to do now? Thanks anyway. Okay, bye." Eric sighed in defeat. He collected up the strewn mess of policy documents on his bed as a knock sounded at the door.

"What's going on *boet*?" Johan's enormous presence filled Eric's small bedroom.

"I'm trying to get Rachel onto my medical aid. They won't allow it." Eric shoved the papers into the bedside table drawer.

"*Boet*, they'll never add someone who's already pregnant onto your policy. Even I could've told you that."

"What now *bru*? She's going to have to go home." Eric ran his hand down his face.

"Look, I'm sorry *boet*, but it's better than using one of these government hospitals."

"*Ja*, I know. If I can find a way to finance this, we could drive down to Durban. There's only one foetal surgeon in the whole country *bru*, and he's operates right here at Parklands. This is all assuming I'm a match of course." He sighed. "I don't even want to think about the possibility that I'm not."

Johan edged himself down onto the side of Eric's bed. "I've been praying for you *boet*. And Rachel and JJ."

"JJ?" Eric frowned.

"Johan Junior." He nodded.

"What am I going to do now *bru*, I can't let her go back. What if she decides she doesn't want me in her life and I never see her and... EJ again?" Eric collapsed onto the bed beside his friend.

"EJ?"

"Eric Junior."

"Touché." Johan smiled. "Listen *boet*, that's not gonna happen, she loves you. Even Johan can see that."

"Anything can happen, Johan. I don't want to let her out of my sight. Ever." Eric rubbed the back of his neck.

"Well then you have to marry her *boet*."

"Not even marriage is going to get her onto my medical aid *bru*, it's too late for that. She needed to be on the policy *before* she fell pregnant. She's going to have to go home."

"Maybe you can go with her."

Eric shook his head. "*Bru*, you didn't see how upset Uncle Kobus was... *is*... with me, and we're short-staffed now with so many away for the Christmas holidays."

"*Boet*, just let her go." He slapped his hand on Eric's knee. "What's that story about the bird? If you have a bird and you let it go, and then it comes back and it's yours or something."

"Well it doesn't seem like I'm going to have a choice. She has to go."

"*Ja*, you're going to have to pray and trust God with this *boet*. Johan is praying also."

***

Eric's Land Rover pulled up as Rachel stepped out her door the following morning. She smiled and gave him a wave. He looked so handsome in his khakis. He climbed out the car and trudged towards her. Something was wrong.

He greeted her with a kiss on the forehead. "Morning Rach, you look beautiful." He ran a hand down her arm, his fingers finding her hand.

She frowned. "What's wrong?"

"It's the medical aid. They won't put you on my policy, I tried everything. I'm sorry."

"It's okay Eric, I'd prepared for this."

"I wish things could be different. I wish I could go back to Wales with you, but it's just not possible right now. I'm sorry." He sighed.

"It'll be fine Eric. The operation is actually the least of our worries. We need you to be a match. We need those test results."

"I know. Listen, how about a distraction. I have to work today, but I was wondering if you wanted to tag along." He tilted his head.

"Tag along on your game drives?"

"*Ja*, no pressure, if you'd rather be doing something else."

"Eric, I'd love to!" She squeezed his hand.

"The front seat's all yours for the day then. Are you ready to go? I need to be back there in half an hour."

"I haven't had breakfast... I was just about to get some at the main house."

"I've got a bag of food packed and ready for us."

Rachel smiled. "I'm all yours then!"

***

This was exactly what Rachel needed today. It was the most beautiful distraction. Instead of sitting around waiting anxiously for the phone to ring, she was out in the African *bushveld* with the man she loved. Of course they weren't alone, but the tourists made for amusing entertainment with their outlandish questions. Rachel had never seen Eric like this. He was in his element; charming, confident, it was no wonder these game drives were doing so well.

"And that elephant there, is the pride of our reserve, Thandi. She's the matriarch of the herd, an excellent mother and a strong leader. And... the desire of all the bulls!" He laughed and everyone joined in. "She's not short on male attention, that's for sure!"

"Where are the bulls, Eric? These are just females here, am I right?" asked a man at the back of the land cruiser.

"*Ja*, once the bulls reach a certain age, they get kicked out the herd to fend for themselves. They might become loners, or join up with another bull herd. But they hang out with the ladies when it's time to... um..." Everyone laughed. "Once they've had their fun, they leave and go back to doing what they were doing before."

The day passed quickly, and once they'd dropped off their final group back at the reserve, they were both hot and exhausted. Eric's mom came out to greet them as they climbed out the vehicle.

"Hi Eric."

"Mom, it's about time you meet Rachel. Rach, this is my mom, Janice."

"Rachel, it's so lovely to meet you! Eric's told me all about you." Janice skipped the pleasantries and gave Rachel a hug.

"I've looked forward to meeting you too, Janice." Rachel smiled.

"And congratulations. I'm so excited that I'll be a grandmother soon!" Her eyes sparkled.

Rachel laughed. "Thank you."

"Why don't you two come for supper? I've got meat, we can have a little *braai*."

Eric looked over at Rachel for an answer.

"I'd love that," she beamed.

"Okay it's settled then! How about six thirty or around then?"

"That's perfect mom, it'll give us time for a quick swim before then."

"That sounds wonderful!" Rachel cooed. "But I don't have my swimsuit."

"I'll lend you something to swim in, unless you want to go straight to the pool now, and then I'll have something ready for you to change into after?" offered Janice.

"A swim in my dress? Sounds like fun, I'm rather desperate right now. I'm not made for this type of heat!"

Janice laughed. "Okay, well then enjoy your swim and I'll see you both later."

"Thanks mom. See you later." Eric winked at her as he headed towards the cabins with Rachel tucked under his arm. When they reached Eric's cabin, he grabbed a couple of drinks and towels, and changed into a pair of shorts and a t-shirt.

***

"Man! This is what summer in South Africa is all about," said Eric, leaning up against the side of the pool. "Sunshine, the bush, swimming and of course, *braaing*!"

Rachel laughed as she neared him. "I could get used to this."

"Could you now?" He smiled as he pulled her against him in the water. He rested his forehead against hers for a long while and held her close. He could feel the swell of her tummy pressing against him. He kissed her shoulder, and then her neck. "Being this close to you makes me wish I could remember our night together," he whispered in her ear as Rachel blushed.

"Me too," she whispered back.

"I don't want you to leave," he spoke as he nuzzled the nape of her neck.

"I know."

He touched his nose to hers. "I can't lose you Rachel."

"It'll be okay. You'll see."

"I won't be okay without you." He held her tighter.

Eventually he eased off, and they moved to the side of the pool. It was nearly time to leave for the *braai* at Janice's. Eric's phone started ringing near his towel. He climbed out the water, dried his hands and answered. Rachel followed, grabbing a towel off the floor.

"Yes doctor, thank you for calling." He looked at her, eyes large.

Rachel, dripping wet, hurried near, anxiety all over her face.

"What? Sorry what did you say?" Eric frowned. "I *am* a match? I'm a match! I'm a match!" Eric dropped his phone, flung both arms around Rachel and lifted her into the air. He spun her around as they celebrated together. Then he jumped back into the pool with her as they laughed and whooped. He'd never felt such relief. Joy and peace flooded his soul.

Eric threw his dripping wet fists in the air. "Thank you Jesus!" he shouted over and over.

***

They were still smiling by the time they reached Janice's thatch-roofed house. Eric knocked lightly on the solid wood door, and entered with Rachel tagging behind him.

"Mom, we're here," Eric called. "And we have very good news!"

"In the kitchen."

Eric smacked the counter of the open-planned kitchen. "I'm a match, mom! I'm a match! Our baby has a chance! A good chance! We just got the call."

She dropped her knife on the chopping board and rushed to hug him. "Thank you Jesus! That is such wonderful news!" The tears shone in her eyes. "I'm so relieved, I can't tell you."

"*Ja.*" He smiled. "We haven't stopped smiling!"

"I'm sure! Praise God!" said Janice as she hugged Rachel. Then she handed her the small pile of clothes that was lying on the kitchen counter. "Shame, you are soaking! I hope they fit! You look about the same size as me, so they should be fine."

"Thank you Janice, where shall I change?" Rachel fingered the shirt on the top of the pile.

"Here, I'll show you." Eric led her to the bathroom and returned to the kitchen.

"So, what do you think?" he whispered to his mom.

"About Rachel?"

He nodded. "*Ja.*"

"Eric, she's lovely! I can't wait to get to know her better. I wish we had more time."

"Me too." Eric's smile disappeared then. Janice resumed her chopping and Eric offered to help chop the tomatoes.

Rachel came through wearing Janice's t-shirt and shorts. "How can I help?" she asked.

"We're just about done, Rachel, thank you." Janice reached for some glasses in the cupboard near her head and fetched a selection of fruit juices from the fridge. "What would you both like to drink?"

"Ooo is that strawberry juice? Wow, I've never seen that before." Rachel turned the box to look at the front packaging.

"Try some, it's my absolute favourite!" said Janice.

"Thank you, I'd love to! One thing's for sure, South Africa has the best fruit juices I've ever tasted!"

"They are pretty special, I'll have the same, thanks mom." Eric pulled out a barstool and sat at the counter.

"I hope you two don't mind, but when I heard the baby was a boy, I had to do just a little shopping." Janice retrieved a blue and white gift bag from the far counter and handed it to Rachel. "I hope you don't mind."

"Of course not, thank you!" Rachel pulled out a tiny cream baby-grow with a giraffe embroidered on the front. "Aaaaw that is so cute!"

Then there were five African-themed bibs, and a pair of soft leather shoes with lions on the front. "Janice, thank you. You've only just met me, and already I feel loved and accepted by you. Thank you." Rachel's eyes were wet as she hugged the older woman.

"That's perfect mom. I can't wait to see him wearing these."

"Well I guess we better get started with the meat! We've got Rachel eating for two, you better get a move on Eric."

Eric laughed, grabbed the tray of tenderised meat and headed out back onto the patio.

The quick-light charcoal was ready for *braaing* on in no time, and soon they were enjoying their meat, salad and rolls in the shade of the patio. The *bushveld* stretched out before them and silhouettes of elephant and giraffe started to form on the horizon as the sun sank.

"Hi, sorry to disturb." Uncle Kobus appeared in the doorway. "I tried knocking but I don't think you could hear." Eric stiffened.

"Kobus, welcome. Would you like to… uh… join us?" offered Janice.

He wrung his cap in his hands. "Thank you Janice, but I'd just like a quick word with Eric please. If you don't mind."

"Sure…"

Eric rose from his seat and followed Uncle Kobus through to the living room. They both took a seat on the couches.

Uncle Kobus shifted and cleared his throat. "Listen my boy. I owe you a huge apology."

"No *oom*, it's fine really." Eric gripped his knee with his hand.

Uncle Kobus leaned forward. "No, it's not fine Eric. I was far too hard on you my boy. I'm sorry."

"*Oom*, I understand. You were shocked and disappointed. And so was I… I was disappointed in myself."

"And now… now we must move on. I want to get to know this lady who's turned your whole world upside down. She must be very special."

"She is *oom*. *Oom*, I'm not sure you know this, but the baby needs a bone marrow transplant. Did my mom tell you?"

"No my boy, this is the first I'm hearing about this. What's wrong?" His bushy brows almost touched as he searched Eric's face.

"The baby inherited a genetic syndrome, it's in Rachel's family. It means he'll have a severely compromised immunity, unless he has a transplant, ideally very soon."

"Oh no, that sounds terrible Eric. Have you found a donor?"

"*Ja oom*. We just found out, I am a match."

"Oh praise God!" He sighed.

"Yes…" Eric nodded.

As Uncle Kobus rose to leave, Eric asked, "*Oom* why don't you join us? There's plenty of food left, and I think there's pudding too. It's your favourite, peppermint crisp tart."

"My boy now you've made it very hard to resist. As long as your mom doesn't mind."

"She won't."

They headed back out onto the patio and Uncle Kobus pulled up a seat. "Rachel, congratulations." Uncle Kobus nodded towards her as Janice brought him a plate of food.

"Thank you," she smiled and tucked a strand of dark blonde hair behind her ear.

"When do you head back home?"

"I'll be leaving in just a few days. I think my doctor wants to schedule the surgery for soon after I'm back."

"Oh I see. You couldn't have the surgery here then?"

"No. Eric couldn't get me onto his medical aid. I'd need private care at Parklands and well… I can't afford to pay privately for the operation. It's quite an involved procedure."

Uncle Kobus nodded and finished up his food.

Eric stood and stacked the dirty plates on the table near the *braai*. "Mom, I'd better take Rachel home. She's had a busy day, and I'm sure she's exhausted."

"Yeh, I need an early night for sure! Thank you Janice, tonight was just perfect!"

Janice rose and hugged her. "It was a pleasure to get to know you a bit better. Hope to see you again before you leave."

Eric tucked Rachel under his arm and walked her around the side of the house, back to his cabin where his car was parked. The stars were out now, but the air was still warm.

"We'll have to do this again… tomorrow, and the next day, and the day after that…" Rachel said leaning into him.

He kissed the top of her head. "Absolutely."

THIRTY-TWO

Uncle Kobus' easy smile was back in place the following morning. He sauntered over to where Eric sat in his car outside the reception. "My boy, I've asked Sipho to do your game drives today." Uncle Kobus leaned into Eric's open car window. "I want you to come with me to check the border fence."

"Okay *oom*," said Eric as he switched cars. He hoped their trip wouldn't last the whole day. He was desperate for more time with Rachel before she left.

Uncle Kobus popped into the reception and came back out with a small cooler box. He handed it to Eric as he climbed in behind the wheel. "Your mom, she's packed us some lunch." He smiled.

"Any progress there *oom*?" Eric asked, settling the box at his feet.

Uncle Kobus started the engine and reversed the car. "*Ja* no, I'm just trying to take it one day at a time. Trying not to rush her my boy. Sometimes it's hard to be patient, but then I pray and ask the Lord to help me."

Eric smiled and nodded. The vegetation was dense this time of year, making the animals, and poachers, harder to spot.

When they finally reached the outer border, Uncle Kobus turned to Eric. "My boy, I didn't ask you to come with me today just because I need the fence checked. I do need to check the fence, but mostly, I need to talk to you."

Eric frowned. "Okay *oom*. What do you want to talk about?" He tapped his fingers on his thigh.

The older man glanced at him briefly. "I want to talk about Rachel."

"*Ja oom?*"

"You shouldn't be apart now my boy. She's pregnant and she needs you with her through this operation. It's a big deal, and it's *your* responsibility. You need to take good care of her my boy, especially now."

"*Ja oom*, I agree, but I can't just leave now."

"*Ja*, that's why I'm going to pay for the operation. You can drive down to Durban, stay there and have the operation, then bring her home to recover."

Eric shook his head. "*Oom* I couldn't ask you to do that, it's too much..."

"I'm not finished yet... and then when it's time for the baby to be born, if she wants to stay here and marry you, then I'm going to pay for the birth also."

Eric swallowed. "*Oom* no. It's too much. I can't accept that *oom*."

"You can and you must. Eric listen to me, my boy. You are like my son, and this baby is like my grandchild. Do you understand? If Rachel wants to stay and marry you, then she'll be my daughter too. *Verstaan?* And no daughter of mine is going to fly across the world, away from her man for an operation, when she can have it right here."

Eric looked down. "It's too much *oom*."

"No, I'm not finished yet." Uncle Kobus dug deep into his pocket and pulled out a dark grey box. "Here, this is yours. For when you're ready."

Eric frowned and took the box. He opened it slowly, and shook his head in disbelief. "No *oom*. No. You can't give this to me."

Uncle Kobus nodded. "*Ja*, I can. It's mine and I can give it to anyone I want to," he said roughly.

"But... it's..." Eric's voice broke.

"*Ja*, it's very precious to me, and that's why I want *you* to have it. You're going to have everything I never had."

Eric put his head in one hand and couldn't stop the tear that slid down onto his lap. Because in his hand was the most beautiful solitaire diamond ring. And more than that, it had belonged to his aunt, Lindie, before she'd died. It was the most beloved thing that Uncle Kobus had, and now it was his.

***

It was New Year's Eve, and Eric was working. He dug his spade deep into the trough and removed the old hay that had collected there. Then he filled both troughs with fresh hay and cleaned and refilled the water troughs. The rhinos were looking healthy. They were relaxed and settled in their new home.

Eric leaned against the fence and watched them like he did each day. But today he noticed something different. Oubaas, the male rhino, appeared to be marking his territory with dung, all around the edges of the enclosure. This was very good news. It was the first step in the mating courtship. Eric smiled watching him go at it.

There were no game drives today, so his work was now done. He was desperate to see Rachel. He had the evening all planned out as a surprise, a big surprise. He'd asked her to be ready at seven, and to pack something warm. He headed back to his cabin for a quick shower, and dressed in a pair of blue jeans and his new button-up shirt his mom had bought him for Christmas. A splash of aftershave and he was rearing to go. He packed the food, drinks and bedding into his Land Rover and headed over to Rachel's *rondavel*.

***

Rachel's heart leapt at the sound of tyres on gravel. One spritz of perfume and a quick check of her make-up, and she was ready. She wasn't sure what to wear, but had eventually settled on blue jeans and a soft pink knitted top. She locked up and met Eric at his car.

"You look wonderful," he said as he leaned in to kiss her cheek.

"Likewise." She smiled as he held the door for her. Once settled in the front seat, Eric reached over and put some music on.

"So I have some news." Rachel drummed her hands on her thighs excitedly.

"Let's hear it!"

"I felt the baby move last night."

Eric grinned broadly at her. "Rach, that's amazing! What did it feel like?"

"It was so weird, like someone tapping my stomach, but from the inside!"

"Let me know when you feel him again, I'd love to feel that."

They drove in silence the rest of the way. When they got to the cabins however, Eric drove straight past and towards the side of the hill. He turned right and took the fork up the mountain.

"Hold on… and trust me." Eric grinned.

Now Rachel could understand why all the rangers drove Land Rovers. She'd never done four by fouring, and it was hair-raising. Eric negotiated the vehicle up the rough, steep terrain, and by the time they reached the top, she was exhilarated. "Wow, that was insane!"

"Not really Rach." Eric grinned at her. "There are much tougher trails out there. That one is relatively tame."

"Show off!" she teased.

Eric laughed as he climbed out the car and fetched the warm blanket and cooler box he'd brought along. The sun was setting in shades of pink against the *bushveld*, and the crickets had started their incessant chirping.

Eric spread the blanket and began to make a small fire for their meat. He collected rocks and placed them in a circle, then laid twigs with paper in the centre.

"So you didn't get invited to any New Year's Eve parties tonight?" Rachel asked.

"Oh I did, quite a few actually. You?" He struck a match and lit the paper.

"Yeh, they've hired a bouncy castle and water slide for the party at the orphanage."

"Sounds like fun. You didn't mind missing it?" He was fishing, but she didn't mind.

"You know I'd pick you any day."

Eric smiled as he broke more twigs over the fire. Once the fire was more established, Eric added some charcoal and blew on it. Rachel loved the fact that Eric could do these types of things, it was so normal for him. He retrieved a small grid from the back of the car and laid it over the rocks. Then he placed potatoes, wrapped in foil, in between the coals.

"All ready for the meat!" He rubbed his hands, then dug in the cooler bag beside him.

"So do you get any South African vegetarians?"

"Um… no. Okay maybe one or two, but it's not easy being a vegetarian in this country. Not easy at all."

"I can imagine."

"So I also have some news." Eric looked over and caught her eye in the light of the fire. "Uncle Kobus has insisted he pay for your operation, in Durban."

Rachel blinked a few times. "Wow, I'm speechless."

"It's a very generous offer Rach. Please tell me you'll take him up on it. That way I can be with you for the procedure. We'll drive down together and be there for just a few days. And then it'll all be over."

"Okay. That sounds good, Eric," Rachel replied.

"We have to get the date set then Rach. I have to start injections for my donation. It takes about four days."

"And I'll have to postpone my flight." Rachel snapped a twig in half and threw the pieces into the bush.

"I like the sound of that... cancel... sounds even better." He wiggled his eyebrows.

Rachel laughed.

The meat was cooked and Eric grabbed two paper plates. "For you... help yourself. There's meat, potatoes and even some salad, just for you."

Rachel filled her plate and took the fruity drink Eric passed her.

Once they'd eaten and cleaned up, Eric got a couple of pillows and an extra blanket out the car. He added some wood to the fire and reclined next to Rachel. He reached over and pulled a bag of marshmallows out the cooler box. Fetching two nearby twigs, he cleaned them off and handed one to her.

"Rustic!" She grinned, examining her twig.

"Watch and learn beautiful, watch and learn." Eric pushed his twig into a marshmallow and held it over the fire. Rachel followed suit and soon they were munching on sticky melted marshmallows.

"So, I have a small confession to make." Eric looked over at Rachel briefly, but couldn't hold her gaze for this admission. "I remember," Eric said quietly, looking into the fire.

"You remember what?" Rachel frowned, searching his face.

"I remember... everything." He stole a quick glance at her.

Understanding dawned in Rachel. "Oh. I see." She bit her lip and looked down.

He placed his hand on the back of her neck in her hair, and searched her eyes. He smiled down at her. "And you are so beautiful." He ran his finger down the side of her face.

Suddenly the New Year's Eve fire works started and they both smiled. He'd thought of everything. They had the perfect view over the whole of Pietermaritzburg.

Eric took both of her hands, and kissed each palm, one at a time. "Rach, you know I don't have much to offer a woman just yet. But I'm a hard worker, and one day, I'll own my own home, I can promise you that. There's so much I want to say, but I don't have the words. You've turned my world upside down Rachel, to the point where I can't imagine a future for myself without you in it." Eric dug into his pocket and pulled out a small grey box. Rachel's heart galloped wildly in her chest. Was he really going to do this?

Slowly he opened the lid and turned it towards her. The large diamond twinkled in the light of the fireworks.

"Marry me."

Rachel saw the vulnerability in his eyes and her heart broke. "Eric," Rachel placed her hand on his cheek, then sighed deeply, "I… can't. I just…"

Eric's countenance dropped as he shut the ring box. "You know I could move to Wales to be with you. I'm not asking you to give up your life Rachel. I have a good degree, we'll be okay," he said, hurt in his voice.

"No you can't Eric, it would kill you. And I'm not ready. There's just so much going on… I'm overwhelmed. I don't even know which continent is home right now. I need to think. I need time to think. I've had so much change… everything is happening so fast." Rachel covered her face with her hands. He wasn't listening to her. He couldn't even look at her. "Eric please. Listen to me." She touched his arm. "I just need some time."

His eyes finally met hers. They were filled with pain. He pulled his arm away and Rachel felt her tears at his withdrawal.

He rose. "Okay Rach. I understand," he answered curtly as he started packing away their blankets and pillows.

Suddenly, Eric was a million miles away, and Rachel didn't know how to get him back."Eric."

"Please don't say any more Rachel. I don't think I could take much more. Sorry."

Eric got Rachel settled in the passenger seat and headed back towards the orphanage. He pulled up outside her *rondavel*, and kept the engine running. "So I'll be in contact about the date for the surgery once I've spoken to the doctors about my bone marrow donation."

This was a side of Eric Rachel had never seen before. Her heart felt like lead as he opened her car door and helped her out. "Okay. I'll postpone my flight and wait for your call then."

"Okay."

Eric climbed back into the driver's seat and left without another word. Rachel felt the tears streaming unrestrained down her cheeks as she unlocked her door. She dressed in the most comfy pyjamas she'd brought, and curled up in her bed. She covered her bump with one hand and cried.

CHAPTER THIRTY-THREE

"Eric, *boet* are you ready to go?"

"Just hold on Johan. Give me five minutes!" Eric yelled down the short passage.

Johan had arrived to take Eric for his bone marrow donation, but Eric was in a state.

Johan sauntered into his bedroom. "*Jinne*, what's happened here *boet*? It looks like you've had a burglary."

"It's nothing, never mind. I'll clean it later." Eric stuffed a pile of clothes into his wardrobe and rammed the door shut.

"And you look terrible! When did you last eat, or sleep or shower?" Johan frowned in concern. "What's happened? And why didn't you tell me?"

Eric huffed. "I don't wanna talk about it Johan. Please. Let's just go."

His friend grabbed him by the shoulder. "That doctor's going to take one look at you, and postpone this donation. I'm telling you now."

"I'm fine, let's just go. Please." Eric pushed past him and marched to the waiting car.

Johan shook his head as he sank into the seat next to him. "I know what happened. It makes perfect sense." Johan looked at him.

"No you don't. Just drive please." Eric pointed to the reserve exit.

"You asked her to marry you, didn't you? And she said 'no'."

Eric sighed. "Johan, please just leave it."

The big man shook his head. "*Ja nee, chicks* are so complicated *boet*. Just when you think you understand them, they blow all your theories to bits and pieces. There was this *chick* once, I promise you, she was stunning. I thought she *smaaked* me *boet*, she was giving me all the signals… all the signals. So I called her and asked her to the movies. And she told me, in no uncertain terms, to take a hike. And that's happened to me on many occasions *boet*. Many occasions." Johan turned the key and the engine sparked to life.

Eric couldn't hide the small smile that snuck up on him. He was grateful to have a friend like Johan around. Especially now. "Thank you for taking me *bru*."

"You might not be thanking me when you have to drag my unconscious body back to the car later, I promise you."

Eric frowned at him, bemused.

"*Boet*, I hate needles, remember? Hate them!"

Eric was relieved when Johan managed to remain upright for the entire procedure. He felt weak and depleted after the hours it took to remove the stem cells from his blood.

By the time he got home, he just wanted to forget the world and sleep. He and Rachel would drive to Durban in the morning. It would be another long day. He took a quick shower and collapsed into his bed. In no time at all, he fell into a deep, dreamless sleep.

***

Rachel had had a horrible couple of days. So far, her new year was proving to be rather dismal. She'd been so overwhelmed and confused by everything that was going on around her, that she'd Skyped her mum and dad for some comfort and advice. They supported her decision to have the operation in South Africa, and when it came to Eric, they'd advised her to put the relationship on hold. She needed to focus on her baby's health right now, that was the priority. It was helpful advice, but so hard to accept. She hated this rift between her and Eric, and now they were driving down to Parklands today. Maybe the time together would be an opportunity to at least ease some of the tension between them.

Rachel packed her pyjamas into her bag as Suzanne appeared at the door. "I came to say goodbye, and I'm praying for you. All three of you." Suzanne embraced Rachel and stroked her hair.

"Thank you Suz. I feel so anxious, thank you for praying."

"Let me know if there's anything else I can do. I have to run now though, I have five babies waiting for breakfast! Love you Rach."

"Love you too." Rachel smiled as Suzanne left quickly and closed the door behind her.

Rachel finished up her packing just as she heard Eric's car pull up. She took a deep breath. This wouldn't be half as hard if there wasn't this chasm between them.

She prayed silently for God's peace to fill her. As she thought about Jesus, she felt a calm in her spirit. Then she picked up her bags and lifted her chin. She was ready to face whatever came her way.

***

Why did she have to look so beautiful? It was like torture, but Eric was determined to hold it together.

"Good morning." He strode towards her, took her bags and loaded them into the back of his car. Once Rachel was seated, Eric looked over at her. "Right, are you ready for this?"

"Yes, let's get it done!"

Eric started the engine and headed for the freeway. The sun was just coming up over the horizon, promising another scorcher of a day. They drove in silence for half the way.

Eventually Rachel started the conversation. "Eric, thank you for taking me… and being with me through all this."

"Rachel, you don't have to thank me. He's my baby too."

"Yeh, but I just wanted you to know I appreciate it. You're not going to like what I have to tell you next, but I need you to accept it."

Eric looked over at her and frowned.

"I need to go back home, Eric. I need time to think about what I want, and to make decisions about my future."

Eric tensed and gripped the steering wheel tighter.

"Please try to understand Eric." Rachel clasped her hands together on her lap.

Eric felt hurt and lost. "*Ja*, okay." He sighed. "I can't force you to stay."

He couldn't even look at her. His heart broke a little more with every word she spoke, until he felt dead on the inside. Resigned and numb. How would he see his son now? Would he be the absent father? The one who came for a couple of weeks in the holidays? And Rachel? He loved her, he really loved her. Perhaps all she needed was a little space and time, and she'd realise her place was with him. Or perhaps she'd go home and not be able to leave the security and love of her family. Either way, it was her choice whether he liked it or not, even though his whole world hung in the balance.

Eric turned up the radio and tapped the steering wheel to get the irritation out. Rachel sat quietly, lost in her own thoughts as they passed through the rolling green hills at the entrance to Durban.

Thankfully, Eric knew exactly where he was going, and within minutes they'd arrived at Parklands Hospital. They had a consultation with the foetal surgeon scheduled, after which Rachel would have some general health observations taken. The surgery itself was set for 2pm. On arrival at reception, they were led straight through into the surgeon's office. He smiled as they entered and Rachel liked him immediately. He was warm and professional, and talked them through each part of the surgery.

Rachel was then led through for a pre-op assessment and an ultra sound. The surgeon had Rachel lie on the bed, while he set up the equipment. He lifted her top and squirted a lubricant gel onto her stomach. Suddenly there was life on the screen, and Eric couldn't move.

"Oh wow. This is incredible." Emotion overcame him and he stepped closer. His little son was moving around, sucking his thumb. His eyes were moist as the reality of being a father hit him. And when he imagined having to live apart from him, Eric felt as though he was being torn apart. He was desperate to leave the room, but knew he couldn't.

"He's looking strong and healthy," the doctor smiled, "and so are you Rachel. I'm happy to do the surgery this afternoon. I just have some consent forms I need you to sign. The sister will set you up in a ward while you wait."

"Thank you doctor."

"I'll see you both later then." He smiled and left the room.

"Isn't he amazing?" asked Rachel as she rose to sit on the edge of the bed.

"He seems like a very capable doctor."

"No, our son, he's amazing!" Rachel smiled.

"*Ja*," Eric said roughly, a lump in his throat.

The nurse came in then to prepare Rachel for surgery. She approached with a consent form and pen. He noticed Rachel's hand shake as she signed her name and returned the forms to the nurse. There were serious risks associated with the surgery, but what choice did they have? Eric prayed silently as the nurse ran through a list of medical questions with Rachel. When the time came for her to be wheeled into surgery, Eric kissed her cheek, touched her tummy, and then she was gone.

***

Emptiness filled the room as Eric stared at the closed double doors that Rachel and his tiny son had disappeared through. He could do nothing now, but pray. So that's what he did. He sat on a chair near the window, put his head in his hands and cried out to God for the life and health of his baby boy.

After a few hours, Rachel was wheeled back into the room. She was pale, an oxygen mask covered her face. She smiled sleepily as he came over to see her.

"You're okay. Thank you Jesus." He ran the back of his hand over her cheek.

Rachel nodded as tears filled her eyes. He took her hand and pressed it to his lips. The foetal monitor sounded loudly through the room as the nurse reattached it. His baby's heart was loud and strong.

The surgeon marched in, green scrub cap in hand. "How are you feeling?" He leaned over Rachel and removed her mask.

"I'm okay, just very tired."

"That should wear off in a little while." He smiled. "I'm very pleased with how the procedure went. Once baby is born we'll run some tests to check whether it was successful. We'll be looking for a normal t-cell count. If for some reason, the bone marrow transplant did not take, we could give baby another one at that stage, so try not to worry. We'd like to keep you overnight for observation. You will probably be discharged around midday tomorrow, all being well."

"Okay, thank you doctor."

He squeezed her arm, smiled at Eric, and left the room.

Eric replaced him at her bedside. "I'm so relieved Rach. That's excellent news."

"Yes." She smiled warily. "Can you get me a drink please? I'm so thirsty."

"Sure."

Eric handed Rachel a Liquifruit. She smiled. "Another great South African fruit juice?"

"You bet!"

Eric felt the exhaustion hit him along with the relief. He hadn't realised how tense he'd been over the last few days. "Okay Rach, I'm going to let you get some rest now. I'll be back in the morning."

He gave her foot a little squeeze over the duvet, grabbed his keys, and left.

CHAPTER THIRTY-FOUR

Rachel awoke early the next morning feeling refreshed. Sunshine streamed in through her hospital room window and she knew it was going to be another hot day.

Breakfast was brought to her in bed and she wolfed it down. After not eating the previous day, she was ravenous.

Once the nurse had completed her observations, the doctor signed her release papers.

She pulled back the covers and examined the plasters on her stomach. Laying her hand over her baby, she thanked God for his protection. After just a little while, Rachel could feel the little kicks and her heart burst with joy. Eric appeared at the door.

"Come quickly!" she waved him closer.

Eric frowned and rushed towards her. "What? Rach, what's wrong?"

"No! Come feel this, quickly." Her green eyes sparkled.

Eric hesitantly gave Rachel his hand. She took it and placed it over an area near a large plaster, skin on skin. Rachel smiled. "Did you feel that?"

"*Ja!*" Eric couldn't stop the grin that stretched across his face. "That's incredible! He feels so strong."

"Yes, his little kicks are getting harder and harder everyday."

Eric pulled his hand back and smiled at her. "So how're you feeling? Ready to get out of here?"

Rachel covered her tummy. "I am so ready! Let's go!"

***

Eric parked his car outside her *rondavel* early the next morning. Why was he putting himself through this goodbye? Part of him wanted to turn around and drive right back out, but another part of him couldn't stay away from her, no matter how painful. In one way he longed to be close to her. In another, he felt upset that she would leave and take his child from him.

Would he even be there for the birth? Perhaps if he flew over to Wales. Everything was so uncertain.

Suzanne met him as she was walking up towards Rachel's *rondavel* herself. She looked at him soberly. "You don't have much time, I was just coming to collect her suitcases. I'll give you ten minutes Eric, then we have to leave or she'll miss her flight."

He swallowed, a knot forming in his gut. "Okay thanks Suz."

Suzanne turned back towards the main house.

Eric took a deep breath and knocked on her door for the last time. The door opened and there she was, vulnerable, beautiful, precious. Eric had never wanted anything more. "I uh… just came to say goodbye."

She smiled sadly. "Thank you for coming, and thank you for yesterday."

"Of course." Eric returned her smile. "Nice necklace."

Rachel's hand went to the pendant and she played with it. "I love it so much, thank you..." Rachel hesitated, a frown on her brow.

"Eric... I wish I could make you a ton of promises right now, but I just can't. I don't know what I'm going to do yet... and I'm sorry."

"That's okay Rach," he said softly, his heart breaking. "Just take good care of yourself, and him." He rubbed the back of his finger against Rachel's tummy.

"Of course. Of course I will."

Eric reached over and touched Rachel's hair. He looked into her eyes and smiled sadly. Then he kissed her on the forehead and left.

CHAPTER THIRTY-FIVE

The emptiness hit Eric like a ton of bricks. And so he filled it in the only way he knew how, he threw his heart and soul into his work.

Today he was servicing the swimming pool pump, and all he could think about was the time he and Rachel had swam there together, celebrating at news that he was a match. Every part of the reserve held memories of Rachel and him together. She was everywhere.

Once he finished with the pump, Eric checked the Ph levels of the pool and added some chlorine to the water.

Next he moved on to the rhino enclosure with Bruno close at his heel. He cleaned out the troughs and refilled them with fresh water and hay. It had been so quiet on the reserve lately, that Uncle Kobus had decided against keeping the security team on. Eric wasn't sure it was a good move, but could understand the financial reasoning behind the decision. The courtship between the rhinos was looking extremely positive, and seeing them together was the highlight of Eric's day. He couldn't help but think that theirs was the only romantic relationship on the reserve that seemed to be headed in the right direction.

He gave Bruno a scratch on the head and headed for the land cruisers. Eric spent the rest of his day servicing all the game vehicles.

He eventually fell into bed too exhausted to think. And that was just how he liked it.

***

"Rachel, you need to think very carefully about what you want honey." Rachel's mum looked over at her intently from the adjacent couch. Her dad had brought her straight over to the family home, where her mom had ordered take out for all of them. "Being a single mum is a very big responsibility… and I know that you love Eric."

Rachel sighed. "Yes, I just need some time, I think… to process and decide if this is what I actually want, for me."

"I know honey. For you and for your baby."

"It would be a big sacrifice to leave you all." She looked up and found her mom's eyes. "I don't know if I could do it. But at the same time… there's Eric." Rachel swallowed down the lump in her throat. Her dad passed her a mug of steaming hot chocolate and she took it gratefully.

"How were things between the two of you while you were there?" he asked taking the seat beside her.

Rachel shifted to look at him. "Amazing really… until…"

"Until what?" He narrowed his eyes.

"Until he asked me to marry him."

The room went very quiet.

Eventually Rachel's mom broke the silence. "I see, well… you can't blame the boy for trying. It was right that he asked you." She nodded and took another sip of her tea.

"But then I hurt him so badly by telling him how unsure I was. And now, well… it's quite strained between us." Rachel's shoulder's drooped.

"That's understandable. The important thing now is that you figure out what you want honey. Of course it will be extremely painful for us if you left, but we *would* understand."

"Thanks mum."

Rachel felt the weight of her decision heavily in her heart. Deep down though, she knew what she had to do. It was actually just a matter of coming to terms with it and accepting it completely. It was peace she was searching for.

Rachel's dad drove her home then. She'd missed her little apartment, and of course, Caswell Bay. She climbed into her oversized pyjamas and tucked herself into bed. Rachel left her curtains open so she could look out at the ocean as she lay there. Then she prayed quietly into the night until she fell fast asleep.

CHAPTER THIRTY-SIX

The days merged into weeks, and the weeks into months. As her little bump increased in size, so too did her longing for Eric. She had made her decision. She didn't feel ready to say goodbye to her family, but would she ever? She knew that her time was short if she was going to fly to her new home before the birth. The doctor had advised that because of her complications, she wasn't to fly after 32 weeks.

She'd closed up her business and referred her many clients on to other accountants. She'd also contacted the landlord and given notice. The apartment was rented as furnished, so she didn't have any furniture to get rid of thankfully.

All that was left to do was to book her flight, pack her belongings, and say goodbye. She wanted to surprise Eric, and so she hadn't told him of her decision. In fact, they'd hardly spoken in any real depth since she'd left. Their calls were brief and consisted mainly of him asking about whether she was taking good care of herself, and how the baby was doing. Rachel opened her laptop as she sat on her bed and booked her flight for a week's time. She'd be just under 32 weeks by then. Her family had offered to take her to the airport, and Rachel was dreading that final goodbye with everything inside her.

As she shut her laptop, she thought about Eric, their baby, and their future together. She smiled. Despite the heartbreaking goodbyes, she knew she was making the right choice.

***

It was the evening Rachel had both been looking forward to, and dreading. It was her last Friday night family pizza night. She pulled up outside her parents' house with a heavy heart and a lump in her throat. Blake, who'd just arrived himself, ushered her inside.

As they neared the back of the house where the kitchen was, Rachel saw a scurry of activity. Her dad was hauling pizzas out the oven while her mom placed flowers on the table. The table had been beautifully laid with baby blue decor and a bunch of balloons hung from the light fitting.

Rachel's heart warmed at the sight. "Aaaaw mum this is beautiful!"

"We wanted to give you a special send off my sweetheart. Hope it's not too much."

"Thank you mum." Rachel's eyes grew damp.

Her mom clapped her hands together. "Right let's get started!"

Deb brought the final pizzas through and laid them on the large table. Once everyone had their fill of pizza, and the plates were cleared, Lyn reached for a gift bag on the floor beside her chair. "Okay Rach, we just wanted to spoil you before you left, so we've all bought you a little something. Some things are for you, some are for the baby."

Rachel took the bag her mom held out to her and peeked inside. She pulled out a pale blue newborn winter suit, along with three newborn baby grows. One had a little Welsh dragon embroidered on the front. Rachel held them up for everyone to see and thanked her mom. As the night went on, and Rachel opened more and more beautiful things from her precious family, the reality of what she was doing set in.

By the end of the evening, when coffee was served, Rachel was emotional.

Her dad smiled over at her and started his speech. "Rach, I speak for all of us, when I say that we are so proud of you. It's been a difficult eight months, and I know that much has not gone to plan. But sweetheart, you have handled yourself and the situation so well."

Rachel's mum leaned over and took her hand as her dad continued. "You've had faith in the most difficult times, and have faced every challenge head on. You are going to be an excellent mother, and hopefully someday an amazing wife also. As our final gift to you and our precious grandson, we have bought plane tickets for all of us to come and visit you once the baby is born."

Rachel's face twisted as the tears started. "Thank you dad, you don't know how much that means."

"You don't have to thank me, sweetheart. There's nothing that'll keep me from meeting my first grandchild, and seeing you become a mother." He came over then and hugged his youngest daughter.

Rachel was exhausted by the time she got home that evening. It was her last night in Wales. In the morning, her family would take her to Heathrow, where she'd fly through the night. The following day, she'd land in her new home, South Africa, where Suzanne would collect her and take her straight to the reserve.

Her lips held a bittersweet smile as her eyelids drooped closed. Soon she'd be in his arms. That truth would keep her going every leg of her journey.

CHAPTER THIRTY-SEVEN

Autumn was creeping up on the game reserve. The days had cooled slightly, and the fields were alive with cosmos, butterflies and insects. The *bushveld* was drying out, making the animals more visible, and that meant more visitors. All the staff had been working longer hours than usual to keep up with the demand. In addition to increasing their pay, Uncle Kobus also decided to host an elaborate spit *braai* to thank them. The upcoming winter months were the busiest of all, and the morale of the staff needed to stay high as they approached.

The pool was uncovered, the sheep on the spit was almost cooked, and the music was pumping. Janice had spent the afternoon making salads and puddings, and Eric had been tasked with helping Johan with the spit.

"So, I've got a date for tonight." Johan slid his hands into his shorts' pockets and rocked on his heels.

"Oh really, wow! Who's she?" Eric tried not to sound too surprised, but it wasn't easy.

"A girl from church, Ursula," he grinned.

"Oh the keyboard player?"

He nodded proudly. "*Ja*."

"Hmmm… I'm impressed *bru*. How did you manage that?" Eric crossed his arms, a smile tugging on his lips.

"Johan just turned on the charm and voila!" He clicked his fingers on the final word.

Eric laughed. "So where is she?"

"She'll be here any minute *boet*."

The *lapa* buzzed with activity. As some swam, others sat around the edge of the pool chatting. Uncle Kobus appeared with a large metal basin of ice. He placed it to one side, and filled it with canned soft drinks. When Janice arrived with the puddings, he helped her lay them on a table near the *lapa*.

A little red car pulled up outside Johan's cabin.

"She's here, I'll be back now."

Eric had never seen Johan move that fast without a rugby ball under his arm. He smiled to himself.

In a few minutes the pair were walking awkwardly towards the *lapa*.

Johan gestured to the redhead. "Eric, this is Ursula, I'm not sure you've officially met?"

Ursula was no taller than Johan's shoulder. She was petite with freckles and pale blue eyes.

"*Howzit, ja*, I've seen you at church but we've never really chatted. It's good to finally meet you. Welcome!" said Eric.

"Thank you. This is amazing! Wow, the watering hole is right here!" Ursula turned to admire the view.

Eric chatted to them for a short while before receiving 'the look' from Johan. He chuckled softly as he strolled over to Sipho and the other dateless rangers near the pool.

***

"Oh look at you! You look amazing!" Suzanne rushed towards Rachel and embraced her.

"Suz, thank you for doing this for me."

"Anytime my darling, anytime. Let me help you with those bags."

Rachel was glad to rid herself of some of her luggage. She'd tried to pack as much as she could into her suitcases, and the rest of her things along with all the baby's things she'd collected, would arrive in a week or so via unaccompanied baggage.

Suzanne and Rachel chatted all the way home, and Rachel was glad to have the time pass so quickly. Before she knew it, they were driving down the hill headed into Pietermaritzburg. It was evening now, and she wondered what Eric would be doing when she arrived. She hoped he'd be as happy to see her, as she would be to see him. She imagined him rushing towards her, scooping her up in his arms and twirling her around with joy. She smiled at the thought.

"You're thinking of him, aren't you?" Suzanne glanced at her briefly.

"That obvious?"

"*Ja.*" Suzanne smiled. "I'm so pleased that you guys are going to make it work. You deserve to be happy together."

"I can't wait to see his reaction!" Rachel shivered.

"*Ja,* I might have to hang around for that myself!" Suzanne laughed. "He's been quite down since you left. From what Kobus told me, he's been working extremely long hours, doing way beyond what's expected of him. He's lost weight too. He needs you."

Rachel nodded and retreated to her own thoughts.

As they finally arrived at the reserve, her heart began to thump. Suzanne drove past the side of the rhino enclosure, and right up to Eric's cabin. His Land Rover was there, but the cabin lights were off. A loud commotion came from the *lapa*, voices, music, it sounded like a celebration.

As she climbed out of Suzanne's Beetle, loud blasts sounded nearby. Fireworks? Rachel frowned and scanned the night sky. Nothing.

Another blast sounded. Rachel felt her body turn cold. Gunshots! At least three or four of them. Poachers?

Rachel dove back into the car and slammed the door.

"Rachel what was that?" Suzanne gasped, grabbing Rachel's knee.

"Gunshots Suz…" She panted, terror in her eyes. "That was gunshots! The poachers are coming for the horns!"

Bruno barked wildly in the distance.

Rachel's pulse raced as dread filled her. "Oh Jesus, Jesus… protect Eric…"

***

Everyone heard the gunshots.

Eric shot to his feet. The rhinos!"

Uncle Kobus raced for his rifle in the main house. Johan, Sipho and Eric ran for theirs in their cabins. Adrenalin took hold of

Eric as his body shifted into another gear, blood throbbing at his temples. The men hurtled for the rhino enclosure, reflexes on high alert. Eric scurried down beside Johan at the fence. Oubaas, the male rhino, was down. In the dark, Eric could just make out two figures near his body. "Quick Johan, call the vet. If we can get rid of these guys, we could still save Oubaas. He could still be alive."

Eric edged closer, wishing now that he'd had more firearms training. There were two men removing Oubaas' horn. Another was in the Land Rover, ready to make a quick getaway. Eric scuttled to where he could see Uncle Kobus hiding behind a bush.

"He's taken Oubaas down," his uncle whispered. "I'm going to try and maim him. As I shoot toward him, you aim for the tyres of that Land Rover."

Uncle Kobus wasn't content with just chasing them off the reserve, he wanted these guys caught, once and for all.

He stood and took aim. Eric rose next to him and did the same. As Uncle Kobus discharged his gun, so too did Eric. Eric's bullet missed its mark, but Uncle Kobus managed to nick the one poacher on the leg. The man yelped in pain and hobbled towards the vehicle, carrying the horn. As Uncle Kobus was about to fire again, a fourth man came from the darkness behind them.

"Don't move!" The man stood firm with his weapon pointed at Uncle Kobus. His accent was one Eric didn't recognise. The man sneered. "You're going to let us take this horn and go."

Eric felt a righteous anger rise inside him. "No, we're not!" With that Eric aimed his gun directly at the poacher and pulled back the safety to discharge. The poacher redirected his aim towards Eric and fired.

"Nooooooo!" Uncle Kobus launched himself towards Eric and took him down hard onto the grass. The poachers seized the opportunity, dashed for their vehicle and sped off into the night.

Eric felt the weight of his uncle's limp body over his chest. "*Oom! Oom?*" He shook his shoulders.

Nothing. Eric felt warm liquid seep onto his stomach. He twisted his body underneath the weight as he struggled to turn his uncle onto his back. "Help! Help me! Call an ambulance! Now!" Eric yelled, crouched beside him, his ear at his uncle's mouth. "Okay, he's alive."

Janice came running up, frantic. "No! No! Nooooooooo! I can't lose him! Kobus, Kobus, no!" Her face was white. Her fingers trembled as she dialled the private ambulance service.

Eric ripped off his shirt and used it to put pressure on the bleeding abdominal wound. "Hang in there *oom*. Hang in there, the ambulance is on its way."

Uncle Kobus opened his eyes. "Eric," he rasped, "tell your mom, no matter what, I still love her. And you, my son."

Eric's panic turned to heartache at the words coming from his beloved uncle. "Don't try to talk *oom*, there'll be plenty of time for that later."

Janice crouched near as Uncle Kobus lost consciousness. "Kobus stay with us! Stay with us!" Eric thought he himself was losing consciousness when he saw Rachel running towards him through the darkness, Suzanne trailed behind her.

"Eric! Are you okay?" she was breathless.

Eric was stunned. All he could do was stare at her, perhaps the trauma was making him hallucinate.

"Eric! What happened? Are you alright?" Rachel bent down next to him and touched him on the shoulder. He was still applying pressure to Uncle Kobus' wound.

"Rachel?"

"Yes, it's me, I'm here. Are you okay?"

"What are you doing here?"

"We can talk about that later. Are you hurt Eric?"

"No, just Uncle Kobus. He needs help, fast." Eric checked if he was still breathing. He was, but it was very shallow.

"Mom, CPR! Now!"

Janice quickly tilted his head back, put her mouth over his and gave him a breath, then she spread her hands together over his chest and started compressions.

Johan bolted up. "What can I do?" he asked breathlessly.

"Go and show the paramedics where to come, quickly!" shot Eric.

"The ambulance will be here any second," said Janice.

Rachel suddenly gripped her stomach and sucked in a sharp breath. Suzanne ran up and hunched down next to her. "Rachel, breathe. It's just a contraction. Probably from all the excitement. Just breathe."

"Rachel! Are you okay?" Eric looked at her with worry. She couldn't speak, but slowly nodded as the contraction eased.

An ambulance screeched up and two paramedics jumped from the vehicle.

"He's been shot! He's losing a lot of blood!" said Janice as she and Eric moved aside.

"We've got it." The paramedics continued with CPR. They lifted his body onto a stretcher and moved him to the back of the ambulance. Janice climbed in the back and scurried to his side. She took hold of his hand and held it to her cheek. The paramedics jumped in after her as the ambulance sped off through the dirt roads, sirens blaring.

CHAPTER THIRTY-EIGHT

Eric collapsed to his knees. Rachel drew near and held him tightly. "It's okay. It's going to be okay." She stroked the back of his head.

"It's my fault Rachel. Uncle Kobus… he can't die Rach… he can't die."

She pulled back and found his eyes. "It's not your fault, Eric. It's going to be okay," she whispered hoarsely.

"That bullet was meant for me, Rachel. He saved my life." Eric rubbed his face with both hands.

A sharp pain radiated through her. Rachel stiffened, clutching her stomach. It wasn't time! It was too soon! How could she have the baby now?

"Rachel?" Suzanne gripped her shoulder. "Breathe, breathe! Eric, we need to get her to the hospital. I think she's going into early labour. I'm not sure what your doctor has advised, but if she needs a c-section, then we need to get there now!"

Johan drove up just then and rolled down his window. "*Boet*, what can I do?"

Eric shook as he tried to stand, his head fuzzy. "Oubaas, you help Oubaas. I'm going with Rachel to the hospital, I… I don't know what's…" Eric looked to Suzanne, a dazed look in his eyes.

Suzanne took charge. "Eric, I'm going to fetch my car. Wait here with Rachel. I'll drive you both to the hospital now."

Suzanne ran towards the cabins. In a few minutes she was back with her Beetle. Eric climbed through into the back while Suzanne settled Rachel in the front seat.

Rachel yelped as another contraction hit her. "What if he's not ready? Suz, what if he's not ready to come now?" she panted.

"Rach, you are 32 weeks, he has a very good chance. We have to trust the Lord now. And for Uncle Kobus. Eric," Suzanne looked at him in her rearview mirror. "I keep a spare t-shirt in my gym bag in the back if you want to borrow it."

Eric moved slowly to retrieve it. Another contraction shot through Rachel and she moaned and twisted in the passenger seat. It was too much. "I can't do this!"

"*Ja*, you can! We're nearly there Rach, hang in there!" Suzanne rubbed her knee.

They pulled up to the emergency department and Suzanne rushed around to help Rachel out the car. Once the staff had seen Rachel's file, they prepped her for surgery. A nurse handed a pile of scrubs and booties to Eric, and showed him where to change.

They took Rachel's blood pressure while Suzanne held her hand and prayed. "Father you know all that has happened tonight, and we pray that your peace would comfort us all. We pray that Kobus would be okay, and that this baby would be delivered safely. In the name of Jesus. Amen."

"Thank you Suz." Rachel sucked in a shuddery breath and tried to relax.

Suzanne squeezed her hand. "Eric will be with you, and I'll be right out here, praying. You are going to meet your baby now!"

Rachel smiled as Suzanne made way for Eric. He was dressed from top to toe in greens and managed a wonky smile down at her.

"You've been praying," she said as she looked into his calm eyes.

He nodded, squeezing her arm. "I feel His peace now. Uncle Kobus is in God's hands. It's time to meet our baby. Thank you for coming back Rach." He bent down and kissed her on the forehead. "I've been going crazy missing you."

Rachel's body tensed as a sharp pain ripped through her. She clenched her jaw and pulled her knees up. Eric squeezed her hand as the surgeon arrived and wheeled her into theatre. The anaesthetist administered the spinal block, and Rachel felt her body relax completely as she lost sensation from her chest down.

Eric stood near her head and stroked the net that covered her long hair. She looked up into his eyes, and he smiled.

"I hope he's ready for this," she whispered anxiously.

"He's going to be fine Rach, you'll see."

Within what felt like minutes, the doctor held a tiny, but perfect baby boy up in the air. "You have a beautiful son!" He smiled at them both and passed the baby to one of the nurses.

Once weighed, measured and wrapped up, the nurse brought the baby to Rachel to hold. She took one look at his little face and the tears started falling. God was certainly not punishing them, He was blessing them. As she held her baby and stroked his little face, all she could see was Eric. Her little son was the image of his wonderful father.

In that moment, Rachel wondered how she'd ever thought of a life without Eric in it. It seemed incomprehensible. Eric beamed and lowered his head to kiss his baby son on the forehead.

"He's perfect Rach. Thank you for giving me a son." Eric ran his fingertip down the feathery cheek.

"How can I love him so much already?" she whispered.

The paediatrician strode into the room. "Miss Wright, I need to run those tests on baby now, if I may?"

As the doctor left with their baby in his arms, Eric turned to Rachel and looked in her eyes. "Can I…?"

"Go," she said, "we'll be fine."

Eric kissed her cheek and rushed out towards the surgical reception.

***

"Can you give me some information on my uncle, Kobus Pieterson? He was brought in by ambulance with a gunshot wound."

"Let me have a look for you." The receptionist scratched through a pile of papers on her desk. "He's in surgery at the moment. Would you like to have a seat in the waiting area."

As Eric turned towards the guest lounge, he saw his mom. She was crying in the corner of the room, looking small and frail. He rushed to her side and enfolded her in his arms.

"Mom, it's going to be okay. Please don't cry. I have good news." He pulled away and found her red eyes.

"Rachel?"

Eric smiled sadly. "Congratulations mom, you're a grandmother."

She returned his smile and hugged him. "Thank you, Eric. That's wonderful news. Is the baby okay?"

"*Ja*. He's very small, but he's doing well. He looks like me mom, he's blonde! They're just running some tests now, and then he'll go up to the neonatal ICU."

"And Rachel? Is she okay?"

Eric nodded. "*Ja*, she did great mom."

Janice took a deep breath, her gaze shifting to the double doors of the theatre. "I'm desperate to go and see him Eric, but I just can't leave your uncle right now."

"It's okay mom." Eric squeezed her shoulders. "The doctors are probably still busy with the baby anyway. There'll be plenty of time later. Do you know any more about Uncle Kobus' injuries?"

"No, they haven't told me anything Eric. I'm going crazy with worry."

Eric ushered her to the couch and put his arm around her shoulders. "He's a strong man mom. He'll be upset that we were all so worried."

The theatre doors flung open and a surgeon stepped into the waiting area. "Are you relatives of Kobus Pieterson?"

"Yes, please tell us he's okay," answered Janice anxiously.

The doctor took a step closer, his face grave. "He's stable, yes. The bullet was lodged between his T11 and T12 vertebrae. Unfortunately there's been damage to his spinal cord. We managed to stop the bleeding, and we've removed the bullet. There wasn't only damage from the bullet though, there was also indirect damage to the spinal cord from the fractured vertebrae. We were able to drain the hematoma, and we repaired the damaged vertebrae as best we could. Whether or not he'll walk again though, remains to be seen. He faces months of physical therapy. It's a long road ahead for him I'm afraid."

"I'm just so relieved he's alive doctor. Thank you." Janice covered her face and cried into Eric's chest. He held her as her body shook. Eric had no idea that his mom harboured such strong feelings for Uncle Kobus. And his uncle? What if he couldn't walk? That outcome would not bode well for any man, but particularly a man in his profession.

"When can we see him doctor?" asked Eric.

"I'll show you to his room, but just one at a time please." The doctor led them down a short hallway to the ICU. He took a sharp right as he entered, and behind the glass in the first cubicle, lay Uncle Kobus, unconscious. A range of machines surrounded him, but no ventilator. He sighed with relief, the man was breathing on his own.

Janice went in to see him while Eric waited near the door. Eric couldn't help but hear the one-sided conversation.

"Kobus, I'm so relieved. I thought I'd lost you again." She laid her head on his chest and stroked his balding head. "I can't lose you again, ever."

Suddenly Eric felt like he was intruding, and took a step back.

When it was his turn, he didn't know what to say. He squeezed Uncle Kobus' hand, "*Oom* I'm so glad you're going to be okay. Don't worry about anything. We are going to take care of you. Also I have some good news. My son has arrived, early, but safe and sound. He's waiting to meet his great uncle. Rachel is right here in the maternity section, she's come back to me."

Uncle Kobus' eyes fluttered slightly. Eric could see a small smile forming on his lips, but his eyes remained closed.

A nurse appeared at the door with a file under her arm. "I think it's time to leave now, sorry. He needs his rest."

"Okay. Thank you for letting us see him. Please take special care of him."

The nurse looked at him tenderly. "Of course I will. You can visit again tomorrow."

As Eric left the ICU, his emotions were in conflict. He was so excited to be a dad, and to have Rachel back, but he was concerned about Uncle Kobus' prognosis. Who would run the reserve in his absence? It would have to be him. But he was a new father. Rachel was going to need his help, at least for the first few weeks. Where would she stay? He needed her to be closer to him. There was no way she could stay at the orphanage, how would he be able to help her from there?

Uncle Kobus was in no condition to be concerned about these things, he would have to take charge of everything to do with the reserve as of now. Rachel could stay with the baby in the guest cabin if she wanted, at least just until he could convince her to marry him.

Eric found his mom in the seating area. She looked weary and pale. He sat next to her and put an arm around her shoulders. "Why don't I take you home for a rest mom, you've been awake through the night."

"I can't leave him Eric. I can't."

"I understand mom, but he's going to need you rested when he wakes up."

Janice sighed and nodded slowly. "Can I see the baby before we leave?"

"Of course, I can't wait to show him to you."

***

Eric watched the smile spread across his mom's face as she looked at her tiny grandson through the glass windows of the neonatal ICU.

"He's just beautiful Eric. That's just how you looked as a baby, that silvery blonde hair."

Eric smiled and rubbed her shoulder. "Hopefully he won't be in here for very long, I can't wait to hold him."

Janice nodded and squeezed his hand as they turned and headed for the exit.

CHAPTER THIRTY-NINE

Rachel sat on a nursing chair cradling her son. Even though he was connected to all sorts of monitors and she was in pain from the c-section, her heart was filled with joy. The doctors had run the blood tests, and the baby's t-cell count was normal. The bone marrow graft was a success.

Rachel quietly sang a worship song to her new son in her arms.

She looked up as Eric rushed through the door. "I'm so sorry I've been gone so long Rach. I had to take my mom home, she was dead on her feet."

"How's your uncle?"

"He's stable, but the bullet hit his spinal cord. The doctor isn't sure he'll walk again."

Rachel frowned. "Oh no, Eric. I'm so sorry."

"At least he's alive. He's a strong man Rach. If anyone can overcome something like this, he can."

Rachel nodded. "I… have excellent news…"

"You got the blood test results?" Eric asked eagerly as he crouched near her.

"Yes, Eric his count is normal. The graft worked!" She smiled into his eyes.

"Praise Jesus!" Eric exhaled. "I'm so thankful. Our boy is healthy!"

"So do you want to hold him?" she asked. "You just have to be careful with these monitors."

"Oh *ja*, hand him over!"

As Eric took the swaddled bundle from Rachel's arms, his whole body warmed. The baby was awake and looking straight at him. His intense little gaze took Eric's breath away. His chest felt tight as he stroked his baby's silky hair. He smiled down at him tenderly.

Rachel laughed to herself. "Looks like he's got you wrapped around his little finger already!"

Eric didn't take his eyes from his baby's face. "You bet, just like his mom does."

"Do I now?" she teased.

He looked down at her then. "You know it… I'd do anything for you Rach."

Rachel smiled as he handed her the baby. "So have you thought of any names yet? Our boy needs a name!" said Rachel, studying the sweet little face.

"Can't say that I have a first name in mind, but I do have an idea for a middle name."

"Oh let's hear it." Her eyes found his.

"Not sure you'll agree because it's Afrikaans… I'd like Kobus to be his middle name."

Rachel nodded. "Okay, so if you get to pick the middle name, then I get to pick the first name?"

"Oh is that how it works, hey? Okay let's hear it then."

"Matthew, it means gift from God." Rachel looked up at him hopefully.

A huge smile filled Eric's face. "Matthew. That's perfect. He'll be Matthew Kobus."

Eric helped Rachel to her feet and took her and Matthew in his arms. "You've made this bachelor so happy Rachel." He bent down and placed his forehead against hers. Then he kissed her like he'd been longing to kiss her for months. He never wanted to stop. Matthew squirmed and they both laughed.

"Embarrassed by his parents' kissing, and at such a young age too." Eric clicked his tongue playfully.

"He'd better get used to it." Rachel laughed, their foreheads still touching.

"Marry me Rachel. Marry me because you love me. Marry me because you can't live without me. Marry me because no man will love you like I will."

"Eric, yes! Yes I'll marry you!" A huge smile lit Rachel's face. As tears started down her cheeks, laughter bubbled out her mouth.

Eric placed his hand behind her head and kissed her with passion.

Rachel couldn't believe how much God had blessed her. It was way beyond what she deserved. Eric and Matthew, her precious little family, God's gift to her.

***

Eric arrived at the surgical reception the following morning to find Johan already there. Johan rose when he saw his friend. "*Howzit boet.*" He slapped him on the back. "Congratulations man. I heard you're a dad now."

Eric nodded. "Thanks *bru, ja*. I can't wait to show him to you. I also have more news." His eyes sparkled.

"*Ja?*" Johan frowned.

"We're getting married!" A huge grin spread across his unshaven face.

"Really hey? I'll have to have a word with Rachel. Clearly she's not thinking straight right now with everything that's going -"

"Very funny..." Eric raised an eyebrow at him.

"No seriously, that's awesome *boet*. You've got yourself a great *chick* there."

"Thanks *bru*. Listen, what are you doing sitting out here in the waiting area?"

"They won't let me in there, it's family only."

"Okay, I'll go in and see how he's doing. Sit tight."

As Eric neared the room, he heard voices and held back. His mom was talking to his uncle in hushed tones. He was awake! Eric sighed in relief. He couldn't hear what they were speaking about, but it sounded intense. Hopefully they were working things out. The love they had for each other had never been more obvious, particularly with his mom's reaction to his injury. His mom's days of hiding her feelings for his uncle were long gone.

He knocked gently on the door and edged in. "Sorry, I hope I'm not disturbing anything."

"Eric, good morning!" said Janice.

"Morning! *Oom* you are looking so good! You gave us quite a scare." Eric walked over to the end of the bed.

Uncle Kobus laughed hoarsely. "My boy, you can't get rid of me that easily!"

Eric noticed that his mom held his uncle's hand. She looked a little strained. What had they been discussing? Perhaps it was his prognosis. "I'm sorry to hear about your legs *oom*. Have you had any feeling back at all?"

"Not yet my boy, but I'll walk again. You'll see. I've got excellent staff at the reserve to fill in for me. It's just a matter of time… and I'll be back in the saddle!"

"I don't doubt that *oom*, if anybody could do it, you could."

"Congratulations my boy, I hear you're a father now. I wish I was out this bed so I could see him. I hear he looks just like his dad."

"He's amazing *oom*. We are very blessed." Eric smiled, slipping his hands into his pockets.

"*Ja* there's much to be thankful for today my boy."

"*Ja oom*, God is so good. Rachel and I got engaged last night also."

"Oh that is wonderful news!" Janice gushed. "I can finally start the wedding planning!" she teased as she came around and hugged him tightly.

"Well done my boy, I'm so happy for you. I hope it'll be a short engagement too."

"*Ja* me too *oom*. The shorter the better!"

"Definitely," Janice agreed.

"*Oom*, before I leave... Johan is out there, he's concerned about you, but they won't let him in because it's family only. Just so you know."

"Johan, what does he want? A raise or something?" joked Uncle Kobus in his raspy voice.

Eric laughed. "Okay *oom*, I need to go now. I'll be back soon."

"Take your time my boy. You need to be with your new family now. I understand. Thank you for the visit."

***

Eric couldn't wait to get the ring in his pocket onto the finger of his fiancé. As he entered the room he found Rachel in the nursing chair with her laptop. Matthew was sound asleep in his incubator, skinny, red arms up above his head.

"Eric." Rachel smiled up at him.

"Good morning beautiful." As he kissed her on the cheek he discovered that Rachel was on a video call with her entire family.

"Eric!" A voice called from the computer. It was Rachel's mom, Lyn. "Congratulations! We are so excited about our new grandson!"

Eric hunched down next to Rachel where he could be seen on the feed. This was awkward. He hadn't faced her family since they'd found out the truth about his drunken night with Rachel. He cleared his throat. "Hi Lyn, thank you. Yes he's so perfect!"

"And congratulations also on your engagement!" Rachel's dad added. "We are thrilled for you both."

"*Ja* it's been a very happy and eventful few days!" Eric laughed as he started to relax.

"We also heard about your uncle. We are praying he makes a full recovery."

"Thanks very much Lyn. He's conscious now and joking around, so he's going to be fine."

"We booked our tickets to visit after the baby was born, but now he's arrived early! We can move the dates to whatever's convenient. Perhaps once you've chosen a wedding date we'll have a better idea," said Lyn.

"I'm hoping for a really short engagement!" Eric grinned at Rachel. She reached out and touched his cheek.

"Well okay you two, we'll let you go now. Keep in touch Rach, I need all the news on my new grandson to keep coming!"

"Yes mum, I'll be calling for advice often! You don't have to worry about that! Love you all!"

As Rachel ended the call with her family, Eric pulled up a chair next to her bed. "How was your night?"

"A bit rough to be honest. I'm quite sore and Matthew was up all hours wanting food. So I was up having to pump milk for him. Sorry if that's too much information."

"Sorry you're in pain Rach. Looks like we have a hungry boy… How's the feeding going?"

"Yeh, he's taking the milk well. I don't know how I'm going to leave him here." Rachel's eyes travelled the length of the little bundle.

"I know." Eric sighed. "He seems so small to leave. We'll have to trust God."

"Yeh, he's overcome the odds already. He's tougher than he looks!"

"That's exactly right."

Eric reached into the gift bag at his feet and pulled out a bouquet of pink roses. "These are for you," he said and walked over to fill the empty vase near the sink with water.

"They're beautiful, thank you!"

"And this is for Matthew." Eric pulled out a little brown bear and placed it on the table next to the incubator.

Rachel smiled. "That's cute."

"And one last gift." Eric drew near and pulled the ring box from his pocket. He opened it and removed the diamond solitaire ring. Rachel's face beamed.

"I've been desperate to give this to you, for months now. Thank you for saying yes." Eric took Rachel's left hand and pushed the ring onto her finger.

"It's incredibly beautiful Eric." Rachel held her hand out admiring it.

"It's a special ring Rach. It used to belong to the wife Uncle Kobus loved and lost. He insisted I take it, for you."

Rachel smiled. "It's perfect."

Eric kissed her palm, and laid it against his cheek.

Seeing that ring on her finger made all that was about to happen very real. She was really his… his soon to be wife and the mother of his child. Eric's heart could hardly take any more joy.

CHAPTER FORTY

After two more days, Rachel was ready to be released from the hospital. It was a fresh autumn day, and Eric was up early to check on last minute arrangements and to clean his car.

"*Boet*, you've never been too bothered about the cleanliness of your car before." Johan leaned lazily against the car Eric was trying to clean.

"Come on *bru*," Eric said as he brushed crumbs off the front passenger seat, "I'm going to fetch my fiancé. I have to up my game a bit."

"I'm impressed *boet*. Are you going to start brushing your hair now too? It's a whole new Eric I'm seeing here before my eyes."

"Very funny. And I wouldn't talk if I was you. At least I have hair."

"Hey, that hurts *boet*. And I've got plenty of hair, I just like to keep it short. Like a real man."

"Ay, be careful *bru*, Jesus had long hair."

"Okay, okay you win *boet*. You know us Afrikaners, we like to keep it short back and sides."

"And with a comb in your sock hey?" Eric teased.

"Hey! Don't mock the comb! It's like tradition man. Separates the boys from the men."

Eric laughed, this conversation was going nowhere. "Right, I need to go *bru*. Next time you see me, I'll have a beautiful woman on my arm." Eric winked.

Johan shook his head. "That's just wrong *boet*, rubbing it in like that."

Eric smiled, winked again, and drove off.

***

"Is my fiancé ready to go home?" Eric popped his head into the neonatal ICU and found Rachel bottle-feeding Matthew. She'd changed out of her hospital gown, and was now dressed in her own clothes. She looked beautiful with her hair loose around her shoulders, his baby in her arms.

"Hey! I'd love to be able to say 'yes' to that, but how am I going to leave him?"

Eric bent down and kissed Rachel on the lips. "He's in very capable hands Rach, and we'll be back tonight to see him."

"Well I'm all packed and ready." Rachel removed the bottle from Matthew's mouth and passed him to Eric for winding and a cuddle.

Eric placed him gently over his shoulder like the nurses had shown him, and patted his back. "Hey Matty, did you have a big breakfast little guy?" Eric rubbed his little head. "Rach, I've organised the guest cabin for you. I need you near me. Is that okay?"

"Sounds perfect, I'll just let Suzanne know I won't be coming back to the orphanage."

Rachel called Suzanne as Eric placed Matthew back in his incubator.

The doctor arrived then with Rachel's discharge papers and pain medications. "So obviously, Rachel we'll need you at the hospital several times a day. Have you left milk with the nurses?"

"Yes, I've done that."

"Great well then, you're free to come and go around here. Matthew will probably need a few more weeks in the NICU. We'd like him to be over 2kgs by the time he's discharged, so he needs to keep gaining weight as well as he is right now."

"Okay thank you doctor."

Rachel and Eric said their goodbyes and tore themselves away from their little boy.

***

"I've finally got you all to myself." Eric pulled her towards him for a quick kiss as they walked down the hallway. Rachel felt as though she could fly she was so happy.

"So, I'm hoping you have the rest of my suitcases?"

"*Ja*, I got them all out of Suzanne's car. All your things are waiting for you in your cabin."

"Great, thank you! I'm looking forward to a full night's sleep tonight in that comfy bed!"

Eric looked at her with a deep longing in his eyes and smiled softly. She knew what he was thinking, because she was thinking the same thing; they didn't want to have to say goodbye tonight.

"It won't be long, and we'll be together like that." She squeezed his hand.

Eric laughed. "Rach, it's already been, way, way too long!"

He tucked her into the passenger seat, placed her bags in the boot of the car and took her home.

***

That evening, after Rachel had had a nap and a shower, they headed back to the hospital. Johan had popped into Eric's cabin to update him on Oubaas' progress and the general goings-on at the reserve. Oubaas had pulled through, but was still critical due to the blood he'd lost. Eric was so thankful that Johan was willing and able to take the reins for a few days while he found his feet.

"Favourite colour?" Eric asked Rachel on the way to the hospital.

"Green, you?"

"Yellow."

"Favourite food?" asked Eric.

"Uh... pizza, yours?"

"It's has to be cockles and lava bread." He winked. Rachel laughed.

"Okay, favourite flowers?"

"Aaah, I like the sound of that question! Yellow roses."

"Man, I was so close!" Eric slammed his palm against the steering wheel.

"Yes you were."

"Okay, here's a good one. When did you first realise you loved me?" Eric glanced over at her briefly with a smile.

Rachel thought for a while. "When I had to say goodbye to you in Wales. You were sleeping, and I still owed you a kiss…"

Eric nodded. "I remember."

"So when did you realise you loved me?" Rachel asked.

"At your farewell party… I guess with the reality of you leaving. I was a mess that night." He smiled sadly.

Eric pulled into a parking space, and opened the door for Rachel. He took her hand as they headed towards the NICU. After a quick cuddle, Eric excused himself. "Rach, I'm going to go and see my uncle quickly while you feed. Johan gave me an update on Oubaas, that he'd want to hear." Eric kissed her on the top of her head and left.

As he arrived at the entrance of his uncle's room, he saw his mom was there again.

"Here he is now, Jan… okay?" Uncle Kobus looked intently into his mom's face.

"*Ja*, okay. I'll go," Janice answered sadly.

As Eric's mom passed by him, she put her arms around his waist and held him tightly. He frowned. Something was going on. She reached up to kiss him on the cheek and whispered in his ear, "I love you my boy."

Eric moved hesitantly into the room and came to stand beside Uncle Kobus. "*Oom*, is something going on here? Something I need to know about?"

"*Ja*, there is. You might want to pull up a chair." Uncle Kobus looked nervous. His hand shook as he reached for a drink of water.

"Is everything okay *oom*? Are you okay?" asked Eric as he took a seat close to his bedside.

"*Ja*, I'm healing up nicely my boy, this is not about that."

"Okay, so what is it?"

"My boy, I know you've been through a lot lately, and so I wasn't sure that this was the right time to tell you all this. Forgive me if it's not, but when a man has a near death experience, it changes things. I've wanted to tell you this for many years, but out of respect for your mom's wishes, I haven't. When I was a teenager, I knew your mom from school. She used to hang out with my brother, André and me. And well, the truth of the matter is, that I was in love with her even then." He smiled to himself. "She had me hook, line and sinker."

Eric frowned. "I had no idea."

"And so it was extremely painful when your mom chose to marry my older brother quite suddenly. I didn't understand the reason for her decision until André's funeral, many years later. She gave me a letter at the funeral explaining everything. That day was life-changing for me.

"You see my boy, she'd discovered that she was pregnant. She was only 18, she was very scared, and without the support of a loving family. André also loved her, and he was a very good marriage prospect at the time. He was nearly qualified as a lawyer, and set to inherit the reserve one day too. It was long before his problem with alcohol."

Eric felt his heart trip into an unfamiliar rhythm. "Okay, well, that makes sense that she'd want to get married to my dad, being young and pregnant." Eric was still frowning.

"*Ja,* only it wasn't André that got her pregnant my boy." Uncle Kobus went quiet.

Eric's jaw dropped. "It was you?" His eyes started to burn as he looked his father in the eye.

Uncle Kobus nodded. Eric could see the love mixed with fear and vulnerability in his face. The tears started down Uncle Kobus' face, and he didn't try to stop them.

"I love you my boy. I wanted to tell you as soon as I found out. Please don't be angry with your mom, she did what she thought was best at the time."

Eric came to him hesitantly. He put both arms around his father and felt the tears start to fall.

Uncle Kobus held him tightly and patted his head. "My boy, I've wanted you to know for so long, and now you do. I know I've missed a lot, but I'm going to be a very good father to you." Uncle Kobus said roughly.

"You already are," Eric replied into his shoulder.

Uncle Kobus looked into Eric's eyes then and patted his cheek. He couldn't hide the smile that was slowly growing on his face as he saw the love and acceptance in the eyes of his son.

Janice stood at the door, tears streaming down her face. She came over to Eric and stood before him. "Can you ever forgive me? I should have told you. At first I thought it best that you believed André was your dad. Then when he died, you were grieving, so I didn't want to tell you then… and then I was so afraid to tell you, in case you never forgave me."

Eric could see the fear and longing in her eyes, and he knew what he needed to do. Forgive. "Mom, I... I wish you'd told me. I grew up so afraid that I'd one day turn out like my dad. But if I'd known..." He looked over at Uncle Kobus. "Well if I'd known, I would've been so proud to turn out like him."

"Please forgive me Eric. I couldn't bear to live if you didn't forgive me for this." Her chin quivered.

"I forgive you mom." He wrapped his arms around her and held her close.

In that moment, all the turmoil within Eric merged into a beautiful rest. He could feel God's love on him. It was as if somewhere deep down inside, he'd known. He felt such a connection with his real dad, that he'd never shared with André.

God had prepared him for this moment, and all he felt was the purest peace.

CHAPTER FORTY-ONE

"So I had my first round of physio this morning." Uncle Kobus looked pleased with himself. He'd been making such great progress, that he'd been moved from the ICU to a private ward.

"How was it?" asked Eric.

"I'm not gonna lie my boy. It was tough, really tough. But I can't let myself think that I might not walk again. I have to keep believing."

Eric nodded. "I know you will." He wasn't sure whether he should call him 'Dad' just yet. He didn't feel nearly ready for that, yet it felt wrong to call him *'oom'*. So Eric found himself not calling him anything, which was equally awkward, but Uncle Kobus didn't seem to notice.

"So how is Oubaas?" the older man asked.

"He's doing well now. It was touch and go there for a while, but since he had that transfusion, he's improved so much."

"That's good to hear. And is Johan coping with managing the reserve?"

"I help where ever I can, but *ja*, he seems to be holding things together quite well. Sipho has taken over the management of the game drives entirely now, and it's working well."

"And Bruno, how is my boy?"

"I'm feeding him, don't worry. He misses you though… looks a little miserable, whines at night."

"I need to get out of here Eric. I must work even harder tomorrow at my physio."

"Just don't overdo it. If you injure yourself, that will set you back. Take it nice and easy."

"*Ja*, it's hard to be patient. And, while we're on the subject of patience, I need to ask you a serious question."

"Okay," Eric answered hesitantly. "Do I need to sit down for this?"

Uncle Kobus laughed. "No my boy, there's no more surprises from me, I can promise you that. I just wanted to ask you how you felt about your parents getting married."

"She said 'yes'?" Eric beamed.

"She said 'yes'!" His dad nodded as an enormous grin spread across his face. "When she saw how well you took the news, there was nothing holding her back. Thank you for forgiving so easily Eric. I know it must've been a big shock."

"I'm just so happy for you both. You deserve to be happy… together this time."

"Not even this wheelchair can make me feel down now my boy. We must set a date, soon. As soon as I'm out of here!"

"Sounds like a plan."

"I don't want to take the attention from you and Rachel, and your big day. So when you have a date, let me know and I'll try to avoid that time."

"You and Mom have been waiting so long for this day, we can celebrate your wedding first. Rachel still needs time to heal and adjust, and Matthew will be in the NICU at least until he's two kilograms. So don't wait for us! You two go right ahead!"

"Right, that's very good motivation for me to get mobile, thanks Eric. Listen, one more thing, you need to start getting a bit more sleep between now and the wedding, my boy." Uncle Kobus reached over and squeezed Eric's arm. "I can't have such a tired best man."

Eric looked over at his father and smiled. He couldn't imagine a better man. How things would have been so different had his mom chosen to marry his dad instead. But it was pointless to dwell on what could have been, particularly when what was, was so good.

"Okay then, let me know what I can do to move these wedding plans along!"

Janice walked in then, a beautiful combination of peace and joy, a woman in love.

"Mom! Congratulations! We were just talking about the wedding. I'm so happy for you!"

"It's about time I marry the man my heart has longed for for so long," she said as she put the flowers she'd brought into a glass vase. "If I'd have known you'd respond this well to the truth Eric, I would've told you years ago, and married him a lot sooner!"

Uncle Kobus looked over at her with a tender smile. "Let's not think about that. We're still young my darling. We have plenty years left ahead of us."

"So that whole story about not being able to see him as more than a brother-in-law?"

Janice pulled a face. "Uh… sorry about saying that Eric, that's never been the case. He's always been the love of my life."

Janice came over to Uncle Kobus' bedside then and kissed him on the cheek.

Eric laughed and shook his head. "I'm going to have to get used to seeing you two like this! I feel like an embarrassed little kid watching his parents kiss!"

They laughed together, and Eric wondered how he'd never put it all together before. Uncle Kobus had always been more than an uncle, and he'd never seen anyone care for his mom as much as he did.

After so many years of waiting and yearning, it was going to be a most beautiful wedding celebration.

CHAPTER FORTY-TWO

"Okay Eric, I can wheel myself to the front."

"Just let me help you, that's what I'm here for."

"No my boy. I need to feel like a man today, let me do it." His dad took hold of the wheels and propelled himself forward.

"Okay, I understand. I'll be here if you need me." Eric patted his dad on the back.

The small church had been beautifully decorated with hundreds of sunflowers. Sunlight streamed in the windows, even though the air outside was cool.

Eric's dad sat in the front, facing the aisle. He fidgeted with his cuff links, then tugged at his collar. It wasn't hard to see that he wasn't at all accustomed to wearing anything smarter than his daily khakis. The congregation of close friends and extended family grew more vocal as the time went on until the church was alive with excitement.

Uncle Kobus checked his watch again. "Eric, you'd better go wait for her at the door now."

Although Eric was the best man for the day, he'd also been asked by his mom to walk her down the aisle. He winked at Rachel as he passed her and stood waiting at the back of the small church.

The buzzing crowd quieted as the piano music came to an end. Eric snuck out the door just in time to see his mom arrive with her younger sister, Cari, and Suzanne. Cari and Suzanne wore knee-length brown satin dresses, while Janice wore an elegant, fitted cream gown with lace. She was exquisite. Her blonde hair was pinned up with flowers, her face, radiant with love.

Eric went over and kissed her on the cheek. "Are you ready? You look stunning!" he whispered.

She placed her hand in the crook of his arm and smiled. "*Ja* I'm so ready. How is he?"

"Nervous." Eric smiled.

"Well then, let's put the man out of his misery!"

Eric laughed as they entered the church reception area behind Suzanne and Cari. They cued the sound man, who in turn started the music for Janice's chosen song, A Thousand Years by Christina Perri. He handed Janice the microphone, and she sang behind the closed door of the sanctuary.

Eric knew his mom had a lovely voice, but he'd *never* heard her sing like this! It was passionate and tender, and filled every corner of the building with intense emotion. The bridesmaids entered slowly, and then when the chorus came, Janice and Eric followed.

As they neared the front of the church, Eric's dad bowed his head. Eric wasn't sure then if he was praying or crying, but as he lifted his head to look at Janice again, Eric could see the tears streaming down his face.

When they reached the front, Eric brought a chair over so his mom could sit next to his dad. Uncle Kobus held his hand out on the arm of the wheelchair, and she took it. He lifted her hand to his lips, and kissed it, smiling at her through the tears.

As the young pastor began his message, Janice and Uncle Kobus hardly took their eyes off one another. When they got to the vows, they'd each written their own personal promises. Janice nervously took the microphone and note offered to her by Cari. She slowly unfolded the paper and looked intently into her love's eyes. "Kobie, you are the man of my heart, and I am very blessed to be marrying you today. I promise to keep on loving you with everything I am and everything I have. I promise to always put the Lord at the centre of our marriage. To respect you and cherish you as the head of our home, my partner in life, my lover and my very best friend."

He smiled at her softly, then pulled a folded piece of paper from his shirt pocket. Unfolding it, he read. "Jan, this is a dream come true for me. I promise to remember how blessed I feel right now in this moment. I promise to love and cherish you completely, as a precious gift from God. My prayer is that our marriage would be a picture of Christ and His church. And when people see how much I love you, Janice, I pray they will catch a small glimpse of how much Jesus loves them. Psalm 34:3..." Eric's dad took his mom's hand, lifted it in the air, and looked her in the eyes. "Come glorify the Lord with me my love! Let us exalt His name together!" Janice's eyes were wet as she squeezed his hand.

As the pastor pronounced them husband and wife, Uncle Kobus took her face in his hands and kissed her passionately. The congregation cheered as the couple turned to face them. Eric came up and hugged them both simultaneously, one arm around each of them.

"God is so good." He smiled at them, then watched them start down the aisle together. He scanned the crowd for Rachel and found her looking at him. The longing in her eyes tugged at his heart. As he moved towards her, he held out his hand.

She took it and drew close to him. "That was incredibly beautiful."

"*Ja*, it was."

"I feel privileged just to have witnessed that."

Eric smiled. "It's so crazy to be at my own parents' wedding!"

"I can only imagine!"

They passed by the crowds to spend a quiet moment alone. Eric led Rachel to a bench outside, where they could watch the guests give their best wishes to the couple. The sun was starting to sag behind the hill now, and the air held a chill.

"We're next, I can't wait!" Eric whispered in her ear. "We have a lifetime of loving ahead of us Rach." He played with her fingers on his thigh.

"I never dreamed I could love someone like I love you Eric." She looked down and then caught his eye.

"I'm not sure I've thanked you?" said Eric.

"For what?"

"For sacrificing so much of your life to be with me. It's hard to believe that we haven't even known each other for a year yet."

"Yes there's still lots that you don't know about me!" She wiggled her eyebrows.

"Oh *ja*? Anything that I need to know urgently?" he joked.

Rachel laughed. "All my past boyfriends might come back for revenge, you'd better be prepared!"

"All your past boyfriends ay? Just how many are we talking about here?" Eric gawked.

Rachel laughed at the expression on his face, but then went quiet. "Actually Eric, maybe you'd like to know that I haven't been with another man."

"You haven't? I was your first?" Eric searched her face.

"I'd made the same promise you had, to keep myself for my husband." The edge of her mouth curled up.

He smiled and looked deeply into her green eyes.

"When Tomos left me, I never thought I'd recover. But I soon saw God's hand in it all, even though there was pain. And then when I fell pregnant, I was so humiliated. I felt like God was punishing me. But then, again, He turned it all for my good… blessing upon blessing. His ways are not our ways. He makes all things work together for the good of those who love Him." She smiled with wonder, blinking back her tears.

Eric put both hands in her loose hair, and gently pulled her mouth to his. As he kissed his future bride tenderly, he knew beyond any shadow of doubt, that God had brought them together. This was the work of His hands, and He had turned even their shortcomings for His glory.

And all he could do in response was to love and cherish her completely, and to live a life that glorified Him in return. And he could hardly wait to get started.

THE END

If you enjoyed this book, please take a moment to REVIEW it on AMAZON.

THANK YOU!

Preview

Deborah's Choice

By

Ashley Winter

** Love in South Africa - Book Two **

CHAPTER ONE

Deborah had never felt so excited. She was almost giddy as she picked up another t-shirt, rolled it and packed it snugly with the others into her deep purple suitcase. She'd heard that a typical South African winter's day was hot over midday and cold in the mornings and evenings, which meant packing for both seasons. But, as long as she didn't have to pack any scrubs or a lab coat, Deb was thrilled.

She took a deep breath and smiled to herself. For as long as she could remember, she had longed to visit Africa. And now, her dream was coming true. And not only that, but she got to share this dream with the man she loved.

Deb emptied the carrier bag of all she'd purchased especially for the trip; sun cream, mosquito repellant and a new straw sun hat, and packed the items carefully.

"Hey." Gavin pushed wide the half-open door and trudged into her granny flat above her parents' double garage. He gave her a quick kiss on the cheek.

"Wow, you look exhausted!"

"Eighteen horrible hours straight." He yawned as he collapsed onto her sofa in the small open-plan living area. He grabbed a nearby cushion, folded it over and lay his head on it. His eyes closed and his breathing slowed within minutes.

Deb marvelled at how easily Gavin could fall asleep anywhere, and wished she could do the same. She smiled at him still wearing his green scrubs, his long, lean body spilling off the end of the couch. Deb picked up the throw that was hanging over the other sofa, opened it and gently covered him with it.

With their upcoming trip to South Africa, both she and Gavin had been working extra hours to make up for their absence, and it was definitely taking its toll on both of them. Rachel's wedding had come at the perfect time. They were so ready for some time away together. Of course they wouldn't be alone though; her parents and brother were booked on the same flight, and would also be staying at the game reserve. But Deb hoped for many romantic moments, where they could steal away together, go on some adventures, and make some lasting memories.

Deb heard a face-call come through on her iPad and quickly answered. It was Rachel.

"Hi sis," she whispered loudly.

"Hey. Why are you whispering?" Rachel whispered back.

"I've got Gav passed out on the sofa over here." Deb checked to see if he was stirring. His dark hair covered over his one eye.

"Oh right!"

"But he's not even flinching, I think we can talk normally now."

"How's the packing going? I can't tell you how excited I am to have you all here!"

"I'm almost done! Gavin's got quite a bit still to pack, he's just come off a long shift."

"So, your dress is ready! Please don't gain or lose any weight!"

Deb laughed. "I'm trying my best! But my meals have been really irregular with these crazy shift patterns. I can't wait to get away from the hospital!"

"You'll love it here Deb. It's another world!"

"Not long to go now and I'll be there in the flesh! So, when does Matty come home?"

"We're expecting it to be any day now, he's just under 2kgs. So he should be home well before the wedding. I can't wait. I need my little boy home now!"

"I can't wait to meet him!"

"Well, I'll let you go finish up the packing sis! See you soon!"

"Yes!"

***

Gavin was so relieved to have had some solid sleep at Deb's. He unlocked the door of his house and trekked up the stairs. His shift had been a really tough one.

He sat on the edge of his double bed and opened the bedside table drawer. He pulled out a velvety box, opened it, and smiled at its contents. He'd bought the diamond ring weeks ago, and he'd been biding his time, waiting for the right moment. When Rachel's wedding had come up, he knew Africa would provide the perfect backdrop for his big question. He and Deb had been together since Deb was in med school, and they'd been almost inseparable since.

He remembered the moment he'd first noticed her. She was doing her training rounds, and he, a senior doctor, was attending the patient in the neighbouring bed. She was confident and precise, comfortable in her own skin, and strikingly beautiful. She'd rattled him like no woman ever had, and he knew he had to meet her, somehow. His opportunity came soon after when he was asked to supervise the training doctors in the ER.

"I'm Doctor Gavin Evans, and I'll be supervising you on your shift this evening." He looked around the group and briefly caught her eye. Deb had appeared completely unaffected by him. She was professional and efficient. That was, until the child she was seeing to in the ER, took a rapid turn for the worse and passed away. It was the first patient she'd lost, and she was broken. Gavin didn't want to take advantage of her grief, but he felt he had to at least try to comfort her.

"Can I come in?" he'd asked as he knocked cautiously on the changing room door. When there was no answer, he'd entered slowly and found her slumped on a bench, head in her hands, weeping softly. His heart broke. Seeing the depth of her compassion, his admiration for her tripled. He sat next to her quietly as she cried.

"Do you need me to drive you home tonight, Doctor Wright?"

Deb lifted her head and looked into his green eyes with her big brown ones. He could hardly breathe as she studied him.

"I'd appreciate that Doctor Evans. Thank you."

They'd never looked at each other the same again after that night. It was as if he'd seen into her soul for a moment. And something deep inside her called to something deep inside him.

They'd been chatting about possibilities in Africa for many months now. There was such need amongst the local people, and they both felt like they had so much to give. Perhaps one day in their future, they could do something important together and make a real difference to the people who needed it most.

CHAPTER TWO

Eric had just arrived back at reception after his final game drive of the day. Even though it had been a long day, and he was tired, he couldn't stop the perpetual smile that occupied his face these days.

He turned the engine off and collected his backpack as the guests vacated the vehicle. Eric's dad came out to greet him then on his crutches, his mom following behind. He was still getting used to seeing them together like this, but it always warmed his heart. His dad was making good progress with his physio. Eric was proud of him.

"My boy, it's been a long day, I know," he leaned in Eric's open car window, "but your mom and I have a little surprise for you and Rachel. Call it an early wedding gift."

"Oh really? Okay, wow! Thank you. Rachel's down at her cabin I imagine."

"*Ja* we can take my car and fetch her quickly."

It was dusk and the sky was slowly turning pink. Eric was ravenous to the extent that he hoped this wouldn't take too long.

As they pulled up outside the guest cabin, Eric went to fetch her. He knocked gently and entered. "Rach?"

"Hello you!" The beautiful blonde emerged from the bedroom.

He took her face in his hands and kissed her. "My parents have a gift for us. They want us to come with them."

"Now?"

"*Ja*. I don't think it'll take long."

"Oh okay, exciting!"

Eric put his arm over her shoulders and walked her to the car. He opened the back passenger door for her and scooted in alongside her.

"Hi Rachel!" His parents greeted her in unison.

"Hi! This is all very unexpected, thank you for spoiling us!"

"We hope you're going to like it!" Eric's mom looked at the younger woman over her shoulder and smiled gently. Eric's dad, with one hand on his new wife's knee, drove up to the thatched-roof face-brick house where Eric's mom used to live. It was fenced off with its own private garden all the way around. Janice's furniture was still inside, but the house hadn't been lived in since their wedding.

"It's in there," Eric's dad pointed towards the house. "Come on."

Rachel and Eric followed his parents inside. As they walked into the living room, they froze. They looked at each other in disbelief, and then, at his parents. Across the wall above the wood burning fireplace was a huge banner which read, "Welcome Home!"

"What? Are you serious?" Eric stared at them.

Eric's dad came up behind him and place a hand on his shoulder. "A hundred percent serious. We've had the title deed transferred into your name." He grinned. "We hope you and your family will be very happy here my boy."

Eric wrapped his arms around his father tightly, a lump in his throat. "Thank you dad, thank you." His dad held him tighter still when he heard the word "dad" come from Eric's lips.

Janice hugged Rachel. "If there's anything you want to change, you go right ahead. You're welcome to keep any of the furniture you'd like to, or you can get rid of it if you'd prefer to get your own. We have painters and decorators coming in tomorrow morning if you'd like to change the paint colours, or just to freshen things up a bit."

"Wow, I'm speechless." Rachel's eyes were wide. "It's too much..." She swirled around taking in her future home.

"You might want to do up a nursery for Matty, they can do that for you also. Just let them know what you'd like," said Janice with a huge smile. "I know you've got a lot going on now with the wedding so soon, so I'm hoping the painters can take the stress out of it for you, and you'll have a lovely home ready to live in once you're married."

"I don't know what to say..." said Rachel.

"You might want to show your fiancé around her new home, Eric! We'll leave you two now. Oh and we know how hungry you are this time of night Eric, so we've ordered you pizzas, there's champagne in the fridge, it's non-alcoholic, for Rachel. Listen out for the delivery guy," said Janice as she gave Eric a quick squeeze.

Eric shook his head in disbelief as they left. He turned to Rachel. She gawked at him, mouth open. He enveloped her in his arms and spun her around as they laughed together.

***

"Can you believe this?" Eric asked as he showed Rachel from room to room.

"No, it feels like a dream."

Eric paused as he reached the entrance to the main bedroom. "And this is us..." he said as he swept the door open. The room was spacious with a plush carpet. It had a large wooden bay window overlooking the watering hole, and a full en-suite bathroom.

Eric took a deep breath. He couldn't stop his mind from imagining the two of them together here in this room, and all they'd share as husband and wife.

Rachel walked slowly through the room and ran her hand over the high quality finishings. When she walked past him, Eric pulled her towards him and placed his hands on her hips. He bent his head into her neck and kissed her there.

"I'm trying to be patient here, Miss Wright, but it's not easy," he whispered. "And being alone in this room with you is not helping..."

"It will be worth the wait, Mr Pieterson, I can assure you," she whispered back.

"Oh I have no doubt about that..." He smiled cheekily.

There was a knock on the front door. Eric sighed and released her, then strode to the entrance to collect the pizzas and tip the driver. The smell of melted cheese and garlic drifted through the house.

"I'll get the champagne and some plates," Rachel called and disappeared into the kitchen as Eric opened up the pizza boxes to cool a little. Rachel reappeared with glasses, plates and a bottle of ice-cold champagne tucked under her arm.

In a few minutes they had their shoes off and were cuddled on their new couch together, in their new living room, in the home they owned, munching on hot pizzas and celebrating with thankful hearts.

***

"We have excellent news. It's home time!" The paediatrician looked at them and smiled. "Matthew is ready to go home with mom and dad today."

"Oh really? That is fantastic news!" Rachel beamed as she picked up their little son.

Eric rubbed his back as he lay against Rachel's chest. "Well done my *boytjie*! All that eating has paid off hey?"

Eric pulled Matthew's bag from the bedside cupboard and packed up his bits and pieces. They thanked the doctors and nurses, signed the discharge papers, and said their goodbyes. He was all theirs now.

Rachel strapped him into his car seat carefully, and together as a family, they took the slowest, most cautious drive of their lives, home to the reserve.

***

"*Boet* are you serious?" Johan held up the silky tie as if it was contaminated, and frowned. He'd expected nothing less than being asked to be Eric's best man, but he hadn't anticipated the attire associated with the honour.

"It's a wedding *bru*, of course it's going to be smart." Eric huffed.

"*Ja*, but, how'm I gonna breathe in this thing." Johan turned to face the full-length shop mirror and held it up against his neck.

"It's just a cravat, please Johan." Eric perched his hands on his hips, exasperated.

Johan looked back at his friend over his shoulder. "Okay *boet*, for you, I'll make this great sacrifice. Just to make you happy, because I love you."

"Great, thank you," Eric said wearily.

"But I'm not wearing a waistcoat, do you hear me?" Johan's brown eyes turned large. "Those things are not manly *boet*."

"Okay, I promise, no waistcoat."

Once the shop attendant had measured them both, he brought out the suit trousers and jackets for them to try on. After finding a style they both liked, the attendant packaged the suits up and Eric settled the bill.

"So, remind me now, what does the best man have to do again *boet*?" Johan turned to Eric on the drive home.

"Johan, I've told you this three times." Eric, faintly amused, kept his eyes on the road.

"Okay, just one more time, please *boet*. Last time, I promise."

"Okay, simply put, you plan the bachelor party, you carry the rings and stand next to me during the ceremony. Then afterwards, you walk the maid of honour down the aisle. You give a speech at the reception and you dance with the maid of honour."

"And that's Deb, Rachel's sister." Johan looked anxious. "*Boet*, I only know how to *sokkie*, nothing else hey."

Eric caught his eye briefly as he took the offramp onto the freeway. "Deb is great, I'm sure she'll be happy to learn how to *sokkie* with you. And she has a serious boyfriend, who'll also be at the wedding, so you don't have to worry about anything. It'll probably only be one dance and then she'll want to dance with Gavin for the rest of the evening."

"Do you think I'm worried she's gonna try something *boet*?" Johan frowned.

Eric sighed. "I'm just saying, it'll be like dancing with your sister *bru*, safe, no pressure."

Johan looked only slightly relieved, and nodded.

"Actually, I wanted to ask you *bru*, if you wouldn't mind taking them under your wing as it were. After the wedding, maybe take them out, show them around, give them a taste of South Africa. That would really help me."

"*Ja*, I can do that *boet*, no problem. I'll think of some ideas. When do they arrive?"

"Well, the new guest cabins are finished just in time, because they arrive tomorrow evening. I imagine they'll be very tired for the first day or so, and then it'll be the wedding, so if you can plan something for after that maybe?"

"Sure *boet*, leave it to me."

CHAPTER THREE

Deb was about to burst! She clutched Gavin's hand on the armrest as the power of the engines pushed the plane like a lightweight toy along the runway.

"This is going to be awesome, baby." He grinned. "We're going to have the experience of a lifetime. Together." He lifted her hand to his lips and kissed it.

Deb smiled and nodded as she looked out the window in time to see the plane lift off the ground.

They chatted about their hopes for their trip until late into the night, then slept on and off until their plane touched down at King Shaka International Airport.

The family dropped their luggage as they reached Rachel and Eric at arrivals. She was beaming, cradling a baby boy in her arms. The family took turns holding her close and cooing over their new family member.

Her mum was the first to hold him. "Oh wow, he's the image of you Eric! He's so perfect!" Lyn had tears in her eyes as she touched his little cheek and held him close for a cuddle. Everyone wanted a turn and Matty was passed around until each family member was satisfied that they'd had their fill for now.

"It's so amazing having you all here, I can't tell you!" Rachel was emotional as she walked them all out towards the hired *combi* in the parking lot.

"*Ja* guys, thank you for coming," added Eric. "It really means so much."

"Wow, and this is your winter!" Peter paused, looked up into the full African sun and closed his eyes. "I think I'm going to enjoy this." He smiled.

"We might have to plaster ourselves in sun cream," said Deb. "I'm not going down the aisle looking like a lobster!"

"Lobster skin would look lovely with your soft pink dress." Gavin teased and kissed her on the cheek. She elbowed him back and continued towards the car, pulling her cases behind her.

Eric had packed a cooler box full of snacks and drinks, and soon they were homeward bound, chatting, joking, eating Simba chips and drinking Liquifruit.

"Was there a fire here Eric?" Peter asked looking out at the black field to his right.

"In the winter months, when it's so dry, we do controlled fire breaks. Burning stretches of land purposefully in a controlled way protects areas that are vulnerable to fire damage, like towns, or any infrastructure. We do them on the reserve also, every year."

"Oh I see, interesting."

"So when an accidental fire reaches the firebreak, it can't go any further, and that's the end of it. But fires are very important for the ecosystem also."

As the men chatted about ecology and conservation, and some of the many challenges facing the country, Deb leaned back in her seat and took Gavin's hand in hers. She soaked everything in with a contented smile on her face. She could hardly wait to experience all the mystery and adventure that this spectacular country had to offer.

***

The reserve was bustling with activity as Eric pulled up at the newly built guest cabins down near the watering hole. Uncle Kobus had employed a couple more rangers to fill in for them over this chaotic, but exciting time. Game drives would be continuing as normal, with Sipho in charge, though there were no overnight guests booked in until after the wedding once the family had returned home to Wales.

"This is incredible. Just look at that!" Gavin was blown away by the rugged landscape and the South African *bushveld*. The sun had started to drop in the sky, creating the silhouettes of the animals and acacia trees, that so often took visitors' breaths away.

"Absolutely beautiful!" Lyn was awestruck as she looked from one end of the reserve to the other. "It's no wonder you love this place so much, Rach."

"And they say there's no God!" added Peter, shaking his head at the thought.

Eric smiled and handed out keys to the cabins. "Lyn and Peter, you're in the far cabin, number 3. Gavin and Blake, you're sharing number 2, and Deb, you have this one here all to yourself, number 1."

"Come I'll show you!" Rachel grabbed her sister's hand and led her into the cabin.

Eric helped Lyn and Peter with their bags and settled them into their cabin. "These are brand new, any problems with hot water or electricity, please just tell me and we'll sort it out. I hope you'll have a very comfortable stay."

"Thank you Eric." Peter shook his hand. "While I have you here, I just want to tell you that I'm looking forward to getting to know my future son-in-law a whole lot better while we're here."

Eric smiled and nodded. "Hopefully I can redeem myself a little."

Peter shook his head. "There's no need for that. We don't hold anything against you, Eric. We are thrilled with Rachel's decision."

"That means a lot Peter, thank you."

***

"Rachel!" Deb clutched her sister's arm. "This is even more incredible than I'd imagined! It's beyond my wildest dreams! How did you even *think* of coming home after this?"

"It is a very special place, and there's lots more to show you, so you'd better have a good night's sleep tonight!"

"Oh I plan to!"

"You'll have to get used to the crickets and frogs, they are very loud at night. I'm so used to them now though, I can't sleep without their noises!"

"So, is this *the* cabin?" asked Deb, a glint in her brown eyes.

"Huh?" Rachel frowned.

"*The* cabin…" Deb wiggled her eyebrows, "where it all… went down?"

"Deb!" Rachel gasped.

"Well *is* it?"

"Yes okay, now nothing more about that. You are something else!" Rachel blushed.

"I'm going to check out the bedroom." Deb winked, strolled past with her hand on her hip, and sprawled out on the double bed. "Ooooo comfy!"

Rachel followed her in. "You are seriously too much!" She shook her head.

"I know, but you're stuck with me I'm afraid! And that's all there is to it," Deb replied with a cheeky grin.

***

After an early dinner of Debonaires pizzas in Gavin and Blake's cabin, Deb was ready for bed. She was physically exhausted and emotionally drained from all the excitement and travel. As soon as her parents retired for the evening, she excused herself.

"Right boys, I'm off to bed!" She stretched, yawned and gave Gavin a quick peck.

"Hang on you." He pulled her in closer and gave her a real kiss good night. "That's better." He grinned at her.

"You two are shameless!" Blake laughed, pulling on his coat. "Gavin and I are going out to explore for a bit."

"Okay, you lads be careful out there, and don't stay out too late!"

Once in her cabin, Deb turned on a bedside light, undressed and climbed into the shower. She soaked her hair and allowed the hot water to soothe her achy muscles. She hummed as she massaged shampoo into her long dark hair. Once she was all rinsed off, Deb reached for the white fluffy towel that hung near the shower. She wrapped it around herself and padded through to the bedroom.

Suddenly Deb's heart leapt in her throat. She sprung onto the bed and let out a blood-curdling scream.

***

Johan arrived back at his cabin desperately needing to unwind a little before bed. It had been a hectic day, and the business was not set to let up anytime soon. He threw on a pair of jeans and a hoodie, grabbed his helmet and keys and hopped onto his motor bike. He didn't usually ride at this time of the evening, but he knew the path well, and it was just what he needed, some alone time, peace and quiet.

He rode past the rangers' cabins and towards the guest cabins just at the start of the hill incline. When he reached the first guest cabin he heard an almighty scream. It sounded as though someone was being violently attacked. Rural attacks were not uncommon in the area, and Johan immediately felt his adrenaline kick in.

He turned his bike around and sped to the front of the cabin where he'd heard the screams. He jumped off the bike, yanked off his helmet and ran towards the entrance. Johan tried the cabin door, it was locked.

"Help! Help me!" came a woman's frantic cries.

Johan had no choice but to kick the door down. The door swung open and he raced in ready for anything. Anything except the scene before him.

A naked lady in a towel, standing on the bed, plastered to the wall, and a harmless, brown house snake slithering around the bedroom floor.

"Get out!" she shrieked at him. "I'm half naked!"

"Okay, okay, lady." Johan balked and retreated. Shutting the door swiftly, he leaned up against it. His breathing came hard and fast, and not just from the adrenaline. Was this Deb? If so, he had a serious bone to pick with Eric. Safe? This girl was *not* safe. Those big, brown, feisty eyes, that prim and proper accent, that silky hair, those long legs. She was anything *but* safe! Eric had not prepared him for any of this!

"Okay lady, you need to decide," he called through the keyhole. "Do you want help or not? Are *you* going to catch that snake? I can tell you now, it's highly venomous." He couldn't hide the cheeky smile that grew on his lips.

"Okay fine then, but don't you *dare* look at me. I'm warning you!"

"Lady, I can promise you, I don't care what you look like. I'm just going to come and catch that snake for you. Nothing else, okay?"

"Okay," she answered shakily.

With that Johan re-entered the cabin and approached the snake. He could feel his heart thumping hard in his chest as he anticipated carrying out a little prank.

He suddenly grabbed the snake with one hand, turned and shouted. "Ouch! Ouch! *Eina! Jislaaik!*" Johan threw the snake out the open door, clutching his hand as he buckled down in pain.

Deb sprung to action with her doctor training. "Oh no!" She gripped her towel with one hand and hurtled towards him, jumping off the bed and landing with an ungraceful thud. She gripped the hand he held. "I can help you, I'm a doctor! Let me see! Quickly!" She flicked her wet hair over her shoulder.

"Lady, if I let go now," Johan panted, "the poison… will travel… to my brain, and I'll be dead… in twenty minutes." He could see the wild panic in her eyes and wondered how long he should let this go on for.

Deborah ran to her bedside table for her phone, towel now barely in place. "What's the number, quickly, I'll call an ambulance! Quick, you idiot!" she yelled.

Johan couldn't hold back any longer. He clutched his stomach and started laughing, softly at first, and then harder and louder.

Deb marched over to him. She grabbed his hand and ripped it off the area he was covering on the other hand, where he'd supposedly been bitten.

Johan could almost see the smoke rising up from her ears as she realised she'd been had. She turned redder and redder until he thought she might explode. He stopped laughing then. "I'm sorry, just a little joke." He snickered, holding up both hands.

"Get out!" she growled. "Get out *now!*" She stomped her foot, grabbed the sleeve of his hoodie with two fingers and dragged him towards the door.

"Look I'm sorry, I couldn't help it, just let me expla -"

She slammed the door, but because the latch had been broken, it simply swung open again. Johan watched in delight as she reappeared, covering his mouth to stem his laughter. She angrily hauled a large suitcase over and rammed it up against the door with a loud thump.

***

Johan found his bike and helmet, and headed back home. That was all the drama he needed for one night. How could someone be wanting help and not want it at the same time?

He shook his head and laughed to himself. Women were complicated. And it was just a harmless joke. She was begging for it… being that highly strung over nothing… a house snake… he snickered.

As he arrived back at his cabin, Johan threw his helmet down on the couch and pulled off his *takkies*. Should he tell Eric what had happened? He might be a little upset with him, but even so, it was worth it. It was better than anything he could've hoped for. The way she pulled him by the sleeve, slammed that door, it was totally priceless. He was going to be smiling for weeks over this. But man, was she beautiful! He couldn't deny that. She'd probably be even more stunning when she didn't have a red, angry face. What a handful! Her poor boyfriend.

He laughed out loud as he climbed into bed for the night. He'd sleep on it. He could hardly wait for their next encounter.

***

END OF PREVIEW

Ashley Winter is a South African Christian Fiction writer living in Wales, United Kingdom. Ashley and her husband Grant, along with their three sons, immigrated to Wales in 2009 to help with a church plant in Swansea. They have since had one more son added to the chaos, and they spend their days chauffeuring the kids and kicking them off their screens and other electronic devices. They have not been brave enough to add any pets to their collection of living things, as they already have so many to keep alive. Ashley finds her escape from the overwhelming masculinity in her home by disappearing into her wonderful world of fiction.